DADDY'S GIRL

Also by Julia McDermott

All the Above: My son's battle with brain cancer

Underwater

Make That Deux

JULIA MCDERMOTT

Julia McDermott

DADDY'S GIRL

ISBN–13: 978-1530250523
ISBN–10: 1530250528

For Dennis,
my girl's daddy

Table of Contents

1..................Cash Poor
2..................Agreements
3..................Trust
4..................Holiday
5..................News
6..................No Complaints
7..................In the Family
8..................A Control Thing
9..................A Slam
10..................Assessments
11..................Tension
12..................Engaging
13..................Getting Away
14..................Baby
15..................Stand off
16..................A Zero-Sum Game
17..................The Heebie-Jeebies
18..................Surprise, Surprise
19..................Epiphany
20..................Killed
21..................Changing Ways
22..........,..................Lies
23..................Seeing Someone
24..................Betrayed

25....................Disclosures
26...........Future Endeavors
27................Ulterior Motive
28..........................Perfect
29........................Halftime
30......................Truth Told
31....................Crime Show
32.......................Snapped
33.............Falling Dominoes

1

Cash Poor

Josh Wilson knew exactly what his mom would say about this situation: *It was a bloody mess.*

The CEO of PriceUtopia sank into a black vinyl chair at one end of the oblong glass table in the conference room. He turned to his left to face the two women, as different from each other as a diva and a groupie. He cleared his throat. "Graham and I just got off the phone with the investment banker, Stewart Young over at Geneva Securities, and here's what he told us. Apparently, Cornucopia got cold feet after the markets closed last night, and they pulled their order. So Stewart had to cancel our IPO."

Valerie Mitchell, the company's head of sales and business development, gave Josh a cold stare. "Because of *one investor?*"

Graham Woodcock, co-founder and Chief Technology Officer, leaned forward and trained unblinking eyes on her. "Not just *any* investor. Cornucopia. Our anchor in the IPO. They had the biggest order in the book—they'd been in it for twelve million."

"But—what do you mean, they got cold feet?" asked Sophie Prejean. Sophie was in charge of social media and public relations.

Josh glanced at Graham and then looked back at her and Valerie. "Stewart said they told him that they took another look at their portfolio, saw that they had a bunch of technology exposure—evidently, much more than they realized—and decided that they didn't want to add any more to it."

Sophie's mahogany, crayon-like eyebrows shot up over bulging green eyes. Like Graham, she was in her mid-thirties and single; unlike him, she was short and on the pudgy side. "Didn't they *know* we're a technology company?"

"Of course they did," said Graham. He leaned back in his chair and ran a wiry hand through his head of thick, dark hair. "And they knew that we're a product-driven company. Not your typical tech startup, with nothing tangible to show for ourselves."

"So what they told Stewart was bullshit, then," said Valerie.

Josh glanced around the table. "Look. We grilled Stewart for over an hour. He said *no one* knows the real reason they pulled. So the story is going to be that they backed out due to, quote unquote, market conditions."

"*More* bullshit," said Graham.

"In any case—" began Josh.

"This is *unbelievable*," said Valerie. She began working her jaw, and a throbbing vein split her otherwise still, smooth forehead. "My staff is going to freak when they hear."

"Graham and I pointed out to Stewart that before Cornucopia backed out, he had a hundred and twenty million in orders. So, even without their twelve, that still left a hundred and eight."

"More than enough for the IPO," Graham interjected.

"So we told him that he needs to solve this problem for us."

"Can he do that?" asked Sophie.

"Honestly, I don't know," Josh mumbled. Sophie had a talent for asking irritating, stupid questions. "He said that once they pulled, lots of other investors started doing the same thing, and doing it quickly. Like a domino effect."

"Basically, everyone panicked," added Graham. He crossed his arms in front of his chest. "Stewart said that most of the other orders were from what they call average investors. Guys they felt weren't going to be long term stockholders, but just in for a quick flip. Apparently they all got scared and canceled their orders, too."

"But is this normal?" asked Sophie.

"*No,*" said Josh. "The thing is, Cornucopia was our most well-respected investor. As Graham said, our anchor. And, according to Stewart, they've *never* backed out of an IPO. When they did, and then when word hit the street, things got ugly. In the chaos, Geneva felt that they didn't have a strong enough book to take us public."

Sophie pulled nervously at her scarf. "What do we do now?"

Josh puffed his cheeks and blew out some air. "We get Stewart to figure out who else he can get to take Cornucopia's place. Another blue chip fund that's willing to invest in a future IPO."

Valerie scoffed. "Seriously? After this, aren't we seen as damaged goods?"

Josh winced. "We're as good a company as we ever were. It's not our fault that some idiot investor didn't know what was in their portfolio."

"And didn't have an understanding of what we do," said Graham. "We don't know who's going to believe the story, but Stewart Young has some skin in the game, too. He's *got* to want to work with us, to plan another offering."

"Right. But today, we need to regroup," said Josh. "Needless to say, salaries are frozen, company-wide. Indefinitely." Josh's ice blue eyes locked on Valerie's hazel ones. He rubbed his wide forehead. "Obviously, we're all in shock right now. But we need to get on task. Sophie, get with your team, update them, and come back here in an hour to discuss the message. Valerie, let's meet at three and talk about the sales and implementation teams. Graham and I have already met with the finance team, and we're meeting with the tech team and the product team next. We're scheduled to talk to Stewart later this afternoon. After that, we'll have a company-wide meeting. We'll keep both of you apprised. Meeting adjourned."

Wordlessly, Valerie and Sophie stood up and walked out of the conference room. Josh shut the door behind them, and then turned to his partner.

Almost three years ago, the two men had founded the company based on a concept, a belief, and a dream. That concept was a new device—a point-of-sale solution response to show-rooming, the growing customer practice of checking out products in stores, then buying them online for less. Josh and Graham believed that PriceUtopia would become retailers' must-have to survive and to stay competitive, and that it would revolutionize the industry. With the device installed at each store point-of-sale

(POS), associates–salespeople–could scan a competitor's link on a shopper's phone or tablet, match the price, and make the sale.

It sounded simpler than it was. Graham had developed the technology and created the hardware, and Josh had known how to market it. Back in the fall of 2009, they went out to the field to validate the need for their product. Friends in the industry connected them with their business contacts. Everyone agreed they had hit on something, and that PriceUtopia was the next big thing. That there was a huge market for it, and all they had to do was get it out there–fast–and develop client relationships. That if they didn't hurry up, someone else would come along, steal their idea, and do it first. They threw in fifty grand apiece, created a prototype, and set out to demo it to several wealthy individuals looking to invest in new companies.

One took a risk on them, and more investors followed. They worked hard to refine and improve their product, and even harder to sell it. Success seemed like a given, and so did their IPO.

Until an hour ago.

Graham regarded his partner, took in a deep breath, and exhaled. "My God. After everything we've been through, all those roadshows and pitches, all those private equity rounds, our fucking IPO gets *canceled* at the last minute. Swift has *got* to be pissed, and so does Ferguson. Adam can't be too happy, either."

Adam Langford was the company's angel investor, the first to take a chance on them back when all they had was the prototype and one non-paying client. Like Josh and Graham, Adam believed that retailers were losing untold millions in sales to show-rooming. The San Francisco venture capitalist invested $500,000, and in fall 2010, Ferguson Venture Partners put in $5 million. Swift was a late-stage VC, with a $10 million investment.

"I'm sure he's upset," said Josh. "The whole thing doesn't make sense. We go and get a west coast boutique investment bank for the IPO, specifically because their whole focus is on high-growth technology startups. Then, at the eleventh hour, our biggest investor backs out, claiming they have too much *tech* exposure?"

"I don't think *anyone* is going to buy that."

"*I* don't buy it, either. Meanwhile, here we sit in Atlanta, and we still need the funds."

*

Valerie entered her private office and closed the door. She sat down at her laptop, pushed a stray lock of silky blonde hair behind her ear, and fingered one of her diamond studs. Though she could feel its weight, making sure that an earring was in place was a nervous habit.

She had a phone call to make, and she couldn't put it off any longer. She cleared her throat and dialed her step-mother's number.

"Hello! You've reached June Mitchell. I'm sorry, but I'm unable to take your call. Please leave a message, and I'll call you back."

Damn it. She had no choice but to leave a message. She couldn't just hang up and expect June to know to call back.

"Hey, June," she said, forcing a cheery tone, and speaking slowly. "It's Valerie. Give me a call when you have a minute. Thanks!"

She scowled, and then smoothed her slim navy Ann Taylor skirt. When she woke up this morning, she had anticipated at least *feeling* wealthy again by this afternoon. She had planned to celebrate the long-awaited initial public offering alone with Josh tonight. She had never dreamed that the company's anchor investor would pull their order, disrupt everything, and throw her life into disarray.

She had risked a lot last August when she quit her job at Lallique and took a 50 percent pay cut to join PriceUtopia. She had been with the trendy, unisex apparel chain for a decade, and had risen up in the ranks. As head of merchandising, she had walked away from a $165,000 salary, plus bonuses.

But on her first day at the startup, she had been issued 80,000 stock options at a strike price of $8, to be vested over a period of five years. Josh and Graham had assured her that the stock price would increase by no less than a factor of five from an IPO price of about $12.50 over that future period. So, five years hence, her 80,000 options would be worth $4,360,000. Net.

Now—best case—that timetable was indefinitely delayed. Worst case, it was out the window.

What if the startup never went public? That was certainly possible. If it didn't, her precious options would be worth absolutely nothing.

Zero.

Damn it. How could Josh and Graham have allowed the IPO to collapse? Evidently, they were complete fools for trusting Stewart Young in the first place. They walked around the small office swaggering, as if their precious product was brilliant, and the retailer's version of the iPhone. As if failure was impossible. And yet, today, they had failed—miserably.

Valerie clasped her hands behind her and stretched. Her world would be so different now if she hadn't left her stable, highly paid position and accepted this uncertain one.

Her inbox dinged with several new email messages, and she scrolled through them. As she had predicted, her sales staff was in panic mode about today's news. Rumors were flying, obviously begun by employees in the finance team, the product team, or someone in Sophie's group. Everyone knew about the big meeting this afternoon, but the salespeople were asking her for direction, ahead of it.

She ought to wait until she met with Josh about strategy before she replied to anyone. But over the next few hours, her team needed to chill, and to continue working as best they could. She changed her mind and decided to craft a short, cryptic response to the team, without disclosing any details.

There. After hitting Send, she tried to allay her own fears. Today's disaster shouldn't affect sales—at least, not yet. Clients were still waiting to be called on, and deals were still out there to be closed. Soon, she would have a clearer vision about how to lead her team through the next several days and weeks. It was Sophie's job to deal with PR and to come up with a narrative, and it was the co-founders' job to approve it. None of that was Valerie's responsibility.

But it was frustrating trying to manage people through a crisis. She didn't like having to depend on the other company executives for leadership in order to do her job. She had never been in that position before. Noted and admired for sinking all of her time and energy into her work, she just wasn't accustomed to stepping back, even temporarily. It wasn't in her professional nature.

Though incredibly energetic, she wasn't impetuous. She had worked hard over the years to achieve career success, and until last year, she had successfully navigated company politics. She had quickly learned how to channel her charm and intensity, and she expected others to ask for and to value her opinion. Why shouldn't they? She was skilled, intelligent, and widely recognized for being able to keep up a frenzied pace at work. Like her father, she was driven, and felt she had inherited her strong work ethic from him.

Before she left Lallique, she had come to him for advice. In his decades-long career, Jim Mitchell had risen to the top through a combination of hard work, risk taking, and seized opportunities. President and CEO of a Fortune 500 company, he had built a fortune in the medical device industry. Last year, Valerie disclosed her job offer to him, and had described her situation at Lallique.

Her boss there was an arrogant man eight years her junior and hand picked by the CEO. Critical and mean-spirited, Gary Trigger had verbally abused her for months, often in front of peers. He routinely dismissed her views, and shouted at her when she didn't parrot his. For the sake of her career, she remained calm and professional, and avoided a public clash. Then one day, they had an unexpected showdown at a meeting with subordinates. Afterward, he promptly called her into his office and threatened to fire her unless she backed his latest, inane idea. She capitulated only because she believed she had no other choice at the time. But with Gary for a boss—and he wasn't leaving anytime soon—she felt very discouraged about her future at the company.

Jim Mitchell had counseled his oldest daughter to take a chance on the startup, assuring her that a year or two of reduced income was a sacrifice worth taking to be a part of something big. He also promised to lend her a half million dollars whenever she told him she needed it. He would get his financial advisor to issue her a low-rate note with annual interest-only payments, and said he would give her the money to cover those until she paid the loan off, sometime in the future, when she was ready.

In essence, he had offered her a $500,000 gift.

Because of that, she felt secure enough to quit her job and join the startup. When she did, she set out to make her father proud. She threw herself into her new position, working harder than she ever had. Though the future of PriceUtopia looked rosy, by the end of October, she began to think she ought to take him up on his promise.

But she waited too long. Two days after Thanksgiving—and an hour after he finished a cycling race—Jim Mitchell died of cardiac arrest.

When his will was read, Valerie was stunned. She and her siblings, Frank and Melody, inherited equal shares of his beach home, Sea Gem, valued at $6 million. But his $8 million Atlanta mansion and all of his money—over $30 million—went in a trust to his current wife, to be passed on to his children...eventually.

Seven months later, Valerie's finances were a mess. With a salary of $80,000, her net income was under fifty grand. She had ignored the problem and focused instead on the dangling carrot of the IPO. She hadn't cut her lifestyle at all. She had been raised in a wealthy household, and was accustomed to buying what she wanted, when she wanted it. And she wasn't going to stop now.

She pulled up a spreadsheet of her annual expenses on her computer. Payments and expenses on her luxury Buckhead condominium came to about $55,000 a year. She spent about $15,000 on clothes, and over $18,000 on food, entertainment, and leisure. Vacations cost nearly $20,000 a year, and annual credit card payments hovered around $8,000. An expensive new car every other year translated into yearly transportation costs of $40,000.

It all added up to roughly $156,000 a year, a good bit over her net income at Lallique. So she had charged what she wanted, and used her father's yearly $13,000 tax-free gift to pay the difference. But since she left Lallique, her credit card debt had risen exponentially. For the past several months, she had been juggling her charge cards, transferring balances, and vainly trying not to add to them. Lately, though, she had been neglecting the issue. She needed an infusion of cash to pay down her debt, and to supplement her income going forward.

But as things stood, she was property-rich and cash-poor.

She closed Excel and massaged her temples. It was time for her Botox injection, and she hadn't yet called to make an appointment. She would have to charge it.

She stood, closed her office door, and gazed out the window, full of rage. *She'd been fucked.*

Why hadn't she asked her father for that $500,000 as soon as he offered it? And—why hadn't she made her inheritance wishes clear? She would have told him that she'd much rather have money—a *lot* of money—than own a third of Sea Gem.

Perhaps he had mistakenly believed that the house meant something to her, but her fond memories of vacations there when she was young had faded considerably.

Back then, she loved spending hours on the beach, sunbathing, swimming, and playing tennis with her father. He'd thrown a sweet sixteenth birthday party for her at Sea Gem during spring break, and hosted her friends for the week. But after he married June, things changed: she made him renovate it to suit her taste, and now the decor was gaudy and ostentatious. It used to be an elegant estate, and now it looked like a kitschy hotel.

Since he passed away, Valerie detested being there. She rarely went down to the Georgia coast anymore, and she hated being entangled in the property with her brother and sister. In recent years, the entire family had gathered there for a week every Easter. Frank and Melody were both married with kids, but she was single, with none. Spending time with them at Sea Gem wasn't exactly her idea of a good time.

Far from it.

Worse, she was now responsible for a third of the yearly taxes and maintenance costs, a total estimated at $60,000. An annual obligation of twenty thousand dollars for something she never wanted in the first place was like adding insult to injury. Last fall, she had politely proposed putting the house in the area rental pool to defray expenses, but Frank and Melody immediately vetoed her idea. Melody had gotten hysterical about what the neighbors would think, and Frank had moaned that renters would trash the place.

Valerie's phone buzzed. She looked at the screen and picked it up. "Hello, June."

"Hi there! Sorry I missed your call. I was having a massage."

"You know, I need a new masseuse. Do you like yours?"

"She's wonderful."

"Would you do me a favor, and text me her number?"

"Be glad to!"

"Thanks. Listen, I called because I need to ask another favor. It's something that Daddy and I talked about last summer."

"What is it?"

"He promised me he'd lend me some money."

"Oh my goodness. How much?"

"Five hundred thousand."

June paused. "Hm. Jim never told *me* about this."

Valerie shut her eyes. "He probably didn't think about it again, after we talked."

"Your father was such a generous man. I miss him dearly."

Valerie put a hand on her forehead. *I knew him a lot longer than you did.* "I'm sure you do."

"Well, tell you what. Let me call David this afternoon, and see about what to do. I'll get back to you. Sound good?"

"Wonderful. Let me know."

Valerie put her iPhone down. David Shepherd had been her father's wealth management advisor for years, and now he was June's. David had always been an agreeable sort. Surely he would have a note drafted and sent over to her in no time. She would have to bleed the principal in order to pay the annual interest payments–June couldn't be persuaded to gift her that amount every year to cover them. As for paying off the loan, she would do that eventually–but not until many years after PriceUtopia went public, and she had made millions.

If it didn't, and she didn't, she would figure that out then.

June could easily part with half a million, anyway. The woman was fifty-three years old and had absolutely nothing to do. She could live very comfortably for the rest of her life on income from the trust. Jim had married her when *he* was fifty-three, less than a year after he had lost his wife, Ginger, to leukemia. June had been thirty-three at the time, about the formulaic age for a second wife: half the man's age, plus seven.

They had dated for only three months. On the day before Mothers' Day, with no family or friends present, they tied the knot in Sea Island. Valerie had been twenty-three at the time, on her own and living in southern California. A year later, she got a marketing job at Carter's and moved back home to Atlanta. She was regularly promoted at the children's apparel company until she hit the inevitable glass ceiling. She broke through it at Lallique with a much better position. Over her years at the retailer, she'd had some conflicts with bosses–and, of course, with other employees. Who didn't? But then, one day, Gary Trigger appeared on the scene and began his quest to make her life miserable.

Now she was up to her eyelashes in debt and earning a fraction of her worth at a company whose future was in serious doubt.

She needed the money her father had promised. Thank God she went over to the house on Sherwood Circle last December and took what she could find of her mother's jewelry. She had sold a sixteen-inch strand of antique pearls for over fifteen thousand dollars. A diamond tennis bracelet went for eight, and a sapphire ring yielded five grand. A collection of rings and necklaces sold for ten thousand. She had thought there was more, but Melody or June—or both—must have hidden or sold the rest.

She wouldn't put it past them.

Valerie fingered the emerald ring on her right hand. She had plenty of her own jewelry, but she wasn't going to part with any of it. She couldn't dick around with small change, anyway. She needed some serious funds, to ease her mind and to help her sleep at night.

2

Agreements

"Hello, June. David Shepherd, returning your call."

"Hi, David. Thanks so much for getting back to me before your weekend begins."

He smiled. "No problem. What can I assist you with?"

"Well, I've got a bit of a sticky situation. I hope you can help me with it. It's Valerie."

"What's going on?"

"She called me today and claimed that Jim promised her he would lend her some money, and–well, now she's asking me to do it."

"Hm. He never mentioned anything like that to me. How much money?"

"Me neither, so you understand why I'm a little suspicious. She said she wanted five hundred thousand dollars."

David paused for a second. "Was this a verbal promise? Or was it in writing?"

"I didn't ask. But she didn't mention it being in writing."

"Okay, then let's assume it was verbal. In either case, he left no such instructions with me."

"That's good to know."

"Did she say what she wanted the money for?"

"I didn't ask that, either. We're not very close, as you know. I don't quite know what to do now, though."

"Well, whether she has it in writing or not, I would advise you not to make her a loan. A promise from Jim is not a promise from you. More important, I feel that it's critical to enforce financial boundaries among family members. Lending money to family just doesn't work. I've seen it done before, and it's *never* a good idea. Either the loan's not repaid, or the relationships are destroyed—or both. If Valerie wants a loan, she can go to a bank."

"I guess you're right. What if I don't make her a loan, though, but just give her the money?"

That's much less problematic, but only if you do it with no strings attached. "June, you could do that. But if you do, you would have to pay a hefty gift tax. For that reason alone, I would strongly urge you not to."

"Oh, no. I certainly don't want to pay a gift tax. And I agree with you about financial boundaries. The thing is, I don't really know how to tell her no."

"Would you like me to call her for you? I could just say that the terms of the trust don't allow you to make any loans."

"Oh, that would be perfect, David."

"And if the topic of a gift comes up, I'll handle that too. I'll be straight with her, and I'll keep emotion out of it."

"Yes, maybe that is best."

"Did you say when you'd get back to her?"

"No, but I think Monday would be fine."

"You know, June, if it makes you feel any better, Jim always told me that he wanted all of his children to earn their own money. He didn't want to rob them of initiative, or spoil them with their inheritance."

"Yes, I know. That's *exactly* how he felt. Well, let me know if you have any problem when you talk to her. And thank you so much."

"You're welcome." David put his phone down and cleared his throat. Yes, he would definitely wait until Monday to call Valerie Mitchell. No need to do it today.

He shook his head. What a predicament June was in—at least, that she felt she was in. It would be just like Valerie Mitchell to claim that her father promised to lend her a substantial sum. Over the years that David had served as Jim's financial advisor, he'd observed some troubling family dynamics. Although Jim had often said he didn't want to spoil his children, he seemed to have done just that with Valerie.

It wasn't only the yearly cash gifts he made to her, all of them the maximum amount allowable without being subject to tax. It was the numerous other gifts: computers, jewelry, clothing, even expensive appliances and gadgets. But, evidently, Valerie spent a lot of her own money as well, because Jim had quietly paid off her credit cards several times. David had helped him do it within the legal guidelines. Though he hadn't particularly agreed with his client's decisions, he had kept his opinions to himself.

Over the years, David had been amazed at how Jim Mitchell was able to keep on fooling himself about his oldest daughter. No matter how many times he lectured her, she believed—rightly—that he would continue to write the checks and fund her lifestyle. When it came to Valerie—and David had no idea why—nothing was too good, no sacrifice too great. As a result, she had grown up to become someone who spent a lot more money than she had. Truth told, Jim had raised Valerie to be a spoiled brat, who believed she was entitled. He had enabled her behavior by either turning a blind eye or making excuses for her. David had often witnessed the same thing when wealthy individuals made large financial gifts to family members, or funded them indefinitely. Sometimes, before very long, the benefactors began attaching strings and exerting power, while the recipients became resentful, and even deceptive.

Many times, David had kept silent when he wanted to shout that it was a disservice to do *anything* for another person that he or she could do for himself. David had watched enabling patterns like the one Jim had established with Valerie become entrenched in families, cementing their relationships. He had seen the resulting bad behavior, heard the accusations, and watched the quarrels escalate.

Sometimes, that had led to violence.

*

Melody Perkins turned on the Miele dishwasher and put the tomato-red oven mitt in a drawer. She pushed a lock of long brown hair behind her shoulder and looked around the room. It was great to have her kitchen organized after the chaos of her family's move into this house a couple of weeks ago. A few unopened boxes still dotted the other rooms, but at least the kitchen was functional and clean. The kids' bedrooms were a mess, though. Hopefully, she and Jeff could get everything under control by the time school started in August.

She glanced out the bay window at the cluster of bluish-purple hydrangeas blooming in the back yard. This house was a big jump up from their Charlotte home, a four-bedroom, two-and-a-half bath built in the nineties. This all brick traditional had six bedrooms and five baths, and though ten years older, was better built. With so much more space, none of the kids would have to share a bedroom anymore. The two-and-a-half car garage meant more space for bikes and skateboards. The kitchen and bathrooms had been updated, and the hardwood floors had just been refinished. And there was a bonus: a second set of stairs. A spiral staircase led from the kitchen straight up to the hall right next to the master bedroom. It reminded Melody of the one down at Sea Gem, which her father had installed when the home was updated.

The location was perfect, too: convenient to Jeff's Buckhead office, shopping, restaurants, and schools. The kids were already Braves fans, and now they could go see them play at Turner Field. Travel would be easier for Jeff, out of Hartsfield. And Atlanta was the same distance from Sea Gem as Charlotte was: about a five-hour drive.

Before Jeff started at Marsh Consulting—and while the moving van filled with their belongings was traveling on I-85 South—the family had spent a week at Sea Gem soaking in the sun. It had been a great vacation: the kids had had a blast, and everyone came home with a tan. The annual family gathering there had been canceled last spring, so it was the first time the Perkins had been to the beach since Melody's father passed away.

Her eyes watered at the memory of last November. June had been in total shock, and had been consumed with grief. The evening of the funeral, the entire family had gone to her house on Sherwood Circle in Buckhead. After too much wine, something had set Valerie off— Melody couldn't recall what it was, exactly—and Valerie had gone ballistic, shrieking at June.

"Why weren't you with Daddy when it happened? Why didn't you know he had a heart condition? Why wasn't he seeing a cardiologist?"

Valerie was grieving, too, but there had been no excuse for the way she behaved that night. Instead of showing support, she had been incredibly hostile toward the woman their father had loved, and to whom he had been married for almost two decades.

An earlier memory flashed in Melody's mind, of the time right after her mother's death. Valerie had acted concerned during the months she was sick, but when the end came, she was insensitive and unhelpful. Rather than offer support to her father and siblings, she had been self-centered and aloof. They had all had some time to prepare for Ginger's passing, but Valerie's behavior then was an unwelcome complication and had upset everyone.

Interrupting her thoughts, Jeff stepped into the kitchen and walked over to the fridge. At six foot four, he was ten inches taller than Melody was in her bare feet.

He gave his wife a measured look. "What's the matter, doll?"

Melody mentally chastised herself. She had never learned how to mask her emotions, and Jeff could read her face better than anyone. "Oh, nothing. Just thinking about when Dad died."

His eyes were soft. "Can I pour you a glass of wine?"

Melody looked up at him from under long lashes, framing dark eyes set a bit too far apart. "I'd love one, babe."

He popped the cork of a bottle of sauvignon blanc and filled two glasses halfway. "Want to go sit in the living room and talk?"

"Sure." They walked over and sat down in two yellow armchairs placed across from each other in the formal room, which was next to the den and separated from it by glass-paned French doors.

Jeff glanced at the unhung pictures leaning against a wall, and the boxes stacked in a corner. He took a sip of his wine. "We can get the rest done over the weekend."

"Let's. I've got a lot to do over the next few weeks to get the kids ready for school. I need to buy uniforms for Matt and the girls."

Jeff nodded. "What do you want to do for the Fourth?"

Independence Day was Wednesday. Melody cocked her head. "What about spending the day at the pool? I heard there's going to be a cookout, and games for the kids. It's BYOB, but they're going to have margaritas. We could go down and meet some of our new neighbors."

Like many in this city, this neighborhood was anchored by an Olympic-size pool and tennis courts. "That sounds good. The kids'll have a blast. What about fireworks, though? Should we go somewhere?"

Melody sipped her wine. "Why don't we 'hit the easy button,' and watch them from the deck? Someone told me you can see the ones at Lenox really well from here."

The fireworks at Lenox Square, a flagship mall just a few miles away, were an Atlanta tradition.

34

"Sounds like a plan." Jeff looked at his wife's wine glass, which was almost empty. "Another splash?"

She nodded. She would limit herself to only two glasses tonight.

Unless she changed her mind.

*

With Cole in her arms, Dawn Mitchell peered out the front window as a car passed by the house, and saw that it wasn't Frank. She'd been trying to get the baby on a reliable nap schedule recently, and some days he cooperated better than others. His morning nap was not the problem. After eating, he usually slumbered for at least an hour and a half. Maybe she ought not let him sleep so long then, though, because in the afternoons, she often couldn't get him down until three. The late nap was wreaking havoc with her goal of getting him to bed for the night by eleven.

For the last four days, Cole had slept for six hours overnight. In Dawn's view, that qualified as sleeping through. She had always been a light sleeper, and over the last few months, she had gotten used to fatigue. It was part of being a new parent—what she had wished to be for years. When Cole arrived, she couldn't believe her dream to be a mom had come true. She'd been scared to death that his nineteen-year-old mother, a college student, would change her mind about giving him away once he was born.

But the girl hadn't. What a blessing that, when she'd found herself pregnant last fall, she had chosen to have the baby and to give him up for adoption. These days, most young women who didn't terminate an unexpected pregnancy usually decided to keep their baby, whatever their financial situation. This girl said she had a moral objection to ending her pregnancy, but felt her baby would have a much better chance in life if he had two parents who were married to each other. Her own hadn't been married, and she barely remembered her father, who had never supported her. She had seen her mom struggle, and she didn't want to repeat the cycle.

What a gift for Dawn and Frank to have baby Cole after twelve years of marriage. Frank had been hesitant about adopting, but last year, Dawn had gotten him to accept reality: with her endometriosis, the likelihood of ever having one of their own was very slim. What had happened to Melody's and Jeff's family last year seemed to have affected him, too. Misfortunes were so much easier to bear once you accepted them. Now, her and Frank's misfortune had been replaced with joy.

She glanced at the wall clock; it was almost six. Her phone buzzed.

"Want me to grab something for dinner on the way home?"

"Sure, if you want."

"How's Cole?"

"Great! He's been up since five. I'm about to feed him."

"How are you doing? Tired?"

"Not too."

"Good. What do you feel like? Should I stop at that Greek place?"

"That's fine. Just hurry home, okay?"

"See you soon, babe."

She clicked off the phone and picked up the bottle of formula. Cole sucked it hungrily. He was wearing a cute onesie her sister Helen had given him. On the front, it said: "Thank Heaven for Little Boys" in baby blue.

Dawn thought of Helen and her new life, and hoped she had found happiness. Helen had been through so much torment and heartache during her brief first marriage. Almost two years ago, she had moved back here to Chicago with her three-year-old daughter, Adele. Then last spring, she had married Frank's second cousin, John Caldwell. From what Dawn could tell, John was a good man, and the total opposite of Adele's father.

Dawn gazed at Cole, who seemed to be studying her face. He was almost four months old—he was born on March 2—and he had been steadily gaining weight. Dawn had just started him on cereal this week. The pediatrician said his weight gain would help him go longer between feedings and start sleeping through the night. Of course, he'd been right.

Cole finished his bottle and Dawn shifted him to her shoulder to burp him. Before she could get him to do it, Frank strode through the doorway, carrying take-out and a bottle of white wine. He put both bags on the kitchen counter and gave his wife a kiss. "How's our little man?"

"He's had a good day. Thanks for stopping. How was traffic?"

"Murder. How was your day?"

Cole burped loudly, and Dawn smiled. "Wonderful. I'm getting more and more confident about being a mommy."

Frank flashed a smile back. "You're already a fantastic mother."

Five hours later, Frank fed Cole his last bottle and put him down for the night. Then he slid into the queen-sized bed next to his wife.

Dawn turned on her side to face him. "I'm so tired." She draped an arm over his chest.

Frank turned on his side toward her. "I love you."

"I love you, too." She kissed him. "Let's go to sleep."

He looked into her dark brown eyes, shining in the dim light. He ran a finger down her shoulder. "Are you really *that* tired?"

A current ran through her body. Romance and intimacy had taken a back seat in their marriage since they brought Cole home. With the focus shifted to caring for him, time and energy were valuable commodities, to be guarded and preserved. But the man lying next to her was her lover, her companion, and her best friend. He needed her to make him feel loved, and she needed to feel his love for her.

She scooted closer to him. "Well, I don't know. I could be roused–"

3

Trust

Valerie sank back into the pillows and closed her eyes.

Josh's head was between her legs, his deft tongue doing its magic. *Keep going.*

Then his hands went to her hips and traveled up to her breasts. He raised his head and moved up her body, his warm mouth kissing her all the way. She grasped his upper arms and pulled him up, then slid her hands toward his lower back. He eased in, pulled back, and then thrust himself deep within her. She caught her breath as she came again, in waves, meeting him.

Afterward, he quickly fell asleep. Like it did for most men, sex mellowed him. It was the best sedative in the world, he'd said. When he went without it for more than a few days, he became moody and irritable. She also needed the release of sex, and she needed it often—maybe more often than other women did. A long time ago, she had learned to compartmentalize, separating her emotional side from her physical one. It had worked, and she wasn't apologetic about it.

Listening to him speak at today's company-wide meeting, she had been stressed and tense. His explanation–actually, Stewart Young's fake excuse–that the IPO had been canceled because of market conditions was nonsensical and weak. Everyone in the office knew by then that Cornucopia had pulled their order only the night before. And no one, including the co-founders, knew why.

Valerie lay back in bed with her eyes closed. She listened to Josh's rhythmic breathing, stretched her legs, and felt drowsiness begin to creep over her. Despite her best efforts, memories of their first night together popped in her mind. That day, Josh had made a dazzling sales presentation to Dan Moreland, the CEO of Lallique, Gary Trigger's boss. Valerie and several other department heads had attended the meeting. Once Josh closed the sale–and moments after the other attendees scattered–he approached Valerie, chatted her up, and boldly asked her to go out that night.

Charming, witty, and attractive, Josh was unlike anyone she had ever dated. It seemed obvious that he was taken with her, and his optimism and energy about his company were contagious. After dinner at Jean-Michel's in Buckhead, she invited him to spend the night. Soon after, she plunged headfirst into a relationship with him. A few weeks later, she turned in her resignation letter at Lallique and started working at PriceUtopia.

Josh had told her that, before that first night with her, he hadn't been with a woman for months. She had believed him then, telling herself that it didn't matter, anyway. Now she felt certain that he had lied. It wasn't a deal-breaker, but she longed to be able to trust the man she was with. She couldn't have him telling her lies. Years ago, she had naively trusted another man, and it had been a huge mistake.

She turned onto her side and tried to relax. Without warning, June's words about calling David to "see about what to do" flashed in her consciousness. Valerie would give David until noon on Monday. If she didn't hear back by then, she would contact him herself. He ought to have no problem getting the funds to her; it was his job. Her father's wealth couldn't be allowed to sit around untouched while her situation became increasingly desperate.

The fact that she was going to inherit millions of dollars one day didn't matter. That day could be decades from now, if it ever came at all.

*

On Monday morning, Josh Wilson woke up in his apartment.

He had spent the weekend at Valerie's, but came home last night to get a good night's sleep in his own bed. God knew, he needed all his juices topped off to deal with the events of last week. On Friday night, he had drowned his sorrows in gin with Valerie, and then had gotten her naked and on top of him. The sex was great, as always—she did things to him that no other woman had ever done. It made up for a lot of other things about her.

Not everything, but still.

He stood in the shower under a stream of lukewarm water and willed away thoughts of their weekend romps. Eventually, he would have to part ways with Valerie. He hadn't meant to let it get this far, but unwisely, he had. She wasn't a beautiful woman, but she was definitely attractive. She was alluring. She had lured him in, the day he met her, almost a year ago–with what exactly, he couldn't say. It was weird. She had her faults, but she brimmed with self-confidence, something that he had always found sexy. And, unlike any of the other women he'd slept with, she held a sort of sexual power over him. But damn if he didn't enjoy it.

He had to get that off of his mind, though. He had a boatload to do. The shock of Friday's fiasco was beginning to wear off, and now he had to refocus and get busy. He needed to talk to Adam, and he also had to deal with Ferguson and Swift. They would badger him about the failed IPO. The nagging, burning question remained.

Why had Cornucopia pulled their order?

It was imperative to solve that riddle to ensure the success of a future IPO, if not that of the company itself. A blue chip fund pulling out because they "took another look at their portfolio" at the last minute was utter nonsense. They had obviously heard something–quite possibly something big–that had kept them from investing millions of dollars in PriceUtopia. But what exactly had they heard, and how had they heard it?

As Josh began shaving, his mind raced with worry and suspicion. What if somebody at PriceUtopia had leaked proprietary information, and that had led to Friday's disaster? Everyone at the company knew they weren't allowed to share information; all had signed contracts expressly forbidding it. But it was certainly possible that someone had. If specifics about the new release–plus a myriad of other confidential info–had been divulged, a competitor could be using it to aid in developing their own price-matching product. If so, that company could have approached Cornucopia at the eleventh hour in an effort to sabotage PriceUtopia's IPO, and to buy itself time.

Josh dressed and continued to mull over the sinister scenario. If his suspicions were true, then he had a traitor on his hands. A new nervousness began to invade his body and mind. With effort, he steadied his shaking hands and drew a long, deep breath. He needed to calm down, look at this thing objectively, and figure out what to do.

On the way to the office, he decided on a loose plan. He would talk his worries over with Graham this morning. If there were a traitor in the company, it *couldn't* be his partner–like Josh, Graham had way too much at stake. It could be almost anyone else, though. But who?

Graham knew each of the few people on the tech team upside down. If there was a Judas in it, he could quickly identify that person. People writing code weren't the only ones who could have leaked information, though. Now that he thought about it, Josh felt almost certain the betrayer wasn't one of them. All seemed just as invested in the success of what they were creating as Graham was. But someone on the finance or product teams might have leaked, or even someone under Sophie's charge. That group was the most engaged with what was going on in the technology world. It couldn't have been Sophie herself, though–like Valerie, she stood only to profit from a successful IPO.

Or–might it have been Sophie, or even Valerie?

No. That was irrational. He would text Graham immediately, and get his opinion. Then he could see if he were on to something, or if panic had sucked him in, like quicksand.

Ten minutes later, Graham appeared in Josh's office and shut the door. "You said it was important."

Josh leaned back in his chair and motioned to the one across from him. "Sit down," he said in a low voice.

For the next few minutes, Graham listened intently while his partner unloaded his suspicions. "I'm with you," Graham said. "But if we have a traitor, I don't believe it was someone on the tech team."

"Why?"

"Because I trust them all. And I don't think they would do it, for the sole reason that this is their baby. None of them want to see somebody come along and usurp what they've been working on."

"Unless there's a lot of money involved. Really, it could be anyone."

Graham paused. "Here's what I think. We contain things, for now. We figure out if someone disclosed information, and if so, what it was."

"How?"

"I have some ideas about that. Trust me."

"So—we do a witch hunt."

"What choice do we have? We need to know. Then we decide what to do, and go from there."

"Whatever we do, we still need funds," said Josh. "The offering would have raised seventy-four million, after expenses. We need money to finish the release, to hire more people, and to grow the business."

"We can get the release done without more manpower. The inventory link feature is being tested right now, and we're working on the client pricing systems interface."

"But without more funding, how can we get it out there and get it entrenched in the market? We need to hire more salespeople, and get more staff out in the field, training clients. With more salaries and expenses, our burn rate is only going to increase. The money won't last indefinitely."

"The sooner we figure this out, the closer we'll be to getting the funding side done. Let's get started, and then we can talk about funding, and about planning another offering."

*

An hour later, Josh sat alone in his office. He and Graham had agreed to start by interviewing everyone in the company. But no matter what they found out, if someone had leaked, what was done was already done. Graham was right, though: the sooner they got to bottom of this, the better. And maybe nobody *had* leaked anything. Maybe a competitor had coincidentally come up with a decent product on their own. It was a sobering thought, but it could have happened. Timing could be a bitch, and it was big in this industry.

Getting your product to market *first* was the only way to succeed.

Once you did that, you had to win clients and secure them. And many retailers were in denial about showrooming. For some of them, decisions were ruled by the sunk cost fallacy: the more you spend on something, the harder it becomes to abandon it. Because of emotion, you continue along a path that you know, intellectually, is unwise; you double down. It was a big part of what Josh had encountered so far in retailers' objections to price matching. Over several decades, they had invested millions of dollars into the sacred, so-called "customer experience:" new displays positioned at key locations; carefully chosen background music; well-advertised markdowns; and sometimes, even in-store cafés geared to women.

But shopping had become more of a hassle than it was worth. It took time to drive to a store, find a parking place, wait in line, and drive home. Then there were fuel and opportunity costs. Rather than make a trip to the store, more and more people preferred to shop online and have their items shipped. The big online retailers offered free shipping for purchases over a certain amount, and they were working on same-day delivery. That would mean instant, hassle-free shopping. Why would shoppers choose anything else?

Even so, bricks-and-mortar stores weren't going away anytime soon. The research showed that people who spent money both online *and* in-store spent four times more than those who only purchased in one channel. When the customer came in to the store, retailers had a choice: match the online price, or lose the sale.

It wasn't enough to give associates discretion to override prices on a case-by-case basis. Although policy in some retail chains, that practice wasn't publicized, nor tracked. But individual exceptions didn't earn the loyalty of new customers, nor did they snag those who came in without an online device. The genius of PriceUtopia was that it was advertised—and visible—to retailers and their customers. Shoppers *and* stores knew they were getting the best deal on any particular item. It would no longer be possible for retailers to price-discriminate against people who weren't very assertive, weren't terribly tech-savvy, or both.

Josh sighed. PriceUtopia had been shaken to the core by the IPO's collapse, but it was going to recover. He and Graham were a very good team. They had clicked like brothers in the early days, when they started fleshing out ideas in a framework on Josh's laptop, in his apartment. Together, they would deal with this mess, and then figure out a way forward. Graham was a realist, and terrific at solving problems. Josh was an optimist, and talented at reading people.

Josh had faced adversity and misfortune before. Things didn't always work out the way you planned, or exactly the way that you envisioned. But things still had a way of working out.

*

David Shepherd stepped inside his office in the Jefferson-Sloan Building on Capstone Road and put his dark blue coffee mug on his desk. He had several tasks on his to-do list this morning, one of which was to call Valerie Mitchell.

He wasn't surprised that June had decided not to become financially entangled with her stepdaughter. Although Jim Mitchell had provided her with a generous income from the trust, June was cautious with her money. It was a good quality to have, no matter what your socio-economic level. June had grown up in a middle class family, and after earning an education degree from the University of Georgia, she had lived for years on a schoolteacher's salary. Once she married Jim, she had gotten accustomed to his affluent lifestyle, but she had never seemed very comfortable with it.

Yes, as F. Scott Fitzgerald had said, the rich were different from other people. But June was the most unassuming rich person that David had ever known.

He picked up his cell and dialed Valerie Mitchell.

"Hello, David. I expect you've got a note ready?"

"Not exactly. I need to explain–"

"What's to explain? I'm very busy, and I'm sure you are, too," she snapped.

He tapped a pen on his desk. "I won't take up much of your time. Here's the deal. As you know, your father left his investments to June in a trust. While she receives income from that trust, according its terms, she's not allowed to take any of the funds out to make a loan."

"Not even one that my father promised me?"

David took a quick breath. "No."

"Look. Here's *my* deal. My father wanted me to have this money, and I intend to get it."

"Did he put that in writing?"

Valerie scoffed. "You're kidding me."

David's pulse quickened. "Is that a no?"

"This is ridiculous! My father was your client for years! You need to *trust* me."

"It's not about trusting you. I don't doubt that your father made you a verbal promise. The problem is, he didn't leave any instructions with me, nor did he put anything about it in his will."

"God*damn* it! I cannot believe this!"

"I'm just telling you the facts. June cannot lend any of the funds in the trust," he lied.

"I don't believe you. What *are* the terms of the trust?"

"I can't tell you that."

"Why not?"

"Valerie, June is my client–"

"Fine. Then instruct her to *give* me the money, instead of lend it."

"I'm sure you're aware of the high gift tax rate–"

48

"So what? She has enough to pay that."

David cleared his throat. "June has decided not to make you a financial gift."

"What? What is *wrong* with her? She's got more money than she knows what to do with!"

"Whatever her situation—"

David heard a click. Relieved to have the conversation over, he put it out of his mind, turned his attention back to his laptop, and looked over his schedule for the week.

*

June had the best shopping luck at Nordstrom's.

Years ago, she had favored the old Lord & Taylor at Phipps Plaza. Later, her number one department store was Parisian. Macy's was fine for shoes, lingerie, and casual dresses, but anything else was just too hard to find over there. She also shopped at Neiman Marcus, Saks, and some of the luxury boutiques. But she wasn't fond of dropping a fortune on clothes, and whenever she did, she felt guilty. It was particularly hard to get used to the prices at Neiman's after she married Jim, but it was where he preferred to go for his own clothes as well as for his many gifts to her.

Ever since he'd been gone, though, it was just too difficult emotionally for June to step inside the place. They had completely redone the restaurant a few years ago, too, which irritated her—she had preferred it as it was, and she had fond memories of lunching there with Jim. Packed in a corner of NM's basement level, it was sterile and cold now, with its modern decor. Nordstrom's café was much more inviting, and was June's favorite spot to meet her friends for lunch.

The anniversary sale at Nordstrom's was great, but what June valued most about the store was the service. If you wanted to browse, an employee would hover nearby, but not too close. If you couldn't find your size, they would pull it up on their computer and have it shipped to your door, free of charge. That was so much easier than wading through page after page on a website, having to guess about the cut and the fit, and not knowing how something you saw online would look on you. And here at Nordstrom's, if you needed something tailored, no problem, and no charge for that, either. When you made a purchase, the salesperson would walk around the counter to hand you your bag and thank you. Little things like that made a big difference.

June pulled a raspberry-colored rain jacket from a sale rack and tried it on over her black sleeveless top. The jacket suited her, and the deep red was a nice contrast against her dark shoulder-length hair. It would be perfect for cool rainy days this winter. She looked at the price tag and was delighted that it wasn't more expensive. Decision made: she'd take it.

"That's lovely on you," offered a perky salesgirl of about twenty-one.

"Thank you. Would you hold onto it for me? I'd like to look around a little bit more."

"Of course. I'm Zoe. What's your name?"

"June." She smiled, took off the jacket, and handed it over.

"It's nice to meet you, June. Let me know if you need any help and if you'd like me to start a dressing room for you."

"I will, thanks."

"Good. I'll keep this at the counter for you." Zoe trotted off.

June turned and heard her iPhone chime. She took it out of her Brahmin satchel handbag and glanced at the screen. It was a text message from Kitty, one of her friends at the club.

Looking forward to seeing you at the BBQ on Wed!

June smiled again. All her girlfriends had been so good to her since Jim had passed. It had been over six months ago now, but she still wasn't used to being alone. She was grateful for her years with him, but she doubted there could ever be another man in her life. Honestly, she felt too old for that to happen, anyway. After "a certain age"–an age she had already passed–no matter how trim or attractive you were, how could it? Despite the fact that Jim had been much older, she wasn't interested in even seeing another man near his age. And men of *her* age weren't looking for women in their fifties. They were looking for much younger women. Just like Jim had been, when she met him.

Thanks to him, she had everything she needed materially, anyway, and one true love in life was enough for anybody. She wasn't sure her friends understood; some of them had already tried to fix her up with one guy or another. She had politely declined, but maybe she should tell them all exactly how she felt.

She walked over to another sale rack and found a navy blue Ralph Lauren top that would be perfect for the Fourth of July barbecue at Kitty's. Her phone sounded again, this time with an incoming call. She should have put it on vibrate after Kitty's text. She checked the screen. It was Valerie.

Oh, Lord. She didn't want to answer, but she probably ought to, and get it over with.

"Good morning, Valerie."

"Hi. Listen, David Shepherd called me this morning."

"Okay–"

"No, June, it's not okay. Evidently, he needed written proof of my father's promise. If I had known that, I would have had Daddy put it in writing. I'm *sure* he would have. But I didn't think to. Of course, *I* thought he was going to live a lot longer than he did."

So did we all. June's eyes watered. Valerie was nothing if not brazen. "The thing is–"

"Look. I understand about the trust. David said it didn't allow you to make a loan. So, I want you to give me the money instead. You can take it out of my inheritance."

June paused. "I can't do that. The gift tax–"

"You have enough money to pay that."

June shut her eyes for a second. Valerie certainly had some nerve. "It's not whether I *can* pay it, it's whether I *want* to pay it. I'm sorry, but I don't."

"I can't believe you won't honor my father's wishes!"

"Your father never told me about this, and he made his own decisions about his estate. I'm sure you'll figure something out. Now, I've got to run. Bye!"

She hung up, put the phone on vibrate, and dropped it in her purse. She let out a deep breath. As usual, Valerie had been unnecessarily insolent and unpleasant. June felt more than justified in cutting her off.

It wasn't that June needed all the money Jim had left to her. She would never be able to spend it all. And she was going to be very careful managing it–she owed that much to Jim, and to his other children. He *had* been adamant that they all earn their own way in the world, and he had privately complained that he'd already given each of them enough money. He treated Frank and Dawn to a two week honeymoon in Italy and Greece, and he sent Melody on a Hawaiian vacation for her twenty-first birthday. He bought a Jaguar for Valerie around that same time. And he gave each of his children a large cash gift when they graduated from college. But June knew for a fact that over the years, he gave Valerie a lot more than he did the others. She wasn't about to start writing checks to her or to any of them, "taking it out of" their inheritances. *It's not what Jim would have wanted.*

She chased her thoughts away, glanced around, and spotted the salesgirl, hovering nearby.

"Zoe? I'd like to try this on now."

4

Holiday

Frank looked at the time. It was just after five o'clock, and his day had flown by. Mondays were always busy, but this one was more so, with the Fourth of July falling on a Wednesday. These four-day work weeks were hectic enough when the holiday fell on a Monday or Friday.

He was seeing clients on Thursday and Friday, and the next couple of weeks were going to be nuts. But that was preferable to having nothing in the pipeline. His business was cyclical, and typically, it was either feast or famine. Luckily, it had been feast for the last couple of years, but one never knew when things would change.

Though Frank took some calculated risks, he was a cautious man and was a saver by nature. Twenty years ago, when he was about to graduate from the University of Chicago and enter the working world, his father had taken him aside and given him some unsolicited but great advice: "No matter how much money you take home, save 10 percent, and give another 10 percent to charity. Don't use credit cards, unless you pay off the balance every month. Always put your needs before your wants, live on

80 percent of what you bring home, and *never* live above your means."

It sounded rather difficult. But it was what Jim Mitchell said he had done all his life, and he had died a wealthy man. Frank had taken his advice to heart and had followed it all these years. Before they got married in 2000, he and Dawn sat down and talked about money. She'd been raised in a very modest household and went to college on a scholarship; a lifetime of scrimping had made her a saver, too. Of the two of them, she was actually the more frugal, and she often worried they were spending too much on this or that. But Frank didn't mind buying expensive things occasionally, as long as they could afford it.

Dawn had earned a nice income as a financial advisor at Meridien Wealth Management. But after fifteen years in the corporate world—and five miscarriages—she had decided to stay at home with Cole. Frank supported her decision 100 percent, but if she ever changed her mind, as women often did, that was okay. They would do fine, either way. Luckily, they had banked most of her salary over the years and had used the rest for travel. Both felt secure with the large nest egg they had built.

They hadn't traveled anywhere since they brought Cole home, but just before Labor Day they were going down to Sea Gem for a week. Frank enjoyed it, once they got there; the only problem was that it was hard to get to the place. They had to fly to Jacksonville and then take I-95 north for an hour.

But when they arrived, he always felt it was worth the hassle. It was a beautiful spot, and the home was more like a private luxury resort than a beach house. It was a Spanish style, with cathedral ceilings and tiled floors, and it had been totally redone a few years ago. The home had six huge bedrooms, seven full baths, a pool, a tennis court, and even a separate guest cottage. It was perfect for family gatherings and for entertaining, and was a great place to go to escape the harsh Chicago weather. It would be pretty hot down there in early September, but unlike most Chicago residents, Frank didn't mind. He'd grown up in Atlanta, after all.

He shut off his laptop and rose from his desk. He had done all he could do for today. He put his Blackberry on his belt and turned to pick up his suit jacket. Then he felt the phone vibrate. He pulled it out and saw a new email.

Frank,

I've decided to sell my share in Sea Gem. Can you get in touch with Melody and let me know when the three of us can schedule a conference call?

Valerie

*

Melody woke up early Wednesday morning, but not to run in the Peachtree Road Race. Starting sometime in the early '70s, the popular 10k was held every Fourth of July. She had run in it only once, over twenty years ago, back when she was in high school and living in her parents' house on Sherwood Circle.

It was the year before her mother had gotten sick, and Melody had never run in another race since. She'd been too busy taking care of her mom the following summer, and from then on, she lost her motivation to train. After marriage and kids, it became next to impossible to find time to go running regularly. For exercise, she preferred to play tennis. She was a decent player, and she hoped to join the neighborhood ALTA (Atlanta Lawn Tennis Association) team, if only she could carve out the time.

Today promised to be hot and humid, typical for Atlanta in July. The pool would be filled with kids, and the deck would be loaded with groups of teenagers who would huddle together, away from their parents. Like Melody and her friends used to do.

She walked downstairs and joined Jeff, who was sitting at the kitchen table with a cup of coffee. Four-year-old Nick sat next to him, eating a bowl of cereal. He looked up and flashed a bright smile. "Morning, Mom!"

"Good morning, sweetie." She fished for her favorite mug out of the cabinet, filled it almost to the top, and then added some low-fat creamer. "Happy Fourth of July."

"When are we going to the pool?"

"Hold your horses, bud," said Jeff. "It's still early. We've got all day."

"But the kids' games start at eleven!"

"That's hours from now," Melody said. The dull wine headache she'd woken up with had almost cleared up, thanks to two Advil. Some coffee would finish the job. "I've got some things to do around the house, and then we'll get ready to go. Okay?"

Nick frowned. "O—kay." His face fell.

Jeff smiled at his wife. "I'll take everyone down before eleven, if you want. You can come on down when you're ready."

The pool was within walking distance, if you cut behind some neighbors' yards; Matt had already figured out which ones, and that the neighbors didn't mind. A well-worn path ended behind the tennis courts, next to the pool.

"That would be good. You guys walk, and I'll drive down about noon. I'll bring sandwiches and Cokes."

"I thought there was gonna be a barbecue!" said Nick.

His father put down his mug. "There is. But that's not until dinner time."

Melody gave Jeff a look. "He's going to be exhausted by the time of the fireworks."

"Let's play it by ear," Jeff said. "Nick and I can come home for a couple of hours and chill if we need to."

"I wanna stay at the pool all day long!" exclaimed Nick.

Melody walked over to the table. "We'll see."

*

At just after noon, Melody pulled her bronze Infiniti SUV into the pool parking lot. She grabbed her tote and cooler, and then spotted Jeff sitting by himself at an umbrella table. She walked over to join him.

He took the cooler from her and put it on the table. She sat down in a chair. "Did you remember to put sunscreen on them?"

He nodded. "What did you bring for lunch?"

"Fruit, turkey sandwiches, and chips. Cokes and waters." There were Sprites, Ginger Ales and Diet Cokes in the cooler, but in Atlanta, all carbonated drinks were called Cokes, whether they were Coca-Colas or not. She'd never stopped referring to them as Cokes, and no one down here called them pop or soda. "The kids can eat during adult swim."

The hourly fifteen-minute interval gave the lifeguards a much-needed break on busy days like this one.

"I'm sure they're working up an appetite," said Jeff.

Melody glanced around. "It's so crowded today."

A second later, a petite, thirty-something blonde woman wearing a turquoise one-piece approached their table and smiled. "Hi, there! I wanted to introduce myself, and welcome you all to the neighborhood. I'm Stacy Wagner. I saw the moving truck in front of y'all's house. My family lives two doors down from you."

Jeff and Melody stood. "I'm Melody Perkins, and this is my husband, Jeff."

Jeff smiled. "Would you like to sit down?"

Stacy sank into a tan chair, and Jeff and Melody sat back down. "My husband's name is Glen. He's over there in the deep end, playing with our son, Yardley, and with our nephew, Sonny." She motioned toward the pool. "Our daughter, Waverley, is over there, playing with your girls, I think? Are they twins?"

"Yes," Jeff said. "Pip and Neely are seven. How old is Waverley?"

"She's seven, too. What sweet names!"

Jeff smiled. "Pip's real name is Priscilla, and Neely's is Danielle."

"Even more adorable. Are they your only children?"

Melody shook her head and glanced toward the pool. Should she bring up what happened last summer? How they'd gone from two to four kids, overnight? She glanced at Jeff. *Not now.* "We have two sons, also. Matt's eight and Nick is four. He's in the shallow end."

Stacy glanced at the pool. Her eyes were wide. "Wow, you all sure have your hands full! Four kids, eight and under? Well, they'll all have to join the neighborhood swim team next summer. The season just ended last week. Where did y'all move here from?"

"Charlotte," said Jeff. "But Melody grew up here."

"Oh really? What area?"

"Over in Buckhead. It's good to be back in Atlanta."

"We like it here. I grew up in Decatur. We moved up to Brookhaven when Yardley was a baby."

"Hey, Dad!" called Matt. "Get in!"

"Stacy, it was very nice to meet you. Excuse me, ladies." Jeff stood and slipped off his T-shirt. He headed toward the water. "Coming!"

Melody turned to Stacy. "How old is Yardley?"

"Nine. Sonny's eight."

"Does Sonny live in the neighborhood, too?"

"No. His mom is my sister, Kristin. She and her husband Chip live over in Morningside, but they came up to spend the day with us. They've also got a two-year-old girl, Sawyer. She's in the baby pool." Stacy threw a glance in that direction and looked back at Melody. "Are y'all staying for the barbecue?"

Melody nodded. "If Nick can make it that long."

"Oh, I'm sure he can. Looks like Matt's started playing with Yardley and Sonny now." She motioned toward the boys.

Melody smiled. Kids were such great icebreakers. Over the next hour, she learned a lot about Stacy's family, and more about the neighborhood. Stacy played on the ALTA women's doubles team and told Melody who to contact about joining it. She had five sisters, three brothers, and tons of nieces and nephews, ranging in age from two to twenty-six.

Melody also heard about the local schools. Yardley and Waverley went to a nearby Episcopal school, and Sonny went to St. Bede's Catholic School, where Matt, Pip, Neely, and Nick were enrolled in this fall. Fortunately, all four had been admitted after the official spring application deadline.

The lifeguard blew the whistle for adult swim, and Kristin walked over and joined the women. Stacy introduced her sister, who was a taller, slimmer version of herself with a stronger southern accent.

Stacy gave her sister a stern look. "You ought to get Sawyer out of the sun, Kristin."

Kristin raised her eyebrows. "Don't worry, Sis. I *coated* her with sunscreen. Chip's taking her to play over in the shade. He's watching her now and giving me a break."

Stacy cocked her head. "Isn't she going to take a nap?"

Kristin shrugged. "She doesn't *take* naps anymore. Won't sleep during the day—afraid she's gonna miss something!" Kristin shook her head and offered a what're-ya-gonna-do face.

Stacy smiled. "So, Kristin. Melody's children are going to St. Bede's this fall."

Kristin looked at Melody. "Really? What grades?"

"Matt's in third, and the girls are in second. Nick's in pre-K."

Kristin's brows shot up. "You have four kids?"

Melody nodded and smiled. "We stay pretty busy."

"I bet you do! Sonny's gonna be in third grade, too. Maybe they'll be in the same class!"

Conversation continued and revolved around kids, schools, and families. Before it was time for margaritas and barbecue, Melody learned more about school, the neighborhood, and Stacy's and Kristin's sisters. One was single, and the others were married with kids. One sister had six kids under twelve years old.

"Jody's the nuttiest of all of us," Stacy said, with a grin. "It's *always* crazy over there."

Melody smiled. "It's pretty crazy at our house, too. I can't imagine having even one more child than I have."

"I feel the same way, with just two," said Kristin. "How did you handle having twins, only a year after having your first baby? And then—what were the girls, only three years old when Nick was born?"

Melody shook her head. *Just get it over with.* "I mean, yes, they were. But we didn't have the girls then. They're our nieces. We adopted them last summer after their parents were killed in a car accident."

Stacy's hand flew to her mouth. "Oh my goodness! How tragic!"

"Yes," Melody said. "It was awful. Their mother was Jeff's twin sister, and his only sibling. The girls' other aunts and uncles are much older than us. They all have grown children."

"Oh my Lord. What y'all must have been through," exclaimed Kristin. "I'm so sorry for your loss."

"Thank you. It's definitely been an adjustment, for all of us. But things are a lot better now."

"*Mama!*" called Waverley. "When are you getting in the water?"

Stacy waved at her daughter. "Later, baby. Go play, now."

*

Valerie was furious. She hadn't heard back from Frank since she had sent that email two days ago. She wasn't surprised, though. His pattern had always been to ignore her. All his life, he had treated her with either disdain or indifference.

She was seventeen months older, but with her birthday in March and his in August, he was only a grade younger: Ginger had pushed him into kindergarten days after he turned five. Back then, the cutoff date was in September, so maybe she hadn't had a choice. Melody was still a baby at the time, so Ginger was probably glad to get Frank into school along with Valerie. Before and since then, Valerie had competed with him for the spotlight, and for their father's attention.

When she got it, Frank seemed uninterested; when he did, he acted like she didn't exist. In front of their father, he was the model son, but away from him, he was a jerk and a tattletale. He'd been protective and almost sweet to his baby sister Melody, but he had always been condescending toward Valerie.

In high school, he ceased dealing with her at all. Perhaps he was more secure than she had been then, or maybe he had just been distracted. He avoided her and seemed ashamed to admit that she was his sister. When she got into Duke, he was unimpressed. But he had looked forward to Valerie's departure with as much excitement as she had, if not more. During the years both were away at school, he took every opportunity to bash her to their father, and waged a campaign to best her.

When she moved back to Atlanta in her twenties, Frank was out of college and living in Chicago. A few years later, he married Dawn, and they had been up there ever since. Dawn was one of those people to whom Valerie had taken an instant, strong dislike. Over the years, that feeling had only intensified, and now she could barely stand the woman.

Dawn had probably advised Frank not to respond to Valerie's email—it would be just like her to do that. Valerie hadn't copied Melody on it because she didn't want to invite a crazed, biting reply-all response from her. Now, though, she wished she had. Maybe she could put up with Melody's histrionics, if that's what it took to get a conference call done, and get this discussion over with.

Then again, maybe she couldn't deal with Melody yet. She decided to give her brother a few more days to get back to her about a date and time when they could schedule a three-way call.

Valerie had no plans for the Fourth of July. She had slept late, and her fitness club was closed; the office would be open tomorrow, of course. Last week's disastrous event was still fresh in everyone's minds. Josh was distracted, and Graham and Sophie had darted around for the last two days, trying to mitigate the damage in morale and to keep people on task. Valerie had been shaken to the core and had found it hard to concentrate on her job. Her team was unmotivated, and unsure of what to do.

On top of everything else, she was incensed that she couldn't get the funds her father had promised her. Why in God's name had he left *all* of his money to June? And why was there a restriction on the trust that kept June from making a loan? Surely he hadn't decided to place that condition; maybe it was standard, and he hadn't even realized it was there.

Was it a legal thing? Some law, that prevented a surviving spouse from lending money from a trust? If so, maybe there was a loophole, and perhaps David knew what it was. Not that he would tell her. But even if there were a loophole—or if there *were* no such law—June still had the right to decline making a loan, just as she had said no to giving money to Valerie. But if it *was* a legal thing, June's hands were tied.

Either way, Valerie wasn't getting the money.

Of course, Jim Mitchell hadn't planned to die as young as he did. He had been a fit man, and in good shape. He had stopped smoking years ago, and he drank only red wine. He might have thought he would live for another twenty years, minimum. He had probably assumed that by the time he died, Valerie—and his other children—would have built their own fortunes. Evidently, he had decided that June would need his money the most when he passed. Maybe he had even thought he would outlive her.

If only he had.

5

News

Melody couldn't believe that another week was over.

In no time, school would start, and so would sports, scouts, and other activities. Pip and Neely had been Daisies in North Carolina, and they wanted to join the Brownie troop here. Matt had played baseball in Charlotte, and the fall Little League season started next month. Stacy had told Melody who to get in touch with about it and assured her that it wasn't too late to sign up.

Melody put a load of laundry in the washer and hung the beach towels up to dry. She had met a few other moms in the neighborhood and had seen them at the pool again today. She'd spent the afternoon there with the kids, to get them out of the house and to tire them out. It was boiling outside, too hot to do anything but swim. But this weekend, she had to get busy on the house and get it completely organized.

Jeff would be out of town on business for a few days next week, and he had two more trips scheduled before the end of July. His travel with this new job was going to increase, with frequent trips up north and out west, and sometimes to London. They had talked about it before he accepted the position, and she'd assured him that she would be able to handle things during his absences. The truth was, although she missed him when he was gone, she didn't really mind occasional short breaks from each other. She could make macaroni and cheese for the kids for dinner, and fix a salad for herself. She could leave her bed unmade if she wanted to, and she had more time to read.

When Jeff returned from a business trip though, she was always glad to have him back. They had always been good team, a perfect mix of romance and companionship. Rather than drive them apart, what they'd been through last summer had brought them closer. Years ago, they had agreed to be his sister's kids' guardians, if anything ever happened. And you never knew what life would bring.

Jeff had been devastated when Heather and Keith were tragically killed by a truck driver who fell asleep at the wheel. Of course, Melody had been deeply saddened, too. The months that followed were difficult for everyone. When they brought the girls home, Melody's life had completely changed, and few but Jeff understood the challenges she had faced. Somehow, though, they had made it through the last year.

Yes, she was still in love with the man she married over eleven years ago. Having grown up with a twin sister, Jeff seemed to understand women a little better than the typical man did: his stated aim was to please Melody. He believed in "happy wife, happy life," and of course, so did she.

Melody walked into the den to check on the kids, all of them sitting in front of the TV. They were beat, but luckily not sunburned. Nick looked exhausted. Hopefully, he would go to bed early.

She stepped back into the kitchen to get dinner started. It was almost six o'clock, and Jeff would be home soon. Her cell phone buzzed. She picked it up from the counter.

"Melody, I'm glad I caught you."

"Hey, Frank. What's up?"

"I got an email from Valerie the other day, and I'm forwarding it to you now. I meant to do it then, but it's been a crazy week."

"What's it about?"

"She wants to sell her third of Sea Gem."

"What? You're kidding."

"No. She wants to schedule a conference call with the two of us. I haven't responded to her email."

"Are you saying she wants you and me to buy her out?"

"I guess. I don't know."

Melody sat down at the kitchen table. "How much money are we talking about?"

"Well, last year, the house was valued at six million dollars."

"Meaning, what? She wants a million from each of us?"

"I suppose so."

Melody's jaw dropped. "Why would she want to do this? Dad left the house to all of us, to *use* it. Not so that we could buy each other out."

"I guess she doesn't want to use it. Sounds like she'd rather have the money."

"I thought she was doing fine."

"Me too. But, you know, she quit her job last year and went with a startup. I read in the Journal that their IPO was canceled. It's big news."

"Do you think she's in trouble financially?"

"I can't imagine she is. She's always been a spender, but as far as I know, she's not *that* big a risk taker. I assume she can afford to keep up her lifestyle. Maybe she's just stressed. In any case, I need to respond to her email. Maybe we could schedule a call for next weekend?"

Melody paused for a second. "Do you think she'll agree to wait a week?"

"She'll have to, if we tell her to. I'd like to push it off for a few days anyway, to give her time to chill, and to give myself time to do some research."

"Okay. Weekends are kind of busy for me. But if you tell me what time, I could make sure I'm available."

"I will."

"Frank—if *we* don't buy her out, do you think she'll try to sell to someone else? I mean, can she?"

"I'm not sure. We're tenants in common with equal shares, and there are some restrictions. If she is able to sell to an outsider, it could mean subdividing the property."

"I don't want to do that! Do you?"

"No. But I don't want to part with a million bucks."

"Me, neither."

"Look. I'll call David Shepherd and ask what the restrictions are. I'll let you know what he says before I answer her email."

"Okay. Thanks."

Melody clicked off the phone, took in a deep breath, and exhaled.

What was the matter with Valerie? Didn't she understand that Sea Gem was supposed to stay in the family? She had always liked going down there when they were kids. Even if she didn't anymore, how could she be so selfish and parsimonious about it? She just couldn't be allowed to sell her share—surely, their father had been specific about that in his will. As far as the money, well, Melody knew that Frank and Dawn did very well financially, and Jeff made beaucoup. Pip's and Neely's insurance money was more than enough for their expenses and private school costs, and their parents had put a ton of money aside for them for college.

Even so, a million dollars was a million dollars.

Valerie had had a successful career, and she must have a bunch of money. She'd had no one to support but herself, and she lived an opulent lifestyle. Obviously, she was doing this to exert power over Melody and Frank. If she were allowed to sell her third of Sea Gem to an outsider, then Frank and Melody must at least have some say about who that outsider could be.

As for the two of them buying her out, that could only happen if they both agreed.

*

That evening, Jeff concurred with Melody's take on her sister's motives. "Why else would she be doing this?"

Melody picked up her wine glass and took a sip. "I have no idea. She's certainly not broke. Frank said he read that her company's IPO was canceled, but—"

"It was? That almost never happens. What's the name of the company again?"

"I don't know. I think it's a technology startup."

"I'm going to google 'canceled IPO.'" He grabbed his iPad and began tapping. "PriceUtopia?"

Melody got up from the sofa, walked toward him, and looked over his shoulder. He had found a *Wall Street Journal* online piece detailing the voided IPO. "That's it."

Both of them skimmed the article. A minute later, she said, "What do you think this means for Valerie?"

"I don't know. This is incredible."

"Frank said it was big news."

"It's huge. Wow–a major investor pulled their order. I don't know how I missed this. It's interesting that, right after this happens, she emails your brother about selling her share in the house. I guess it means she could be feeling a pinch."

Melody stared at Jeff. "So, since she's not going to make a bundle from an IPO, the rest of us are supposed to come to the rescue? I'm sure Dad didn't want a scenario where Frank and I could only keep Sea Gem by paying her a million dollars each! And I *know* he wouldn't want it subdivided!"

"I agree. Let's wait and see what Frank finds out. Whatever the restrictions are, she can't *force* you guys to buy her out. I'm sure you have at least some power over what happens to the house."

"I hope so. I want to keep it in the family. I *know* that's what Dad wanted."

6

No Complaints

On Monday, July 9, Josh walked into his office, shut the door, and sat down at his desk. Over the last week, he had spent much more time with Sophie Prejean than he had wished to.

She wasn't all that difficult to manage, thank God. She did as she was told, and she had a real knack for handling social media. Controlling the narrative was more important than ever now. However, afraid to commit a blunder, Sophie had come to him for direction a lot more often than she had in the past. The girl wasn't unattractive, but she wasn't hot, either. She wore too much makeup, and she had a severe, Frenchwoman kind of quality about her, and not in a good way. Her mussy dark hair was cut short and was the opposite of sexy. And she was on the clingy side, especially when stressed. Everyone at the office was stressed though, and with good reason.

Josh had been busy over the last few days trying to calm the company's investors. He had spoken to Adam Langford again late Friday afternoon. Adam had voiced deep concerns about the company's future, and he had expressed more doubt than anger. Like Josh and Graham, he wanted answers. Josh hadn't mentioned the traitor idea, but he wondered if the possibility had crossed Adam's mind.

But if someone *had* leaked proprietary information, what could they do? Fire the person, of course, but not until they knew what exactly had been divulged. He and Graham had already started investigating, and so far they had learned nothing.

Josh picked up his coffee cup and pushed his panicky feelings away. He had to stay the course right now, and it was time to get to work. Checking his laptop, he hoped to see no new messages from Valerie. That woman's behavior made Sophie's appear laid back. Earlier, she had fired off an email asking him about funding. Didn't she realize it was his number one priority?

The door to his office opened. Valerie walked in, shut the door, and perched on the chair across from him. Her lips were pursed, and her thin blouse was open, exposing soft cleavage outlined by a kind of lacy underthing. Those breasts weren't fake.

He gazed at them for a second, and then raised his eyes. "I'm busy right now."

"Take a break. We need to talk."

"No, Valerie, we *don't* need to talk. We need to work, so—"

She raised a palm. "It's been ten days. I don't see us making any progress."

"Let me worry about it, and you get back on task."

"I *am* on fucking task! I'm calling on retailers and getting appointments set up, like I've done for months. But considering our black mark and all the press coverage we've had, it's gotten very fucking hard to get *anyone* to take me or any of my sales staff seriously."

"With the passage of time–"

"What? They'll forget all about it? I don't think so– in fact, I *know* so. You need to apprise me of the plan, so I can do my job."

Josh stared at her, his ice blue eyes stony. "The plan is fluid, and you know it."

Her voice turned shrill. "What does *that* mean? It sounds like you have no clue about what to do."

He set his jaw. "This is ridiculous. You work for me, not the reverse."

Her eyes glazed, and the vein on her forehead throbbed. "Whatever. I took a big chance, coming to work here. I deserve to know what's going on."

It took everything he had not to react. "There is nothing going on that you don't already know about."

"Goddamn it, Josh! Shit needs to be going on! You need to come up with a new plan, *today*."

"I'm working on a new plan, and getting upset at me won't help. Are you worried about money or something? Your money, I mean?"

Valerie bit her lip. "My personal situation is fine."

"I would think it ought to be. You told me a year ago that you were in a very good position. You had just been on a European vacation. You drive a brand new BMW, buy expensive clothes, and live in a pricey neighborhood. You told me you expected to inherit a ton of money from your father one day. When he died last fall, I assumed you did."

Valerie huffed. "It's complicated."

He gave her a measured look. *What did that mean? How complicated?* He hadn't grown up with money, and her extravagant taste had bothered him, early in their relationship. Considering what they were going through at the company right now, her habits and attitudes about money were irritating, and entitled. "Whatever. That's none of my business. Now please, let me get back to work."

"This conversation isn't over," she threatened.

Josh trained his eyes on his laptop, determined not to look at her again. He heard the door open and close, and then let out a relieved sigh, grateful for solitude. He would do whatever he had to do to ensure success for the company. Then, after he made enough money, he could find himself another woman. Hell, Valerie was *his* age, and she was getting older every day. He needed a younger, sexier, and more beautiful woman. But first, he had to earn the money to get one.

It was a crass thought, but that was okay. It was true—women *did* cost money. The younger and more attractive they were, the more they cost. His last girlfriend was five years younger than Valerie, but she wasn't nearly as sexy. Valerie was in shape and had an attractive body, for a woman her age. But the way she made him feel—the way she treated him—had changed over the months they had been together. She had become complacent about their relationship, and she often took it for granted. When she wanted to have sex—which was frequently—they had it. No complaints from him about that. And when *he* wanted it, she almost always consented.

No, his objection to staying with her long term wasn't a physical one. It was mental. When she went off on him at work, the way she had just done, it was one thing. At best, it was uncomfortable. But when she did it when they were away from the office, it was way, way worse.

Like when she'd had a fit over the kind of flowers he gave her for her birthday last March. He had always been a flowers-giving kind of guy. It seemed to work with all women–all, that is, except Valerie. When he walked into her condo carrying two dozen red roses, she had snarled at him. She had screamed that she "couldn't believe he didn't know" that she *hated* that flower.

How was he supposed to have known? And, what woman didn't like roses? They'd had a huge argument, and she accused him of ruining her birthday on purpose. According to her, he somehow should have known that the only flowers she liked were tulips and orchids. And since then, she hadn't let him forget it.

He shuddered. He couldn't tolerate that kind of behavior, at least not permanently. And one day, he might want to have kids. Why not, once he made his own fortune and got rich? Valerie was too old to have children, and, truth told, he wouldn't want to have them with her, anyway.

He pushed away thoughts of a future partner and possible family, and focused on his agenda. Stewart Young had told him and Graham on Friday that finding another blue chip mutual fund to invest in the company was going to be next to impossible. He had suggested they go back to Swift in a few weeks, and ask Julian Stone for a chunk of funds to tide them over. The venture capitalist firm had invested twelve million in them a year ago, so perhaps they'd be open to putting in fifteen to twenty more.

Later this morning, Graham was going to update Josh on the status of the new release, which was planned for early November. The pricing systems interface was going to allow their clients to share price matching data in real time with the rest of their stores nationwide. As for Sophie, she would have to start using her own judgment about social media posts, and stop coming to Josh for approval. He had neither the time nor the desire to micromanage her.

*

On Saturday morning, Jeff took the girls to the vet with him for Napoleon's annual checkup and vaccines. Melody hadn't wanted to take the dog last summer, but the girls had been so full of grief that she couldn't bring herself to say no. The dog was a wheaten terrier, great with the kids, but unused to hot weather. Jeff had promised he would take care of him and that he would have the girls help.

Melody couldn't remember a more awful time than last July—including when she had lost her parents. When her mother died, she was only eighteen and had just graduated from high school. She had helped her father take care of her while she was sick, a period that lasted most of Melody's senior year. Frank and Valerie had been away in colleges far from home. When Ginger finally succumbed to cancer, at least the family had had months ahead of time to prepare for it, and to say goodbye.

But how did you deal with losing both your parents so suddenly and tragically, when you were only six years old? The funerals had been terribly sad, and the girls had been inconsolable. Keith Redmond's brothers and their families came in from out of town, and so did several cousins on both sides of the family. Tears flowed freely in the church, which was packed with relatives, friends, and the girls' schoolteachers and classmates.

It was a blessing that Pip and Neely already knew their Uncle Jeff and Aunt Melody. Between photos, frequent phone calls, and occasional vacations together, the Perkins and the Redmonds had become close over the years. But it was a different thing to vacation with another family than it was to live with them. The girls were jettisoned into a different part of the country, had had to go to a new school, and had to say goodbye to their friends and former life. Now they would have to go to yet another new school, and would have to make new friends all over again.

Melody heard the front door swing open and a scramble of feet and paws on the hardwood floor.

"We're home," called Jeff.

She stepped to the sink to put some dishes in the dishwasher. "I'm in here. How did Napoleon do?"

"He did terrific," Jeff replied. "He's at his ideal weight, too."

Pip knelt down to pet the dog, his big brown eyes partially covered by wisps of fur. "Can I take him for a walk?"

"Yes, but I'm going with you," said Jeff. "Want to come too, Neely?"

"Okay."

"I'll get lunch ready while y'all are gone."

"Come on, Napoleon!" Pip said. "Let's go."

The dog turned around in a frenzied circle, then trotted alongside her toward the door.

Melody walked into the den and found Nick sitting in front of the television. Matt was on the sofa reading a book. "I'm going to make some lunch, and we'll all go to the pool this afternoon."

"I'm hungry!" said Nick.

"It'll be ready soon," Melody assured him. She heard her cell phone ding. There was a text from her brother. *Are you available tomorrow at 2 for the conference call?*

7

In the Family

At one forty-five the next day, Jeff was at a matinee with the kids. Frank was going to ring Melody when he had Valerie on the line.

Later this afternoon, Stacy's cleaning lady, Sonia, was coming over so that Melody could meet her and decide if she wanted to hire her. Stacy had her come to clean her house twice a month. Melody hadn't had a maid in Charlotte, but she and Jeff agreed that it was a necessity here.

Melody started the dishwasher. She didn't mind loading it–she had a certain way of doing that, and she didn't let anyone else put even one cup in. No one–including Jeff–knew how to load it efficiently, not only to get everything clean but to minimize the number of times it had to be run. However, she hated emptying it. She made a mental note to add that chore to the daily task list she was devising for the kids. She planned to make a big chart and put it in the kitchen at their eye level.

She filled a glass with water and sat down at the table with her iPhone. It was almost time for Frank to call.

Then the phone buzzed. "Frank?"

"Hi, Melody. Valerie's on the line."

"Hello," said Valerie.

"Hi," said Melody.

There was an awkward pause. Then Valerie spoke. "So, this is about me selling my share in Sea Gem."

"Frank told me."

There was another awkward silence.

"Valerie, Melody and I have talked about it, and neither of us would like to buy you out."

Valerie huffed. "I don't know why you wouldn't. It can't be because of the money."

"Actually, it can," Melody said, "but it's not just the money. The house is supposed to stay in the family—"

"It *can* stay in the family. All you have to do is buy out my share. If you don't, then I guess it may not."

"Look," said Frank. "I spoke with David Shepherd. He advised me that none of us can sell our share on the open market."

"So you two have a decision to make. Either buy me out for a total of two million dollars, or we agree to sell the property and divide the proceeds."

"That's not going to happen," said Melody.

"I can file a suit—"

"What are you *talking* about?" asked Melody.

"I've already consulted my lawyer. If we can't agree, I'll sue. A court will direct us either to sell it and split the money, or to subdivide it and allow me sell my part."

"Valerie," said Frank, "I can't believe you would do that."

"Well, you need to believe it. Sea Gem is not some kind of a shrine to the Mitchell family, and I own a third of it."

Melody gritted her teeth. "Suing the two of us is not what Dad wanted, and you know it. The world doesn't revolve around you, Valerie."

"Melody, you need to back off."

"*You* back off."

"Hey," Frank said, "Let's stick to the subject, okay? Subdividing the property isn't practical, I think we all know. I don't see how a court could order that done, Valerie."

"All I know is, I want my share of what it's worth. And I'm certain you two can afford to buy me out."

"You *don't* know that," said Melody. "Don't make assumptions."

"I'm the one who's a victim of assumptions here. Everybody–including Daddy–assumed that I wanted to share the house with you. Nothing could be farther from my wishes."

"That's clear," said Frank. "But we have wishes, too. Threatening us with a lawsuit isn't going to help us resolve this."

"It's not a threat. It's a promise."

"Valerie," said Frank, "if you do that, it will drive a wedge between us. I don't think any of us want that to happen."

"Get real, Frank. There's already a wedge between us. You never communicate with me, and even though Melody just moved here, she hasn't reached out to me once, or tried to get together."

Melody's jaw dropped. *Who does Valerie think she is? And since when does she want to hang out?* "I've been busy, Valerie! I know you have, too."

"How long does it take to make a call or send a message?"

"You could have reached out to me, too, but you didn't."

"I was afraid to, Melody! You're so controlling! Obviously, you don't see that about yourself."

*No—*she *doesn't see that about herself. She's projecting, as usual.* "You're the one who's controlling! You're trying to control us!"

Frank cut in. "Let's all just calm down. Valerie, I'm not buying you out, and I don't think Melody will, either. So—"

"So we'll see what the judge decides."

Frank continued, "Fine. I guess we will."

"This is nuts," said Melody. "The house stays in the family, and no matter what you do, we're not buying you out."

"You both have the money to do it, yet you're forcing me to stay part owner in a property that I don't use, and don't want!"

"You're unbelievable," Melody said. "Again, this isn't just about money, and my financial situation is none of your business! This is about keeping Sea Gem in the family, Valerie. It's not something that can be carved up. *We* plan to use it. If you don't, that's your choice. It's not my problem, nor is it Frank's."

"Daddy didn't specifically state in his will that he wished for Sea Gem to stay in the family," said Valerie. "Instead, he chose to leave it to us in three equal shares."

"Exactly. He didn't choose to give *you* an amount of money equal to the value of your share," said Melody.

"Apparently, June manipulated him into leaving all his money to her."

"Whatever his reasons were, I know he didn't intend to put you in the driver's seat, and me and Melody in the back."

"Any one of us could do this, Frank. I have a right to sell my share."

"If we all agree to sell Sea Gem at some point in the future, you'll get your third of the money then," Frank said. "We don't agree right now—"

"So, you'll hear from my lawyer."

"Valerie, can't you see our side? Jeff and I have four children. Where else are we going to take them for family vacations? Don't you want to keep going to Sea Gem for vacations with your nieces and nephews? Now that Frank and Dawn have Cole—"

"Don't presume to know what I want, Melody. I'm not some actor in your little fantasy world. Matt and Nick are my nephews. They're related to me. The children you adopted aren't, and neither is Cole."

"Just a minute. Cole is my son—"

"He's not *my* blood," said Valerie.

"Thank God for that," Frank said slowly, his voice cold. "This conversation is over. Do what you will, Valerie, but you're not getting any money out of me—nor will I allow you to force a sale."

"We'll see about that. I'm hanging up. You two can keep on bitching if you like."

Melody heard a click. "Frank? Are you still there?"

"Yeah."

"God. I'm amazed by what she said about the kids. You know, now it's making sense to me that she still sends birthday presents to my boys, yet she didn't send anything to the girls."

"To hell with her."

"Can she really sue?"

"I'm afraid so," said Frank. "A judge could conceivably force a sale. I don't see how the property could be subdivided, though."

"I don't want it to be sold, *or* subdivided! That property belongs to us. Don't you think it will matter to the judge that two of us want to keep it?"

"I don't know, but I wouldn't count on it."

"What can we do?"

"I guess we have to wait and see what she does. I'm not budging on buying her out, though. I was prepared to pay a third of the annual taxes and upkeep, but that's all."

"Us, too. Twenty grand a year is plenty."

"If the judge does force a sale, I'm not sure it would bring six million, either. The market for luxury oceanfront properties is pretty soft. The judge might even order it to be sold at auction."

"That's totally unacceptable."

"Maybe we can figure out a different solution, and persuade her not to sue."

"What kind of a solution?"

"Let me think about it. Talk to you later, okay?"

"All right. Thanks."

*

Valerie detested having her feelings dismissed by her siblings, both of whom seemed intent on getting their way. They had made her wait over a week for the conference call, and then they had ganged up on her, as they had done so many times in the past. She knew they talked about her, and they didn't care that she did. Neither one of them had an ounce of empathy, nor were they interested in understanding her point of view.

Why shouldn't *they* want their shares of Sea Gem in cash, too? Selling the place wouldn't be very difficult. Then they could buy another vacation home, or do whatever they wanted with the funds. Why did she have to be held hostage to their desires, and to have her own so lightly discarded?

It was just like when they were kids. Their mother had always sided with them, and had believed them rather than Valerie, whenever there was a conflict. Her father had been her constant advocate, but when he was away on business—which was frequently—she had had to fend for herself. She had felt alone and unloved, isolated by the rest of the family. No wonder she had had to lie so much back then—it was the only way to survive. She only told white lies at first, but when she realized how easily others believed them, she told bigger ones, and told them more often. And once she started lying, she couldn't quit.

At some point, that began to haunt her. She had tossed in bed at night, worried that she was addicted to lying, and wondering whether she had created some different reality that would soon implode on her. She would resolve to stop telling lies starting the next day, but then something would always happen to make her do it again.

For years, she had blocked out memories of those nights. Eventually, she had cut way down on lying but never ceased completely. With effort, she pushed her memories away now, and chastised herself for letting them surface. She had to get out of the house—she would go and work out at her fitness club. She needed to relieve her stress and to recover from her conversation with her siblings. Josh was coming over at seven to take her out to

86

dinner. She was looking forward to that. Perhaps she would invite him to stay overnight.

Neither she nor Josh pretended to be in love. Only one man—boy, actually—had ever told Valerie that he loved her, and that was back in college, during her freshman year at Duke. Owen Crawford was three years older and had been her first real boyfriend. She had naively believed that they were meant for each other, and even that he would propose.

Then one winter night, when her roommate was away for the weekend, she and Owen got drunk on tequila shots. With the walls spinning and all her clothes on the floor, they did it in her dorm room. When they were done, Owen opened the door to a waiting line of six fraternity brothers hiding somewhere in the suite, and let each one take a turn with her. She didn't know what was happening until the first guy was inside of her. When she screamed and started punching, two more guys rushed into the room and held her down. She sobbed and scratched and begged for Owen, but he never came back to help her. When it was all over, she lay there bloody and nauseous. She stayed in bed the entire next day, crying and covered with bruises, and nursing the worst hangover of her life.

She didn't go to the police because she felt humiliated, and because she wanted to block out what happened. She couldn't prevent Owen and his buddies from talking about it, but she didn't want what had happened to become publicly known. She avoided Owen on campus, and they never saw each other again; thankfully, he graduated a few months later. She didn't let another man touch her until she was twenty-four years old.

When she did, she rediscovered sex, and she had men gratify *her* physical needs, not the reverse. She had a semi-serious boyfriend in her mid-twenties, and another one when she was in her thirties. But after a couple years, she realized that she couldn't put up with either one of them anymore—the romance was gone, and all they did was disappoint and irritate her. She dated several men in between, but she had hesitated to jump into another relationship until she met Josh.

She had only told one person about that horrible night in college with Owen and his friends—her father. She didn't regret that decision; it was hard to tell him, but it served the purpose she had intended. Then she locked the awful memory into a dark abyss of her heart and buried the key. She vowed to never let herself be used by anyone, ever again. She had also chosen to take full control of her sexuality. Sex was power, and she was going to exercise it, relish it, and enjoy it.

Valerie raced to the club and did an intense workout on the elliptical machine. When she got home, she stepped under a stream of hot water in the shower. At the club, she had willed away her worries about money, but as the bathroom filled with steam, the reality of her financial situation blanketed her consciousness like a thick wall of dense fog.

No one was going to use her or take advantage of her again. Frank and Melody were powerless to stop her from getting her way. She was going to get the money she was due as a third-owner of Sea Gem. No matter what.

8

A Control Thing

Wearing slim, dark jeans and a crisp, sky blue dress shirt, Josh arrived at Valerie's condo just after seven o'clock that evening.

"You're early," she said as she opened the door and ushered him inside.

He shrugged. "We said seven, didn't we?"

Valerie led him to the white galley kitchen and placed two rocks glasses on the black granite counter. "Would you fix our drinks while I finish getting ready?"

"Of course." He filled the glasses with ice as she headed across the adjacent living area and into her bedroom. Finding the Ketel One in its usual spot in the cabinet, he poured the liquid and garnished the drinks with a slice of lime he found in the fridge.

Drink in hand and hers waiting for her on the counter, he sat down on the cream-colored sofa. He sipped his cocktail. He had made a reservation at Ogden's, a hip new restaurant in Midtown. She had selected the place, and though he was fine with it, he knew it was going to be an expensive evening. She was aware that all his money was tied up in the company—and that he was taking little out—but she never offered to pay the tab when they went out. However, that was something he had accepted some time ago. Men paid the bill on dates, and he hadn't been brought up to expect otherwise. Valerie was an inheritance baby, and evidently, she believed money was always available, waiting to be spent on her.

His glass was half empty when she sauntered in, wearing a sleeveless, low-cut dark red dress that clung to her body like a goatskin glove. Did her clothes flatter her so much because they were expensive, or because her figure was nearly perfect? *Maybe it's a cause and effect, chicken or egg thing.*

She grabbed her drink and sank down into a dark leather chair directly across from him. "How do I look?"

Do women ever really want to know the truth? But she did look fantastic, and particularly sexy. "Awesome," he said. It was her favorite word to describe herself.

She flipped her hair back behind a shoulder. "I need to catch up to you, it looks like."

"I might have another little splash before we go."

"Suit yourself." She shut her eyes, then opened them and looked right at him.

"Something wrong?"

"No. I'm just annoyed about a phone call with my sister and brother. Not a big deal, though."

She never talked about her family, and he had learned not to ask; evidently, it was a sore subject. All he knew was that she and her sister didn't get along, that her mother died years ago, and that her father passed away last year. At the time, she'd been very distraught, but within a month, she was over it. He couldn't figure out if she was emotionally tough, or just unfeeling. Or both.

She picked up her iPad and started tapping, her eyes glued to the screen as she sipped her cocktail. He had never known a more distracted yet productive individual. Multi-tasker ought to be her middle name. He stood, walked back to the kitchen, and helped himself to that extra splash of vodka. He needed to relax, and the liquor was helping. He had gone for a six-mile run earlier today, and then played basketball at the gym. He planned to eat a decent dinner.

"Anything interesting?" he asked idly.

"Um," she said, not looking up. "Not really. Did you say Sophie was working on a press release?"

He nodded. "Let's not talk business tonight."

She looked up and cocked her head. Her lips were a tight line, and her eyes blazed.

"Let's down these drinks and get going. I'm hungry, and I'm looking forward to a nice bottle of wine."

"Fine," she said. Taking her glass with her, she rose and went into her bedroom. Josh drained his glass and set it on the coffee table.

Business was the last thing he wanted to talk about tonight. On Friday, he and Graham had spoken to Julian Stone at Swift and had made their appeal for funds. The conversation hadn't gone very well. Before he supplied them with any more money, Julian wanted the sixty-four thousand dollar question answered: What was the real reason Cornucopia pulled out of the IPO? The mystery threatened to haunt Josh and Graham indefinitely. They hadn't discovered a traitor in the company—yet—but neither were they convinced that one didn't exist. They hadn't mentioned their concern to Julian, though.

At Ogden's, a hostess showed Josh and Valerie to a corner table. It looked perfect to Josh, but he stood back and watched Valerie ask–no, order–the poor girl to seat them somewhere else. It never failed–Valerie always demanded a different spot in a restaurant than the one to which they were guided.

It didn't matter that much when they were alone, or when they arrived at a restaurant before another couple that was joining them. But even when they got there after others were seated, Valerie insisted on a different table. The last time it happened was when they met Josh's friend Tim and his girlfriend Lucy at Le Terrain in Brookhaven. Tim and Lucy were waiting for them out on the covered patio, drinking a glass of wine.

When Josh and Valerie arrived that evening, she walked outside, glared at the other couple, and motioned for them to get up and follow her to another table inside. Josh stood by with a sheepish look on his face. Confused, Tim waved them over to where they were sitting and pointed to the empty seats and the wine. Josh stole a glance at Valerie, who wore an exaggerated, exasperated expression. She had made up her mind and wouldn't take no for an answer. It was embarrassing, but Josh had learned to expect it. It was a control thing, but of course Valerie didn't see it that way. And you couldn't joke with her about it. God knew, he had learned *that* the hard way.

The waiter walked up just after they sat down at Ogden's. "Good evening. May I get you started with a cocktail?"

"Kir Royale," said Valerie.

"I'll have a Moscow Mule, please," Josh said.

The waiter trotted off and Valerie perused the menu. "Let's share a couple of appetizers," she said.

"Fine." Josh skimmed the choices. Before he could make a decision, Valerie motioned to another server hovering a few feet away, and caught his attention.

"Tell our waiter we want the shrimp cocktail and the fish tacos, to start with," she called.

The poor guy lifted his eyebrows, nodded, and scurried away. Josh gave Valerie a look, but she avoided his eyes, focusing on the menu again. You'd think he would be used to it by now. She often ordered appetizers for both of them, without bothering to consult him about what he wanted. If he protested, she whined about it. She also seemed to think she could veto his entree selection—if he chose something that she planned to order, she made him change his to something else. He was fine with the appetizers she wanted this time, but that wasn't the point. The point was that she took over, and put her own desires and wishes first.

Constantly.

His drink arrived, and he downed half of it while waiting for the waiter to return with their order. No matter how much Valerie irritated him or how selfishly she behaved, her body beckoned, and the sex was incredible. Was he so shallow that it made up for all the rest?

Maybe.

Hours later, moderately inebriated and satiated with food and sex, he stretched out in her queen-sized bed and fell sleep.

*

Dawn put Cole down for the night in his room, and then crept into bed with her husband.

"He's been a little fussier than usual lately," she said. "I think his first tooth is about to pop through."

"That's early, isn't it?" asked Frank.

"I think so. But it's not all that unusual." She turned off the lamp on her nightstand and snuggled up to him. "Let's pillow-talk."

"I thought you were tired."

"I am. I just want to talk a little, then fall asleep."

Frank let out a good-natured grumble. "I'd rather just fall asleep."

"Oh, come on," Dawn entreated. "Not for long."

Frank snuggled closer. "What do you want to talk about?"

"Well, what are you going to do about Valerie?"

"I don't know. I know she has the right to sue, and get a judge to order a sale of the house. I don't see how they could have the place subdivided, though."

"So, to prevent her from suing–"

"We would have to either buy her out, or talk her into keeping her share. I just can't believe she needs the money this badly."

"I can."

"Why?"

Dawn shifted a little and drew closer. "She's always seemed to spend more money than she has. At least, from what I can tell."

"Do you think she's in trouble with debt?"

"Who knows? Maybe. Or maybe she just wants the money as a cushion, like if she lost her job or something."

"If that happened, she'd get a new job in a month."

"Think so?"

"She's experienced, and she's very connected in her industry," Frank said. "I don't imagine she'd have any trouble. I don't think she's going to lose her job, anyway."

"But–that company. She must not be making all that much, not yet."

"She's set to make a bunch when they finally do go public. Which will happen. At least, I think it will."

"What if it doesn't? Maybe she's panicking right now."

"She's got to have some decent savings, and if she has debt, I'd be surprised if it were out of control. I think she'll land on her feet, no matter what happens at her job. She's like a cat–in more ways than one."

Dawn giggled. "I shouldn't laugh. I actually feel kind of bad for her."

"After how she told me that Cole wasn't really her nephew, since he wasn't her blood? Why?"

"Because–I don't know. Evidently, knowing someone is her blood relative is very important to her. It must have been so hard for her when she found out that your mom wasn't her biological mother."

"But that was over twenty years ago."

"Still. After all that time growing up, and not knowing the truth–"

Frank let out a deep breath. "I guess Dad should have told us all a lot earlier, but maybe he didn't because it was too painful. Back then, people just didn't tell their kids that kind of stuff–not while they were growing up, anyway. I'm sure it was something he tried to block out, too. I mean, he marries his high school sweetheart, and after they have a baby, she gets postpartum depression and commits suicide."

"Thank God he got through all of that, and then found your mom. But just think about how Valerie must have felt when she found out—and not until the woman she had always thought was her mother got very ill. It could be that she's never really gotten over it."

"I'm sure it was harsh, and was a very difficult time for her. I feel like she got worse, though, afterward. She's never been a happy person. But happy or not, she doesn't mind making other people unhappy."

Dawn ran her finger along Frank's jaw. "There's a reason she's doing this lawsuit. It's not just that she doesn't want to use Sea Gem, and I don't really think it's a control thing, either."

"Maybe it *is* about money," he said.

"I just don't see that. She's going to inherit a lot of that, eventually."

"*Eventually*. But not anytime soon." Frank pulled his wife closer still. "Let's not talk anymore. You don't seem as tired, now."

"I'm not," Dawn said, slithering out of her nightgown.

*

Late the next morning, June got a call from David Shepherd.

"How are you, David?"

"I am well. Hope you are, too."

"I'm fine. What's on your mind?"

"Well, I wanted to let you know that I just spoke to your stepson. He had some questions about the beach property he and his sisters inherited."

June sat down at her kitchen table. "Oh? I thought you and the lawyer went over all of that with them, months ago."

"We did. However, it sounds like Valerie wants to sell her share."

June paused. "Goodness. I wonder why she'd want to do that. Is it even possible?"

"It is, as I told Frank."

"I don't really understand. When she wanted money from me, I never thought—well. I'll let you enlighten me."

"Okay. Frank told me that the three of them had a conference call yesterday. Valerie asked if he and Melody wanted to buy out her share."

"Do they?"

"No. So she plans to file a suit to force them to sell the home."

Her pulse quickened. "A lawsuit? She's going to sue?"

"Unfortunately. Frank asked if I thought the property could be partitioned—subdivided, more or less—to prevent a sale. He's going to talk to a lawyer, but he wanted to check with me about Jim's specific instructions as to the home."

"As far as I know, Jim wanted Sea Gem to stay in the family, not only for the children, but also for the grandchildren."

"That's what I believe, too, but there was nothing specific to that effect in his will. In any case, Frank wondered if you might be interested in buying Valerie's share. I told him I'd check with you, but that I didn't think you would. Hope I was right."

June caught her breath. "Yes, you were. I have everything I need, and I don't want to get mixed up in Sea

Gem. Frank and Melody have told me they would invite me to visit sometimes, when they go down there. I don't want to go without being an invited guest, and I don't want to be a part-owner with them."

"I understand. That's exactly what I would advise."

"But—I *could* come to their rescue, I suppose. To keep it in the family."

"You could. If you do, though, it would be fairly complicated. You would have to finance it."

"You mean, get a loan? Why?"

"Because, despite what I told Valerie, though the trust doesn't prohibit you from making a loan, it doesn't allow you to use any of the funds for an additional real estate investment. You can sell your own home and buy another, but if you wanted to buy Valerie out of Sea Gem, you'd have to borrow against your home, or against the assets of the trust."

"No," said June. She pursed her lips. "That's completely out of the question."

"Right. Good decision. Well, glad I guessed correctly as to your answer. I'll let Frank know."

"Thanks so much, David."

*

Late Friday afternoon, Josh left the office early and drove down to Hartsfield airport to pick up Valerie.

She had flown to New York on Tuesday morning to reassure several clients who were upset about the failed IPO. Preferring not to leave her BMW in a lot at the airport, she had taken a taxi that day. Today, though, she had talked Josh into fighting the Friday rush hour traffic and coming to get her.

"Don't park and come wait for me inside," she had ordered on the phone. "And don't drive up the hill and around to the curbside check-in and drop-off area. Follow the signs to the lower level, pull over, and wait for me there. I'll text you when I land."

"Okay. If you don't see my car, I'll be on the way."

"Leave early enough to get there by 5:30! My flight gets in at 5:10, and I'm not checking my bag."

Unwilling to deal with her wrath, Josh had acquiesced to her demand and obeyed. He walked out the door at a quarter to five and joined the throng of cars stacked bumper to bumper heading south on the downtown connector. Forty-five minutes ought to be enough time. Once he got past the turnoff to I-20, traffic should pick up, and he would arrive at the airport on time.

Luckily, it did. He pulled off the highway at five twenty and made his way to the South Terminal for Delta. He bypassed the parking lot entrances, took a left into the lower level drive, and pulled over about halfway down in front of the entrance to an escalator. Ignoring the No Parking signs, he turned off the ignition. Valerie wouldn't be here for at least ten minutes, and he wasn't going to stay here with the motor running that long.

He pulled out his phone. Good—no texts. He opened his Twitter feed and began scrolling. Then he heard a tap on his car window.

It was a policeman—a security guard. The man pointed to the sign. "I'm sorry, sir. You can't park here."

Josh turned on the ignition and pushed the button to lower the window. "Oh, right. Sorry about that. I'm just waiting for someone. She'll be here shortly."

The cop shook his head. "No can do. Gotta move along."

"But, officer–"

He cocked his head. "Sir. I don't want to give you a ticket."

Josh sighed. "Okay, fine. I'll go."

The cop stepped away from the car as Josh pulled away slowly. Once he got to end of the drive, he glanced at his phone. It was five twenty-seven. Still no text from Valerie.

Fine. He would circle around the parking lots very slowly and pull over here again. She would text him soon, and if he needed to, he could circle around two or three more times. He would pull up just as she was walking out, and they would be off.

After the third time around, he began to get impatient. She still hadn't texted him, and now it was five forty. He had checked her flight online before he left the office, and it was scheduled to arrive a few minutes early. Surely it was on the ground and she was in the terminal by now.

He drove around the circle again and entered the lower level drive at five forty-six. There she was, her small red rolling bag at her side. Her face was fiery.

He pulled up and unlocked the doors. She threw her bag in the backseat and got in the passenger seat next to him.

"Where *were* you?" she snapped. "I've been waiting for at least five minutes!"

"I got here over twenty minutes ago. Why didn't you text me?"

"My phone died, but that's not the issue. You were supposed to be waiting for me."

"Valerie, I couldn't wait for you here. The cop wouldn't let me."

She glared at him. "Whatever. I've seen other people do it, so I *know* you could have figured it out."

Josh pressed his lips together and focused on the road. There was no traffic going north. They drove on in silence, and twenty minutes later, he pulled up to her condominium.

Wordlessly, she grabbed her purse and her suitcase from the back seat and slammed the car doors.

He drove away without looking back.

9

A Slam

August 1 was a Wednesday, and it was June's day to play bridge at the club.

Unlike most people of her generation, she had learned to play the card game while she was growing up. Her parents were both math teachers—her mother was an elementary school teacher, and her father taught high school calculus and statistics. Both were very good bridge players, and they taught their daughters the game. Jim had played bridge, too—it was one of the many activities that he and June did together.

Her partner today was Nancy, a redhead in her sixties who was married to Kip Jamison, president of Memorial Bank. Their opponents were Angela Sims, another banker's wife, and Lois Blair. Angela was June's age, but she looked ten years older, with thinning bleached blonde hair and a face weathered by major sun damage. Lois was slim, in her mid-seventies, and had olive skin and dark, dyed hair. Two years ago, she had lost Ty, her husband of fifty years and a top executive at Coke. Lois was recognized as the best bridge player in the group, if not in the whole club.

"June," she exclaimed. She smiled as June walked up to the table and took the seat to Lois' right, across from Nancy. "You look so beautiful this morning!"

June flashed her a warm smile. "Thanks, Lois! You're such a doll. You look beautiful today, too. What a lovely necklace."

Lois laughed. "Flattery will get you nowhere, my dear. Prepare to get beat." She looked slyly across the table at Angela, a sparkle in her eye. "Right, partner?"

Angela nodded. "Whatever you say, Lois. I'll do my best to keep up." She fanned the cards out face down on the table. Everyone picked a card. Nancy drew the highest, a Jack. She slid the other deck to her right for Lois to cut, and June gathered the other cards to shuffle.

Nancy began to deal. "So, what's new with everybody?"

"Well, I just booked a two-week Viking River cruise for Hugh and me," said Angela. She smiled.

"Oh, fun!" June exclaimed. "Where are y'all going this time? And when?"

"In October. It starts in Paris and ends in Avignon. We fly out of Marseille at the end."

"I'm jealous," said Nancy. "Kip and I haven't been to France in ages."

"You mean, two years?" asked June, offering Nancy a wry smile. "Before that trip to Iceland?"

Nancy shrugged as she finished dealing. "That sounds about right."

"Speaking of France," said Lois, "have you met Angela's and Hugh's friend from Grenoble, June?"

June shook her head. "Tell me about her."

"Him, not her," Nancy said. "Pass."

"Him, then."

"One Spade," said Angela. "He's a French George Clooney, June. Only slimmer, and better looking. His name is Antoine." She wiggled her eyebrows.

June rolled her eyes. "You know, I never *have* liked George Clooney. I really don't see what all the fuss is about. Pass."

"You're kidding," said Nancy.

"No," June said. "It's just—he's got some kind of a *look* to him. I don't know what to call it."

"Sexy?" asked Lois, her face straight. "Three Hearts."

"Pass," said Nancy.

"Four Hearts," Angela said, her eyes on her hand.

"Damn," June muttered. "Pass."

"No table talk, girls," said Lois. "Six Hearts."

June and Nancy exchanged glances. *A slam? We may as well lay it down.* After the first card was played and Angela displayed her cards on the table, conversation resumed.

"I just think you ought to meet him, June." Angela sipped her sweet tea. "He's gorgeous."

June smiled and focused on her hand. "I've told all of you, and Kitty, too. I'm not interested in meeting anyone."

"You might want to reconsider," said Lois, taking the trick. She trained her eyes on June. "You're so young, dear."

I'm not that young. "I'm very happy by myself."

"I'm not saying, go out with him," Angela said. "I'm just saying, meet him. He's originally from Grenoble, but he lives in Lyon."

"How nice," June said as Lois took another trick. "Change of subject. Valerie wants Frank and Melody to buy her out of Sea Gem. She's threatened to sue them if they don't."

Nancy looked up from the table. "Oh my goodness. That girl has *always* been trouble, hasn't she?"

June raised her eyebrows. "Y'all don't know the half of it."

"Tell us!" said Angela.

"Yes, do," said Nancy, taking a trick.

"The rest are mine," Lois said. She displayed her hand, showing the rest of the Hearts and high cards left in the deck. "But before you do, tell us something else. How did you find this out?"

"David told me, a few weeks ago. Evidently, Frank called him to make sure I wasn't interested in buying Valerie's share."

Nancy gave June a measured look. "Are you?" She cut the second deck for Angela. Lois gathered up the first deck to shuffle.

"Lord, no. *I* don't want to get mixed up in that! I just hope those two won't think I'm being selfish, not to do it."

Lois' eyebrows shot up. "Selfish? Good God, June. It's not up to *you* to bail out Valerie—or the other two, for that matter. All three of them make very good livings, do they not?"

June nodded. "They do, from what I hear. Melody's at home with the children, you know, but her husband makes quite a bit of money. Frank's been very successful, too. Jim decided to leave Sea Gem to the three of them, anyway—purposely leaving me out of it, and with my blessing."

"That was wise of him," said Lois. "Then *I* say, put this out of your mind. They'll work it out. If they don't, that's what lawyers are for."

"That's what I'm afraid of," said June.

"Tsk, tsk," said Angela, finishing the deal. "I agree with Lois. Now, you said we don't know the half of it about Valerie. I'm guessing there's more to tell us about than just this little dispute."

June picked up her cards and threw a sideways glance at Angela, sitting to her right. "Remember how I went up to Chicago last Christmas and spent the holidays with Frank and Dawn?"

"Yes," Angela said. "What happened? Did Valerie show up?"

June studied her cards, and then looked around the group. "No. But on the day I got back–it was a Sunday–I found her inside my house! She had let herself in, was ransacking around, and said she was looking for jewelry and mementos that had belonged to Ginger–and to Jim's first wife, Beverly!"

"Oh my God!" said Nancy. "She had a key?"

June nodded. "Jim must have given her one, way back when. I had no idea she had it."

"Oh, no," said Angela. "Why didn't you tell us this before?"

"I guess I was just so shocked by it–and so distraught–I couldn't. Anyway, we had an altercation when I came in and found her there."

"I'll bet you did," said Lois. "And I'm glad you did."

June raised her eyebrows. "Anyway, the next day, I had all the locks changed."

"You should've done *that* right after Jim died," said Lois, shaking her head. "Or even before. Just for security."

"I know." June took in a deep breath and let it out. There had been so much she'd had to do, right after Jim's death, and none of it had been pleasant. "The worst part wasn't even that she was in the house. She left a huge mess, of course. The worst part was, she screamed at me and accused me of either giving away or of *selling* all the jewelry, and of throwing out all the photos!"

"Oh, June," said Nancy. "How horrible."

Angela picked up her tea and took a sip. "*Was* there anything in the house that had belonged to Ginger–or to Beverly?"

"Nothing–at least, nothing that I knew of. Jim told me he thought he gave all of Ginger's jewelry to her and Melody long ago–which I reminded her of. Not that she listened to me. He may have given some to Frank, too–I don't recall. But I do know that he didn't have *anything* left of Beverly's, and that before we got married, he gave away all of Ginger's clothes. And he told me he had Melody box up all the photos, keepsakes, and whatever else."

"What happened to those boxes?" asked Nancy.

"I have no idea. I told Valerie to ask Melody if she had them, but I don't know if she ever did. Those two have never gotten along–they've even gone through long periods without speaking. I remember when Jim and I were first married, and Melody went off to college. She was so happy that Valerie had moved out to California."

"So she wouldn't have to deal with her," said Lois. "What do you bid, partner?"

Angela gazed at Lois. "Pass."

"There's more," said June. "But we don't have time right now for me to go through the rest. One Club."

"You can tell us at lunch," said Lois. "One Diamond."

Nancy gave June a sympathetic look. "I'm so sorry you had to go through all that. After you tell us the rest, you need to hear more about Antoine." She smiled and then winked. "Pass."

*

Cole was over six months old now and able to sit up by himself. His Aunt Helen had assured Dawn that in about six weeks, he would also be holding his own bottle. He was growing like crazy, making lots of cute baby sounds, and smiling constantly. Thankfully, he was a good sleeper.

Dawn was excited about the family's trip to the beach over the week after Labor Day, and she was glad that Helen, John, and Adele were going with them. Adele would be five years old next month; with a September birthday, she was just barely too young to start kindergarten. She would be one of the oldest children in her Pre-K class this fall. At this stage, taking her out of school for a week was no problem. Cole seemed enthralled with Adele, and she adored him.

The trip was just two weeks from now. Helen had never been down to Sea Gem, and Dawn knew that she would be amazed by it. The sisters had grown up in a lower-middle class family, and, like Dawn was before her marriage, Helen was unused to luxurious resort communities. The first time Dawn had stepped foot inside Sea Gem, she had been in awe and afraid to touch anything. Now she was more comfortable there, but she had never gotten totally accustomed to it.

Helen and Adele were coming over for dinner this evening. John was out of town on business, and Frank had a business dinner in town. Dawn checked the time. It was almost seven o'clock. She had already fed Cole his cereal, and she hoped he would still be up when his aunt and cousin arrived.

A quarter of an hour later, they did. She picked up Cole from his playpen and went to open the front door.

"Hi, Aunt Dawn!" said Adele, her blonde ringlet curls bouncing. She grinned. "How's baby Cole?"

Dawn smiled. "Hi, sweetie! He's doing great." She leaned down slightly to show him off.

"He's so cute!"

Cole smiled. "He's growing so fast," Helen said.

"I know!" said Dawn. "How was school today, Adele?"

She shrugged. "Oh, you know. Just like yesterday!"

Helen cocked her head and gave Dawn a look. Adele was such a precocious child. "She can't wait to go to the beach."

"I bet you can't. Me, neither! Come on in, you two."

"I brought a bottle of white wine for us," said Helen.

"Great."

Helen and Adele followed Dawn to the kitchen, and Helen put the wine bottle on the counter. "Shall I open it?"

"Certainly. Let me get some glasses."

The sisters chatted in the den with a glass of wine while Adele busied herself with her coloring books, spread out on the coffee table. Twenty minutes later, Dawn put Cole down for the night, then served the meal she had prepared ahead of time: poached salmon and a big salad.

"I love salmon," Adele said. "We have it a lot."

"Well, maybe once a week or so," said Helen.

"That's good," Dawn said to Adele. "It's healthy."

"The only fish I don't like is fish sticks," added Adele.

Dawn laughed. "I don't blame you."

When dinner was over, Adele parked herself in front of the television in the den while Dawn and Helen cleaned up the kitchen.

"We should go home soon," said Helen. "She's getting sleepy."

"Wait just a little bit," Dawn said. "Let's stay in here and talk a little longer." She turned on the dishwasher.

The sisters sat down. "Let me pour a second glass of wine for us," said Dawn.

"I shouldn't."

"Yes, you should." Dawn filled the glasses and put the bottle back in the fridge. Just then her cell phone buzzed. She turned to pick it up. "I don't recognize this, but it's an Atlanta number. 404."

"Could it be a telemarketer?"

"I guess. But what if it's June, and it's an emergency? I'm going to answer."

Helen picked up her wine glass and took a sip.

Dawn tapped the phone. "Hello?"

"Hi, Dawn. It's Valerie."

Dawn threw a glance at Helen. "Hello, Valerie. How are you?"

"I wanted to ask about your trip coming up, to Sea Gem. I spoke to Frank today, and he mentioned you had invited your sister and her family?"

"Yes, that's right."

The line was silent for a few seconds. "I'm amazed that you did that, without asking me first."

Dawn paused. "We don't need your permission—"

"I'm one-third owner in the house, Dawn. I don't approve of you inviting your relatives down there without running it by me."

Dawn kept her eyes trained on Helen. "What are you talking about? We can invite whomever we wish—"

"Before you do, you need to make sure that neither Melody nor I have a problem with it. That's what we agreed."

"No, we agreed to check with each other only as to our schedules, for visits to Sea Gem. You *know* this—"

"Dawn, *you* don't own a share of Sea Gem—Frank does. Those people you've invited aren't his relatives."

Dawn's voice was stern. "Yes, 'those people' *are* his relatives, and—"

"No, they're *your* sister and her daughter."

Dawn's eyes widened. "They're his niece, his sister-in-law, and his cousin! Who's also *your* cousin! Not that that matters. We don't need your approval about who we invite to Sea Gem."

Valerie's tone was icy. "What I'm saying is, you should have passed your plans by me first. In the future—"

"In the future, we will do the exact same thing, Valerie."

"I'll just call Frank, and talk to him about this—"

"Do what you like. I have to go."

Dawn tapped the phone, put it down, and picked up her wine glass. "God, what a *bitch!*"

Helen sipped her wine. "She's angry that you invited us?"

Dawn nodded. "She's always angry about something. The nerve of her to tell us what to do, especially after she's said she wants out of Sea Gem! I mean, why does she care who we invite?"

"Do you think she's changed her mind about wanting out?"

Dawn raised her eyebrows. "No. She made it very clear that she wants her third of what it's worth. Since Frank and Melody won't sell it or buy her out, she's just going to be a bitch. Which shouldn't surprise me."

"She wanted to piss you off. Don't let her."

"I usually don't. I don't know why I am, now. Did I tell you she's threatened to sue, to force a sale?"

Helen shook her head. "Good God. You know, in a way though, I feel sorry for her. I mean, there she is, alone and evidently unhappy with her life. And here you are, a beautiful woman who's in a happy marriage, with a darling baby boy—"

"Did I tell you about how she told Frank that Cole wasn't her 'blood'?" Dawn made air quotes.

"Which is a good thing," Helen said. "Oops. I'm sorry. I mean, Frank—"

"Don't apologize. We're both married to her 'relatives'"—Dawn made air quotes again—"but Frank was *so* *pissed* when she said that about Cole. You have no idea."

"I can imagine."

"But then, we were talking about it, and I said that maybe she's hung up on who's related to her because she's never gotten over the fact that Ginger wasn't her real mother—or because she never knew, when she was growing up."

"She didn't know until Ginger got sick, right?"

"Right. None of them knew about Valerie's mom. I guess their parents were going to tell them one day, but when Ginger was diagnosed with leukemia, the subject of her biological children came up."

"'Blood relatives.'"

"Right." Dawn took another sip of wine.

Helen shook her head. "But—go back to what I said before. I think, deep down, she's jealous of you."

"Ha!"

"No, I mean, really. You have everything she doesn't have: a loving husband, a family, and apparently, more financial security."

"You know, I've felt sorry for her in the past. But she has a high-powered career, and she is attractive, for her age. She travels wherever she wants, and she buys anything she wants. At first, I thought she wanted out of Sea Gem because she needed the money. But I can't imagine that she has any real financial problems. She'd be a total idiot if she didn't have a bunch saved."

Helen sipped her wine. "She probably can't even imagine what we went through, growing up."

Dawn shook her head. "I'm *sure* she can't. She's from a different world. She grew up in a mansion, where servants did all the chores and put fresh flowers in every room—like in a hotel. She got a Mercedes for her sixteenth birthday. She got tons of expensive Christmas presents every year."

"But so did Frank and Melody."

"Yeah, but for some reason, they're not like her. Frank says their father gave Valerie whatever she wanted, but that he didn't do that with him or Melody."

"Did they resent it?"

"I would think so, but Frank and Melody got stuff, too."

"But Frank says Valerie was the favored one?"

"He says that his dad just treated her differently. Not that he complains about it—you know how close he was to his father. But his dad just did more for her, and tolerated her behavior. *I* think he enabled it."

"Maybe he felt sorry for her because of the way her mother died. Do you think he worried that she might have issues with depression, too? That giving her more attention might keep her from going into a tailspin, herself?"

"Who knows? Whatever the reason, the whole family walked on eggshells around her, according to Frank. They all lived in fear of setting her off."

"So basically, they were a dysfunctional family."

"Right. But, unlike ours, they were a *rich* dysfunctional family. Frank says that he and Melody got along well when they were growing up, and they were always united, having to deal with her. After their mother's death, he says they bonded even more. But when they were kids, his parents did everything they could to keep Valerie happy. They kept throwing money at her, hoping she would change. And when she got out of college and began working, Jim was super proud of her. He was glad she was so career-driven."

"Even though his wife wasn't."

"But Ginger was a good artist, just like you. Frank thinks she wished she pursued that, and that she would have loved to work in a creative field. Instead, she took care of the kids and ran the household while Jim was out building his career. When they bought Sea Gem, she was busy getting that set up, too. She had it remodeled, kept it going, and managed the staff and the maintenance people. She went down there a lot, too, I've heard."

"I'm sure that took a lot of time and energy."

"I imagine so. She was pretty hands-on." Dawn finished her wine and put her glass down.

"Here's the thing, though," said Helen. "What *you* have is what Valerie really wants, and it's something that money can't buy. No matter how much of it she got from her father, or how much she's made."

"Oh, I don't know that she wants what *I* have. I'm sure she thinks Frank and I are very boring. And she's never liked me, not from the get-go."

"Who cares? Frank adores you. You don't need her to like you. Or to like *me*." Helen offered a mischievous smile.

Dawn laughed. "Don't worry. Because you're my sister, she doesn't. Plus, I've been pretty blunt to her in the past—but only when she's pushed me. You know how I can be."

Helen giggled. "Yes, I do. But I've always admired that about you."

10

Assessments

On Monday morning at ten o'clock, Valerie walked into the conference room and sat down at the table next to Graham. Sophie was seated across from them. Josh stepped to the door, closed it, and turned around to face the group.

"So, this meeting is about the four of us knowing ourselves–and each other–better, so we can maintain a positive culture," he said. "We've each received our psychological assessment results from Rogers Development Group, and we've had lots of time to digest them. Now, we're going to share our results and talk about what they mean." He glanced around the table. "Then, we'll talk about how we can each improve, and how we can make good hiring decisions going forward."

"Culture is set by the first dozen or so employees," added Graham. He crossed his arms in front of his chest. "We have almost three times that many people working here. Making the right hiring decisions is extremely important–"

"Except, we're not hiring at the moment," Sophie cut in.

Josh turned toward her and raised his eyebrows. *Why does she always have to state the obvious?* "That's true right now, but it won't always be the case. That's why this is a good time to discuss it."

"How is this a good time, after what happened?" asked Valerie.

"There's never going to be a perfect time," said Josh, his voice stern. "So we may as well do it now. Look. The four of us are passionate about PriceUtopia. We've all chosen to come here to work in a collaborative environment. Each of us has an amazing skill set, but we aren't just individual contributors. We're members of a high-performing team with a sole focus."

Valerie persisted. "That's fine. But I don't understand why we're taking time to discuss this, given current circumstances."

"The importance of hiring talented, skilled people cannot be overstated," Graham said. "We can't afford any toxic employees. Finding the right people is the only way we can foster a culture of success."

Josh turned to Valerie. "And to that end, we have to start by looking at ourselves, and figuring out how we can each improve."

"Okay," said Valerie. "I don't see the point in sharing our results with each other, though. What does that accomplish?"

Josh cleared his throat and glanced down for a second. *Will she ever stop challenging me publicly? Why can't she just defer to my judgment?* "Here's what it does. It helps us to know one another better, and to take an honest look at ourselves."

Graham glanced around the table. "Let's get this done."

Josh nodded. "Right. I'll go first, but before I do, I'm going to refresh everyone's memory about the terminology." He looked at his iPad. "We were measured in four areas: Heart, Integrity, Head, and Hand. I'll read the descriptions. They're short."

An awkward silence filled the room. Josh glanced at each person and then continued. "Heart refers to interpersonal abilities: effective communication with others, social skills, persuasiveness and likability. Integrity is about honesty, trust, discipline and responsibility. Head is intelligence, agility, quickness, logic, and to a lesser extent, creativity. Finally, Hand refers to engagement, practicality, stamina, motivation—doing what needs to be done."

He read his assessment results aloud. "So, to summarize, I score high in Heart and Head, medium in Hand, and on the low side in Integrity. Sophie, your turn."

Sophie inhaled, let out a deep breath, and read her results. She registered high in Heart and Integrity, and slightly low in Head and Hand. Graham followed, with results the exact opposite of Sophie's. Then it was Valerie's turn.

"I would rather not participate," she said. She stared at Josh. "Haven't we wasted enough time?"

Graham turned and stared at her. "We read ours. You have to do it, too."

"I would, if mine were correct."

Josh clasped his hands in front of him on the table. "Valerie, you have to participate."

Valerie set her jaw, gave him an icy stare, and then reported her results to the group. Her score in Head was well above average, and she scored just above the mid-point in Hand. In the other two areas, she scored very low.

"Thank you," said Josh. "I've just sent everybody the low score interpretations. Open them up and read them silently. Let's keep in mind that each one of us has at least one low score. Low scores are not meant as criticisms. They're actually positives, because they allow us to pinpoint the areas we need to improve in. When we're done with those, we'll look at the high score interpretations."

All four people opened their iPads and began reading.

*Individuals scoring very low in **Heart** may lack empathy and tend to be narcissists. They often come across as arrogant, blunt, and unfeeling. They seek to control and manage all situations, and can become toxic if left unchecked. These individuals focus on personal achievement and relish performance mode. However, they sometimes use aggressive tactics to get what they want.*

*Those scoring low in **Integrity** tend to claim credit for others' work. They lack tact and have difficulty realizing it when others tune them out. They can be quick to blame others for any problems, and they deflect responsibility for any mistakes.*

*Those low in **Head** are more focused on politics and negotiation than on knowledge and learning. These people are savvy when it comes to relationships, but are sometimes unable to process new information in a timely manner.*

*A low score in **Hand** indicates someone who manipulates others to do the work he or she wants to avoid, and who believes that the rules don't apply to him or her. This individual can be charming and assertive, but may procrastinate, and often doesn't follow through on getting tasks accomplished.*

Valerie looked up and stared at Josh again. Their eyes locked for several seconds, and the vein on her forehead throbbed. Her face was bright red. "This is bullshit."

"Valerie, this is a tool—"

"No, it's not!" she yelled. "It's bullying, and it's a branding iron on each of us!"

Josh held up a hand in an effort to stop her from going off. "Calm down. None of us are perfect. We're going to look at our positives, too."

Graham and Sophie exchanged nervous glances. Sophie turned to Josh. "So are you sending us the high score interpretations?"

"I just did." Josh looked down at his device. "You can open them."

Valerie's eyes were blazing. She spoke steadily, her voice lower now. "I don't need to open mine. I know what my strengths are, and I know my weaknesses. These assessments are bogus, and you know it. I can't believe you used company funds to pay for them."

Josh put his hand on his chin. "Lots of companies do these—"

"So that's why *you* had them done? Because it's the hot new thing to do?"

He shook his head. *Damn her.* "Look. Maybe we should have started with the high score interpretations. But I thought it would be patronizing and disrespectful to begin there, and then focus on negatives and on ways to improve. That seemed manipulative and controlling—"

Valerie pushed her chair back and stood up. "What kind of crap is that, and where did you get it? It's so ironic, it's funny. This whole thing is controlling and manipulative, and it's also abusive." She glared at the others, and spoke quietly. "These results do none of us any good. They're just an excuse for Josh to feed his own ego and to broadcast how brilliant he thinks *he* is."

Sophie raised her brows. "I, for one, think we should have focused on the positives before the talking about the negatives."

Valerie glanced at Sophie, and then trained her eyes on Josh. "None of those descriptions apply to me. As for using these assessments, do what you like, but let the record show that I completely discount them. I think this is a scam." She turned and stormed out of the room.

*

Safely alone in her office, Valerie sat down at her desk and put her face in her hands. Josh had practically called her a narcissist, a liar, and a manipulator. She had been forced to suffer through a personal attack—one that she hadn't deserved in the least, and by a man who purported to be her boyfriend, no less.

Fury settled inside of her and overtook her mind and body. How dare he treat her that way? Her mind raced with thoughts of revenge. Had he hurt her on purpose— was it just hatefulness? Or—more likely—was he just incredibly stupid? Months ago, she had realized that he wasn't as intelligent as she thought he was. He was a pretty good actor, but he wasn't very smart. She needed to be with someone else—a much more intelligent man. A man that she could learn from, and who challenged her mentally.

A man that she could respect.

She fought back her tears and forced herself to calm down. Everyone knew it was ridiculous to waste time on the RDG assessments, since there was so much to do to recover from recent events. Earlier, when she and Josh were alone, he had told her it would be foolish not to use the feedback from RDG. The company had paid a lot of money for that information, he said. She had agreed with him. But that was before she found out the assessments were false, or that the meeting would turn into a bullying session.

She gritted her teeth and pulled up the high score interpretations on her iPad. She skimmed them, looking for the one about "Head," in which she had scored a 7 out of 10. She found it halfway down the page.

*A high score in **Head** indicates more than intelligence. This person can have a deep though perhaps narrow knowledge base in their particular field. This individual is usually very productive and agile, and is able to discern the most important elements in a business and how to apply them. He or she is logical, and processes new information quickly and well. Such an employee can be very valuable to an organization in planning and prioritizing objectives.*

It did properly describe her, but it was still bullshit, since she'd scored only a 7. The positive score interpretations in the other areas included words like team player, diplomatic, and empathetic. All signified weaknesses, not strengths. No wonder she hadn't scored highly in them. Who would want to–especially working in a startup?

No matter what Josh's "positives" were–and she wasn't interested in seeing anyone else's but his–surely he was smart enough to realize that the whole thing was a crock. He had only two high scores, anyway. Valerie couldn't remember what they were in, but it didn't matter.

She sighed. Why did she always have to fight for herself, in every situation? Why couldn't someone else be her advocate, for once? Why couldn't Josh be? He had talked her into taking this job, and had failed to deliver on his promises when the IPO was voided. Now, who knew when she would get paid what she deserved?

She was sick of being conned. Her mind flashed to a memory of the way June had treated her last November, after she had gone to the house to look for jewelry. She had claimed to be searching for old photos and keepsakes as well, but of course she didn't care about all that stuff. When June told her she thought Melody had them, she had feigned anger and indignation, but in truth, she was mad she hadn't found more jewelry. Luckily, no one asked any questions when she didn't follow up about the photos. But she did want the antiques and the paintings her father had promised she could have when he was gone. Unfortunately, for some reason, he never got around to putting that in his will. If she had gotten those pieces out of the house, she could have sold them too and made a lot of money.

That was another time when Valerie had been cheated out of what ought to have been hers. June had screamed at her and ordered her not to come back. Then she had demonized Valerie to the rest of the family. She had painted Valerie as greedy and selfish, and had tagged her as a villain.

Now, Frank and Melody were intent on getting their way about Sea Gem. Other people used Valerie, not the other way around. She was done with being used and abused. She sat down at her laptop and sent her attorney an email requesting an appointment. She had to get the process started.

11

Tension

Josh shook his head slowly. "I don't know what to say about what just happened. I suppose I did make a mistake by starting with the low score interpretations."

"Don't sweat it," said Graham. "She'll settle down." He offered his partner a sympathetic look.

"Yeah, I think she will," Sophie said. "But–do we continue discussing these now, without her? I mean, do you still want to go over the high score interpretations?"

Graham shrugged. "Well, we *could* just read them over privately–"

"Yeah, let's do that. If we stay in here together, she'll probably think we're talking about her, and then she'll get even angrier. It was stupid of me to expect her to stay calm."

Graham cocked his head. "You mean, to expect her to act like an adult?" Everyone knew who Josh was sleeping with.

Josh inhaled and let out a deep breath. "I'll deal with her later. Meeting's adjourned."

Graham and Sophie left the room. Josh leaned back in his chair and stared at the ceiling. What a disaster. He wished he could roll back the tape for a redo. Better yet, bag the whole thing. If he hadn't already paid Doug Rogers for the assessments, he probably would have—or at least he would have postponed the meeting.

Valerie was right, too: God knew there were tons of other things to do that were in need of immediate attention. What she didn't know—and what Sophie was unaware of, too—was that he and Graham had eliminated everyone but them from the list of possible traitors. Graham had done most of the digging; since he knew everyone's passwords, he had been able to peruse their computers without being discovered. Of course, someone may have said something about product features or whatnot on the phone or elsewhere, but the office paper trail was secure, and didn't reveal a traitor.

Graham had accessed most of Valerie's and Sophie's data, but because they were execs, he hadn't been able to view all of it. But he and Josh believed that neither was the culprit, if there was one. Both women had vested interests—literally—in not disclosing the company's proprietary information. Each had been issued tens of thousands in stock options, and each seemed committed to the success of the startup. It wouldn't make sense for either to divulge or peddle anything.

However, just to cover all bases, the men had agreed to follow through with the psych evaluations. Neither believed they would reveal betrayal, but both thought it wise to take a look. The assessments were supposed to be helpful not only in making hiring decisions, but in rooting out toxicity. Though not an investigating tool, the process could shed some light on things.

But if no one had leaked information, then Josh and Graham were no closer to solving the Cornucopia puzzle.

For weeks, people had been peppering Josh with questions he couldn't answer. Was a new IPO being planned, and if so, when? Was some competitor out there about to release a better product? What would happen if someone did? When would more funds be coming in, and how were he and Graham going to get them?

Besides the embarrassment of the failed IPO, it irritated the hell out of Josh that Cornucopia had changed its mind, and worse, that he didn't know why. It seemed unlikely, but maybe their explanation had been true—maybe they really *hadn't* wanted to add more tech exposure to their portfolio. It was possible. But if so, they should have never committed to invest in the public offering.

When Josh made a decision, he stuck with it. He absolutely hated it when people changed their minds. When they didn't do what they said they were going to do. But hopefully, Valerie would change her mind about his intentions this morning. He felt certain that she hadn't read the high score interpretations he'd sent out. Better if she hadn't–she had no really high scores. He would let her have some time today before he approached her about anything. Meanwhile, he would think of a way to fix things. She certainly wasn't the first woman he had ever pissed off.

For the sake of the company–and for the sake of their relationship–he had no choice but to repair the damage. Not that he couldn't get sex elsewhere. But he wasn't ready to end it yet with Valerie. Not while she was still his employee.

He just didn't feel that he could take the risk.

Only this morning, an hour before the meeting, the two of them had met in his office to discuss some retailers' concerns. One of PriceUtopia's first clients, Lane's Department Stores, had reported a major hit to margins since it began widespread use of the PriceUtopia technology. However, its reputation with customers had improved, and the store was now viewed as committed to being a serious competitor to the big online retailers.

Price transparency–and price matching–would attract more customers over time, Josh believed, and in the end, retailers would do better, not worse. Margins would suck initially, but that didn't matter, because shoppers were on a quest for more information, and they didn't intend to stop or to slow down. The more quickly retailers understood that, the better for everyone. And over time, price matching would improve retailers' ability to negotiate better prices from their suppliers, which would in turn help bring margins back up, and closer to former levels. That was the narrative Valerie needed to use, to respond to clients' feelings of unease.

One client she met with recently had told her of its plan to eliminate shipping fees for holiday orders this fall. However, it wasn't ready to match competitors' prices. It had made major investments in its chain of national superstores over the last several years, and management believed customers weren't savvy enough to demand it match prices for any purchases, in-store or online.

"Their biggest rival is Save-Max," Valerie had told Josh, a fact that he already knew. "Save-Max has the pricing advantage, and it also has the edge in e-commerce."

"Look, for the retail world, the transition to digital price matching is going to be hugely disruptive, but it's something they're all just going to have to accept–or they'll go out of business. Tell them PriceUtopia will give them better visibility into price comparisons with Save-Max, as well as with all other competitors," Josh advised. "We need to push the visibility factor. We can't lecture clients about the inevitability of price matching, though. Some retailers want to see what happens to their competitors before they'll agree to participate. But eventually, all of them will jump on board."

"If they're not willing to match competitors' prices, they won't."

"They'll change their minds about that," Josh had declared. "They're going to have to play the game."

Josh had been glad when that discussion ended. Valerie had proved to be great at maintaining momentum when things were going well, but when problems arose—or when others dared to push back—she could become unhinged, and sometimes, even nightmarishly unkind. Josh was blind to that in the early days, when she had lured him in with magnetism and phenomenal sex.

Right now, he needed to clear his thoughts and focus on his agenda for the day. With the new release, PriceUtopia was going to be in a position to seize opportunities that hopefully no one else had identified. But he had to get funding arranged so that could happen. No further delays.

Because money was just as important as passion.

*

At just before five, Josh leaned back from his desk and gazed out the window at the gathering, menacing clouds. Afternoon thunderstorms were an almost daily occurrence in Atlanta in August. Raindrops would soon pelt the city's web of roads and highways, resulting in a blanket of steam rising from asphalt and concrete. Josh shut his eyes. Tension had filled the small office today like an odorless, poisonous gas, creeping around corners and invading every pocket of space. Valerie had stomped around the place fuming, with a "mad on," as Josh's mother used to say about his father, way back when Josh was a kid in Charleston.

"Stay away from him tonight, honey. I don't know why, but he's got a mad on again."

Josh had grown up tiptoeing around his father and trying to avoid him. Paul Wilson had died of a stroke six years ago, and all his life, he had carried a chip on his shoulder. His favorite pastime had been to grumble, and to blame others for his own lack of success. While he was continually passed over at work, his family had lived from paycheck to paycheck. Savings were nonexistent and bills were paid late (but usually within the grace period). Josh had an indelible memory of his mom, Colleen, sitting in the den on Sunday afternoons, looking through the newspaper ads for sales. Every weekend, she spent hours perusing the circulars and clipping coupons. At the time, he had wished for a way to help her find the lowest prices, not just for what was advertised, but for everything.

The youngest of six whose parents were Irish immigrants, frugality was in his mom's blood, and Josh supposed that it must be in his, too. From the age of fifteen, he had worked after school and on weekends, saving his money and looking forward to the day when he could escape. He and his younger brother Andrew got loans to go to public universities, and both paid them off with no help from the old man.

A month after college graduation, Josh took a sales-clerk job at a Sun and Ski Shop that he was way overqualified for with his marketing degree. With zero connections–and without a stellar GPA–it was the only job he could find. His boss was the store manager and a complete jackass. But Josh had put up with him, and slogged in every day for years, perpetually broke, his salary spent before it was earned. He was forced to live on a pittance, working retail, and–short of murdering his boss–with no real way to get ahead.

What an idiot Josh had been not to have studied harder in college. If he had done that–say, if he'd made the Dean's List every semester (not easy, but certainly doable)–he would have had a much different life. He wouldn't have had to waste so much time catching up and looking for better opportunities that others seemed to find effortlessly. Too bad he wasn't twenty-one right now, majoring in computer science and running his company from his dorm room–able to bypass all the crap he had had to go through over the last two decades.

He would have become a millionaire by now.

He was twice that age, though, and what had happened, happened. Somehow, he had moved up the ranks the traditional way, patiently waiting for opportunities and telling himself it would all work out in the end. He had switched companies several times and had learned a lot about the industry in the process. Maybe, when you really looked at it, he'd had to experience all that to get where he was today: co-founder of a startup, selling an innovation destined to permanently alter the retail world, and to reshape the economy.

His thoughts suddenly shifted back to this morning's debacle. Maybe Valerie had been PMS-ing–but he knew better than to ask her, of course. You couldn't mention that to any woman, even if you knew for certain that it was the problem. In any case, being around her all week *and* all weekend could get oppressive.

Valerie's arrogance and wrath were well known throughout the office. Demanding and usually blunt, she was also efficient, astute, and even respected for her work ethic and as a leader. But when things turned sour, she had lashed out at almost everyone over the past year. You actually had to witness her behavior at those times, to believe it. She cut people off and barked at whoever got in her way. She rarely smiled, without it being fake, and she was often impatient and dismissive of others' feelings.

Just last week, a twenty-something girl on Sophie's team, Tina Martin, had complained to Josh when Valerie forgot to wish her a happy birthday.

"She's so *cold,*" Tina said, her eyes brimming with tears. When Josh confronted Valerie about it, she tossed her head, laughed, and said Tina was oversensitive. But many other employees had come to him with stories about the callous way Valerie spoke to them. After silently listening to them, he had always defended her.

Was it only because he was sleeping with her?

Everyone knew that he was, too—at least, he suspected they did. Given her behavior, people probably thought he was crazy. Maybe he *was* crazy. Ironically, when he met her, he had admired what he thought of as her fierceness. The tech side of his business was going well at that time, but sales were weakening, and he needed someone with the right qualifications to take them to the next level. Valerie had seemed perfect for the job. She was tough, relentless, and driven—all qualities he thought would make her a valuable member of his executive team, and a great addition to the company.

He hadn't hired her to wish people a happy birthday.

When she started at PriceUtopia, though, she had charmed subordinates and others with compliments and praise. She went out of her way to do favors, but soon she called them in; her good deeds always had strings attached. She was blunt, abrasive, and even unkind if things didn't go her way, or if anyone pushed back. Maybe that was how she had always handled relationships in her career. Josh knew she had never managed a large group in previous jobs, but she had been entrusted with major responsibilities. Her toughness and ambition must have helped. But during her time at PriceUtopia, her positives had morphed into negatives.

As their personal relationship evolved, and in too short of a time, she began to take *him* for granted. Initially, she was hesitant, but before long she became controlling, pushy, and domineering. Memories of his parents' fights had stopped him from reacting; at a young age, he had learned to keep quiet and to avoid confrontation. But after a while, he called Valerie on her attitude. He protested mildly, even trying to joke about it while secretly hoping she would come around. Instead, she got worse.

Her bad behavior embarrassed him at times. Like when they went to the movies–she always brought some kind of jacket or cardigan sweater, but not to ward off the chill of the air-conditioned theater. When they sat down, she draped it over the two seats just in front of them to make others think the seats were taken, so that no one would sit there and block her view. It normally worked, and the few times it hadn't, he had seen her get belligerent, and order the intruders away. The last time that happened, when they went to see *Argo*, he had quietly slithered away to get popcorn. When he returned, the theater was full, except for those two seats.

That night, he hadn't said a word to her about the altercation. And, pretending someone was sitting in front of you wasn't that big a deal, anyway—she couldn't be the only person who ever did that. It was just one of her bad habits. Like the habit she had of telling him how to drive. He remembered the first time, when they were heading south on Peachtree Road one night, on the way to dinner.

He was behind the wheel of his black Audi, driving in the left lane. She kept ordering him to move over to the right. She insisted that if he didn't, they would get caught behind someone taking forever to turn left. In that section of Peachtree, there was no center turn lane, and the traffic lights had no arrows. He had argued with her, saying he could make better time by staying where he was and changing lanes whenever necessary.

She had screamed at him and had called him an idiot.

He should have broken it off with her then.

Instead, he had put up with her all this time, and had excused her antics. He had done it primarily for the sex, but also because she was so productive. Her work ethic was unparalleled. Besides, you couldn't directly accuse a woman executive of bossiness—it wasn't politically correct, and it wasn't worth the risk.

He sighed, regretting his entanglement with her and where it had led. If she didn't work at PriceUtopia, he would have parted ways with her long ago. As it was, he couldn't.

Not yet.

Maybe he just needed a break from her. But no matter what he did in his personal life, hiring the right people—and being able to trust them—was ultra-important.

Recalling her psychological assessment results, he suspected they were accurate. She was a toxic employee.

But what was he going to do about it?

12

Engaging

Despite her earlier resolve not to date, June was looking forward to seeing Antoine Dugast this weekend.

They'd met on the Friday after bridge. Angela had ambushed her, having set a well-laid trap. Antoine "just happened" to run into the Sims at an art gallery opening they attended with June, after the three friends had dined at Miller Union over in West Midtown. Slightly awkward introductions followed (*"Enchanté, Madame"*), and then the Frenchman joined Angela, Hugh and June to view the exhibit. The Sims soon disappeared, and an hour later, June and Antoine were having a drink at The Jury's Out, a new restaurant off Piedmont Road.

"Tell me about yourself," he'd said.

She smiled. "What do you want to know?"

He leaned toward her, a sparkle in his eye. "Everything."

That night, she had been amazed at the chemistry between them. Somehow he got her to tell him more about herself than she had revealed to anyone in years. He was easy to talk to, and was a very good listener. And she had been fascinated, learning about his past, and his life in France.

She had told herself he wasn't interested in her romantically. That they were becoming friends, and would remain so. She was intrigued by him, but couldn't believe he could feel the same about her. Then, the next week, they met twice for lunch. That Friday night, he took her to La Belle Maison, a French restaurant near Ansley Park. The owner was a friend of Antoine's and was also from Grenoble—one of the many gems of France, both of them told her, but for some reason, not a popular tourist destination.

June closed her eyes now, recalling details of that evening. The way Antoine *did* seem "enchanted" with her ("delighted" was closer to the meaning of the polite French greeting he had used when they met). The way he ordered for both of them *en français,* selecting the perfect wine. The way he displayed the ideal amount of interest in her. The sexiness of his deep voice, and of his scent. Those piercing green eyes beneath his long, dark lashes.

Antoine was a trim five foot eleven with graying hair. He was only fifty-six, three and a half years older than June, and was the youngest of four children born after World War II. His parents were from Lyon, and he had grown up hearing stories about the French Resistance and the *traboules*—hiding places—in *La Vieille Ville,* the "old city."* He spoke perfect English, but with a seductive French accent; every time he pronounced "the" as "zuh" or "they" as "zay," June felt a tingle on the back of her neck.

They had seen each other five times already now. Antoine worked for the French government and, though not fully retired yet, he had much more time to himself now than he'd had in the past. He had been married only once, in his twenties. His wife of five years had died of pneumonia after a seemingly normal bout of the flu. Since then, he'd had just one serious relationship, in his thirties.

"She left me," he said that night at La Belle Maison. "We were together for only two years. I traveled constantly, and I wasn't ready to start a family. The next year, she was married to someone else and expecting their first child."

"I'm sorry," June said. She wasn't *that* sorry, though. If he had married her, he wouldn't be here tonight. With her.

"Ah, well, *c'est la vie,*" Antoine said. "As they say." He smiled and gazed at her. "You've known your share of loss, too." He reached across the table and held her hand.

On Saturday night–three days from now–they were going to a performance of the Atlanta Symphony, and then a late dinner at a spot nearby on 14th Street. She couldn't believe she was doing this–she felt too old to be dating again. But when she was with Antoine, she felt so much younger than she was. It was very different being with him than it had been with Jim. Not better–no, she assured herself–just different. She couldn't betray Jim's memory by deciding Antoine was a better man. Jim had come into her life at a time when she had almost given up on love and companionship, when she had believed that she might never get married. Their years together had been the happiest of her life. But now...

Well, now Jim was gone, and June had the rest of her life to live. Jim had proposed to her just a year after he had lost Ginger. Would he really mind if she found love again?

Of course he wouldn't.

She stopped herself. Love was a strong word—stronger now, it seemed, than it had been twenty years ago. Who knew what would happen with Antoine? The future was indecipherable, and she had learned to live in the present. She barely knew this man, anyway.

But it was absolutely lovely, getting to know him.

*

On Thursday, Dawn started getting organized to go to the beach.

It was too early to pack their suitcases, but there were many other things she needed to do ahead of time. She, Frank, and Cole planned to fly down the middle of next week, a few days before Helen's family's arrival. That would give Dawn and Frank a chance to stock the kitchen and bar, to get Cole settled, and to make sure everything was in order. Mick, the house manager, had been in touch with Frank and had assured him that all was well. The housekeepers were busy doing a deep cleaning today.

Frank had heard from Valerie the day after Dawn's terse conversation with her, but not by phone. Instead, his sister had sent him a blistering email, repeating everything she had said to Dawn. Frank had chosen to delete the message rather than respond. You couldn't expect to have a reasonable dialogue with Valerie, he told Dawn—all she did was make demands and spew her opinions. She didn't listen to him. And she didn't care if she offended anyone.

"I'm not going to engage her," Frank had said. "It would just invite more crap."

"Good," said Dawn. "You know, I don't know why she even cares that we invited Helen and John. Especially since she wants out of Sea Gem."

"She's never been all that rational. She expects other people to follow the rules, but she feels free to ignore them. Remember how she announced last winter that she doesn't respond to 'angry' emails?" Frank made air quotes. "So I'm just doing the same thing–not responding."

Dawn shuddered. For the dozen years Valerie had been her sister-in-law, her behavior had grown from bad to worse. How could anyone live the way she did? Never happy, and always wanting to cause trouble and upset others?

Valerie seemed to have a knack for that. She had no sense of humor, either, unless you included laughing *at* someone, always at their expense. She was sarcastic, but not witty in the least. Oh, well. Dawn never sent messages to Valerie or called her. She had learned to keep her distance and to ignore her rants.

No matter what happened with Sea Gem–whether Valerie sued or not–Dawn hoped to avoid seeing her in the future. As for what would happen if she filed a lawsuit, they would cross that bridge then. It would be two against one (really, four against one). Frank thought the judge wouldn't force him and Melody to divide up the property, because there was no clear way to do it. If they were forced to sell at auction, though, things could get ugly.

*

That afternoon, Melody opened the back door to let Napoleon in, grabbed him by the collar, and wiped off the bottoms of his paws.

"There you go." She wrinkled her nose, and then shook her head. The dog smelled just this side of rank. "What a mess you are. Good thing you're so cute."

She sent him downstairs to the basement, where Pip, Neely, and Nick were watching TV; Matt was at Sonny Duncan's house and was spending the night with him. They were in the same class, and Sonny's mom Kristin was the class mother. Melody was grateful that she had introduced her to lots of the other moms.

On the weekends, Jeff helped with Napoleon as he promised he would, and he enlisted the older children to help out. But when he was at work and they were at school, the pet-care responsibilities landed squarely on Melody's shoulders. Her least favorite task was giving the dog a bath. Maybe she ought to make an appointment for him at the groomer for tomorrow morning. Jeff could drop him off on his way to go pick up Matt at Sonny's.

Melody sat down at the computer to search for the groomer's number, but decided to check her email first to see if there was a message from her brother. She had only talked to Frank once since the day of the conference call. He called her back a few days later, saying he had talked to David and had floated the idea of June buying Valerie out.

"She wasn't interested," Frank had said. "I guess I don't really blame her for passing on it."

"I don't, either," Melody said. "She doesn't need to buy her out. June knows that we'll invite her to come down to visit."

"If she had agreed to do it, she'd just be giving in to Valerie's demands–basically, she'd be rewarding her for threatening to sue us."

"You mean, enabling her behavior," added Melody. "And forking over a couple million dollars to do it."

"Anyway, I guess we wait and see what happens. Maybe things are going better at Valerie's company. If so– and since she's had some time to cool off–maybe she won't file a lawsuit."

"That would make things a lot easier."

Frank had promised to update Melody if he heard anything, so it was probably a good sign that she hadn't heard from him. Maybe he had been right. Maybe Valerie *had* reconsidered, and had decided to think about other people, for once.

*

The next afternoon, Valerie met with her attorney in his office in Buckhead.

She drove over to the office building in the heart of Buckhead, near the intersection of Highway 400 and Peachtree Road. She parked in the underground garage and took the elevator to the fourteenth floor. The doors opened into the lobby of the law practice, and she breezed by the receptionist.

Finding her attorney in his office, she tapped once on his half-open door and entered. He was expecting her. She settled into a black leather chair across from him.

"Are you sure you want to do this?" he asked. "I mean, could there still be a way to arrive at an amicable agreement with your siblings?"

"The chance of that is slim. We've talked, and they've had weeks to let my intention to sue sink in. I don't know if they think I'm bluffing, but as you know, I'm not."

"Okay. Let me go over a few things with you one more time. We're asking the judge for a partition by sale. The judge will appoint a commissioner to go down and see the property, in order to determine whether it's feasible to divide it into parcels of approximately equal value."

She shook her head. "It isn't feasible."

The lawyer cleared his throat. "Right. That's what you've said. So, once that is decided by the commissioner, the judge will arrange for the property to be sold at auction to the highest bidder. Then, you'll get your third of the proceeds. However, you need to remember that there's no way of knowing how much the property will go for at auction. That amount could be much less than what it would bring if it were on the market."

"I understand. But once they realize I'm serious, I'm certain that my brother and sister will reconsider. They won't want a sale at auction, either. They'll do whatever they have to do to avoid it."

"They could look for a third party to buy your share."

"They won't do that, unless they can talk our stepmother into it. She has the money, and she's the obvious choice. But I assume they've already asked her, and she declined."

"Well, unless you want to talk to them again—"

That was the last thing she wanted, whether they had approached June or not. "I don't."

"I'll file the suit, then," he said.

13

Getting Away

That night, Josh showed up at Valerie's apartment with an orchid and a carefully chosen bottle of white wine.

Since Monday's meeting, things between them had been strained, to say the least. After Valerie's emotional display at the meeting, Josh had retreated into his man cave, and he had done a lot of thinking this week.

No, their relationship wasn't ideal. And yes, Valerie could be overbearing at times. But she did have her strengths. When he had first met her, he was mesmerized with her and captivated by her charm. He had seen her turn on that charm many times since, both in business and in personal life. She could be charismatic and was quite alluring. She was also intense, but the trick was to get her to channel her intensity. She didn't like criticism, but then, who did? When she had a good reason, she went into performance mode; rather than drain her, doing that always seemed to energize her.

He was the opposite. Though he was passionate about the company, he could be "on" about it for only so long. He woke up every day thinking about what he could do to make PriceUtopia a success, but he needed frequent mental and physical breaks. He got too fatigued and distracted, otherwise. On the other hand, Valerie seemed to thrive by constantly being on, and by working hard. Her job was her entire life.

And all things considered, it was better to have her on his side than the alternative.

He didn't totally blame her for what happened on Monday. Everyone had their moments. Wasn't she entitled to hers, too? Plus, he held himself at least 90 percent accountable. He hadn't handled the meeting well; as he said, he should have started out with praise. Should have emphasized the positives, and downplayed the negatives. Unfortunately, he had done the reverse.

No doubt, Valerie was responsible for the rest of what happened. But Josh thought he knew how she must have felt. He had grown up with a father who continually disparaged him, who never complimented him, nor recognized his abilities. The old man had given him absolutely no encouragement, and had even laughed at his ideas. Constant criticism made you numb, after a while. And then, you just wanted to get away.

Josh couldn't afford for Valerie to get away—not yet, anyway. He needed her at PriceUtopia. As for their relationship, well, he was a romantic at heart. He was empathetic to a fault. Even his psych assessment had indicated that, with his highest score being in Heart. Still, he didn't quite agree with his results; he felt he was an honest person, despite his low Integrity score, and he didn't believe he deflected responsibility for his mistakes. And his two high scores, in Head and Heart, seemed to contradict one another.

Maybe it *was* all just a bunch of nonsense, like Valerie had said. Maybe Doug Rogers really had scammed him. In any case, what was done was done. And, truth told, he still wanted to sleep with her.

So he had pushed away his earlier misgivings about her, and now he was ready to do a one-eighty and come crawling back. He had texted her late this afternoon, while she was out of the office somewhere. He had begged forgiveness, and proposed that he take her out to dinner. Whatever she had gone to do must have put her in a pretty good mood, because she consented. He knew that she hated surprises, but he hoped the flower she preferred and the wine he had selected would be accepted as his peace offering. He knocked on the door and waited.

She opened it and stared at him, a blank look on her face.

"Listen," he began. "I apologize. I was wrong. I never meant to cut you down—"

"But you still did."

He shut his eyes for a second. "I shouldn't have. And I agree with you that the assessments are bogus."

"Because you don't accept yours?"

"Because I don't accept anyone's."

She took the orchid from him, walked brusquely over to her dining table, and set it down. Josh noticed another orchid, sitting on the coffee table, that she had evidently bought for herself. He followed her to the kitchen, carrying the wine.

"Put that in the fridge," she said.

He did, and then faced her. "Are we over this? I mean, are you?"

Valerie gave him a measured look. "I just want to forget about it. Totally."

That was probably as good as he was going to get. "Sure. Let's forget it. It was a huge mistake on my part—"

"Stop. You don't have to go on. But just promise me that you won't waste any more time or money on bullshit."

He looked into her eyes. "I won't." He leaned in to give her a tentative kiss, placing his arms on her shoulders.

She kissed him back, then turned away and headed to the other room. "Did you make a reservation for dinner, or what?"

*

The next morning, Josh woke up next to Valerie in her bed.

After a little alcohol last night, she'd become slightly less testy. She seemed distracted, though, and Josh had been, too. Their unspoken agreement to have sex later had carried him through the evening. He had gone into listening mode during dinner: smiling and nodding (but not too much), while she blathered on about the company and business. She never got tired of talking about it. At least she hadn't interrogated him about the roadshow he and Graham were about to go on next week. Everyone at the office knew they planned to go to meet with some new VCs to ask for more money.

Last night, once they were back at her place and she was sufficiently drunk, she'd been more than willing to get naked and get after it. Afterward, he had easily fallen asleep. Now, he lay there wondering what to do next. Should he get up and make some kind of breakfast for the two of them? He'd done that in the past, once or twice.

Coffee, at least–he could handle that, and God knew, he could use a cup right now.

He got out of bed and went to the head. Then he washed his hands and threw on his pants and shirt. He could shower later, either here or back at his own place. He ambled toward the kitchen and started searching for the accoutrements he would need to make some java.

Two minutes later, he heard her yell.

"*Damn* it, Josh! You left the toilet seat up again!"

Oh, God. That was an unforgivable sin. Josh mentally kicked himself. "Sorry! I just forgot."

"God! How do you *forget* something like that? Don't forget again!"

Bang! She must have slammed it down, but hopefully she hadn't broken it. Oh well, this was her place, not his. But if she had, she would make him fix it.

He found a coffee filter, added some ground coffee beans and filled the reservoir with tap water. Oops–last time, she'd made him start over and use filtered water instead. He turned around to make sure she hadn't entered the room. Good–he was alone. He flipped the On switch and grabbed two mugs from the cabinet.

She was still in the bathroom. After a cup of Joe, he would finish dressing and get the hell out of here.

*

That night, Antoine picked June up at seven thirty.

Many of her friends dotted the audience of the Symphony performance in Woodruff Arts Center in Midtown, and several of them shot her big smiles and raised eyebrows. Word was out now–she had been seen in the company of an attractive man, out on a date.

During the intermission, she hurried to the ladies' room and rejoined Antoine in the lobby for a quick drink. No one she knew approached them, and after the performance, they took a side exit and quickly walked the short distance to Jolie's, a new restaurant around the corner.

"So, did you enjoy the performance?" Antoine asked once they were seated.

June smiled. "Very much. And you?"

He gave her a sly look. "Yes, but I'm enjoying this part of our evening so much more. Shall I order some wine?"

"That would be lovely."

"What do you feel like?"

"Oh, anything. I'm sure I'll love whatever you select."

She studied his face as he perused the wine list. *Could this really be happening?* Was she attracted to him because she was starved for male attention? No—that wasn't it. She honestly found this man captivating. He looked younger than his age, and had volunteered to her that he had no health problems. The French believe in going to doctors, he had said. *We love our pharmacies.* He was so unlike the other men who had expressed an interest in dating her over the past year, the men her girlfriends had tried to fix her up with—most of them balding and a little overweight.

She had read somewhere that the person least likely to be noticed in American culture was a woman in her fifties. But June didn't lump herself in with other women her age. She had a slender, proportional figure, and was in good physical shape. She did yoga and spinning classes every week at the club. She constantly watched her diet, and she wore a size four. She had taken great care of her skin and had few wrinkles. She didn't have even one gray strand popping out of her dark brown hair. Friends told her that she looked at least ten years younger than her age.

The waiter approached and took Antoine's order for a bottle of champagne and an appetizer to share.

"Now," he said, his eyes shining, "I have an idea that I'd like to present to you."

June lifted her eyebrows. "All right."

"What if you accompany me to Nice during the second week of September, and through that weekend? I have some business to take care of there, but it's very little. We could spend the rest of the time seeing the city, and relaxing together."

"My goodness. That sounds very appealing."

He smiled. "Have you been to Nice before?"

She shook her head. "Never." She had visited France many times with Jim, and they had been to the Côte d'Azur–the French Riviera–twice. But they hadn't ventured east of Cannes.

"Would you like to go with me, then? Get away together? I have a reservation at the Negresco. It's a beautiful hotel, just across from the sea and the *Promenade des Anglais.*"

"I'd love to." *What?* What had she just agreed to? She'd have to figure out if–

"Wonderful." His eyes sparkled.

She gazed at him and asked herself what could go wrong between them. Everything seemed too perfect. Was there something about him that she didn't know? Something that would doom their relationship, that might even end it?

14

Baby

Dawn stopped about fifteen yards from the ocean and looked at her sister. "How's this spot? Or do you want to put our chairs down closer to the water?"

"No, this is fine." Helen and Dawn had walked over to the beach from Sea Gem after Cole went down for his nap. Frank was staying in the house with him, and John had taken Adele out to buy a boogie board.

The sisters set their chairs next to each other. "I can't believe it isn't more crowded, this being Labor Day weekend and all," Helen said.

"Oh, I think it will get a little crowded." Dawn put her tote down and spread their towels on the beach chairs. The cloudless sky was a dazzling shade of blue, and a slight breeze tickled them with the scent of salt water. "Especially tomorrow and Monday. Next week, we ought to have the beach to ourselves, though."

Helen slipped off her cover-up to reveal a one-piece navy blue strapless bathing suit. She sat down next to Dawn, who was wearing a dark purple tank that flattered her height and figure.

"Pretty suit," said Dawn, smiling. "Is it one of Candace's?"

"Thanks, yeah. I got it a few months ago." Helen's former sister-in-law was the CEO of an Atlanta women's shapewear company that designed and sold a line of swimsuits. "It's so beautiful down here, Dawn. And Sea Gem is such a great place to spend your vacation. I can see why you guys don't want to sell it."

"We don't get down here often enough, though. You know how Frank hates to take time off."

"Well, now you have Cole. And, you own the place."

"Part own," corrected Dawn.

"Whatever. Anyway, I bet Frank'll want to come down a lot more often now."

"I think he will. We have to pay a third of the annual maintenance costs, so that right there will make him want us to come."

"Is it a lot of money? I don't mean to pry, but–"

"It's okay. But I won't tell you the amount. Let's just say, we have enough money put away, and can afford it. And Frank has good memories of the times he spent here when he was growing up. I think he feels kind of honored that his dad left it to him and his sisters. As Melody says, he kept it in the family, and wanted it to stay a tradition. The thing is, the house is so *big*. It's almost *too* big."

"Not when you all come down here together."

Dawn grimaced, and then humphed. "That's when it isn't big enough. You know that saying about how your 'relatives'"–she made air quotes–"begin to smell like dead fish, after three days?"

Helen chuckled. "Oops. Sorry we're here for the week."

"Not *you* guys, silly."

"Whatever you say. Anyway, I think the house is amazing. I'd love to come down here on a regular basis." Helen gazed at the ocean. "Would you give me the sunscreen?"

Dawn fished in her bag, pulled out the bottle, and handed it over.

"Thanks." Helen began reapplying it to her shoulders and arms. "So, since we're alone, I have something I want to tell you." She looked at Dawn.

Dawn turned to her sister. "What is it? Is it bad?"

Helen took a deep breath. "No. It's good. Really good."

Dawn raised her eyebrows. "Are you..."

Helen smiled. "I'm pregnant."

Dawn grabbed her arm. "Oh my God! Helen, that's wonderful! How far along are you?"

"I just found out. I'm due in late April."

"I'm so happy for you. Does Adele know?"

"Not yet. John and I are going to tell her in a few weeks."

"Oh. But—can I tell Frank?"

Helen nodded. "Now you know why I didn't have any wine last night when we got in. Even though I wanted it."

"Are you feeling okay this time?"

"Yeah. No morning sickness or anything. So different from last time, thank God, and no problems at all."

"That's great. I'm so excited for you!"

"Thanks." Helen gave her sister a measured look. "So. I know it may be too soon to ask, but since the process takes some time—are you and Frank thinking of adopting again?"

Dawn let out a sigh. "We haven't talked about it. And truthfully, I doubt we will. But you never know. We're just so thrilled to have Cole."

"He's a sweetheart. And he's just getting to the fun age."

Dawn smiled. "You know, I feel bad for June, that she was never able to have babies."

Helen turned to her. "How do you know she couldn't?"

"She told me. She knew how much I wanted Cole, and I guess she empathized. She said she'd had endometriosis so bad, she had to have a hysterectomy when she was only thirty. Before she met Jim, she thought she might never even get married."

"So that's why they never had children."

"That, and Frank always said that he thought his dad didn't want any more, since he was in his fifties when they got married."

"But if June had been able to have kids, and had wanted to, I would think Jim would have agreed."

"Well, evidently he married her knowing that she couldn't. And they were very happy together."

"Does Melody know this about June? Or does Valerie?"

"June said she told Melody a few years ago," Dawn said. "She and Melody are pretty close. She said she never mentioned it to Valerie, though."

"Valerie might have guessed it."

Dawn gave Helen a look. "I wouldn't bet on that."

"Mom!" called Adele. Helen turned and saw her daughter approach carrying a new boogie board. "Look!"

"Great! Hey, did you put on sunscreen?"

"Yep." Adele ran toward the water.

154

"Wait for me," called John. He walked up to his wife, gave her a kiss, and pulled off his T-shirt. "I'll go in with her."

"Good," said Helen. "She might need some help getting used to the waves."

John flashed a smile. "No problem, baby."

*

That evening, Dawn snuggled up next to Frank in the king-sized bed in the master suite. All six bedrooms in the house were enormous, but this one also had an adjacent spacious sitting room. Cole's portable crib sat in it. He was sound asleep, and the door was ajar.

"I'm so glad that Helen's happy," Dawn said. "She deserves it."

"John, too."

"Um-hm," murmured Dawn. "I know. Maybe it'll be a boy."

"I'm sure he'd like that."

"I'm so glad they could come down here with us. Helen couldn't get over how big the house is."

"Do you think she feels intimidated by it?"

Dawn shifted on her pillow and stretched out her legs. "No. And yes. She seemed pretty awed last night when they got in. But I think she's getting used to it. She and I have never really talked about how much money your dad had. Or the fact that you're going to inherit a lot someday."

"You know, since June's only in her fifties, we could be pretty old when I do. I mean, I don't even really count on getting that money. Women usually live longer than men do."

"She's twelve years older than you, though."

"Still. I mean, I do think about the money, for Cole. June may outlive us, but Cole ought to outlive her. God willing."

"This is so morbid."

"Well, even if I do outlive June, I look at my inheritance as something that will come in handy when we're old. We might need it for medical expenses."

"In addition to insurance, you mean?"

"Maybe. Who knows? We might want to pay whatever medical expenses we have ourselves."

"I hope we don't *have* any big medical expenses."

"Me, neither. But we might. And by paying for them ourselves, I don't mean only the big stuff. I mean things like going to the dentist, and seeing whichever doctors we want to see. Having the freedom to do what we want to do."

Dawn turned to her side to face him. "You think of everything."

"Well, it's just that it's been in the news. Anyway, my inheritance can help with medical care, retirement, and as a supplement to whatever amount we save up to leave to our children."

"You mean, child."

Frank pulled her close. "Who knows? He may have a sister or brother someday."

Dawn's eyes widened. "Are you saying you'd be okay with that?"

"Sure," said Frank. He looked into her eyes. "Would you be?"

"Yes," said Dawn. She reached her arm around him. "I'd be *very* okay with it."

Frank grinned. "I love having a family with you."

"Me, too." She leaned in to kiss him. "Don't ever change, okay?"

*

Two weeks later, Valerie drove over to her father's home on Sherwood Circle. June was out of town. Stupidly, she had posted something on Facebook that didn't say where she was going, but did specify when she would return: Monday, September 17.

Why June didn't know better than to make such a declaration on Facebook was beyond Valerie, but it suited her purposes. She planned to go over the house and take another look around. With June safely away, she could methodically search for any more jewels that could be hidden there, and she could also hunt for anything that had belonged to her father. She might even take whatever antiques and art she could carry. When June returned, she could think there had been a burglary, and would call the police. They would file a report, but they would tell June they probably wouldn't be able to recover anything. June would collect the insurance money, and Valerie could sell the items online after things died down.

So—no real harm done to June, and Valerie could get a little bit more of the money she believed her father wished her to have.

She still had her key to the house, and she wasn't worried about an alarm system. June said she never used it; she was afraid it would go off if someone tried to break in, and then what would she do? She was scared the police wouldn't get there in time, and a burglar would get spooked and attack her.

"If somebody takes something from the house, fine," June had said last winter. "Those things can all be replaced. But I don't want somebody to take *me*."

Valerie's amazement was outweighed only by her joy. And today, even if June had changed her mind since then and *had* set the alarm, Valerie could always tell the cops that she was kin, and didn't know it had been on.

She could talk her way out of it, and if they called June, so what?

She parked in the rear of the house and looked around. No one was about–good. She pulled her key out and tried to unlock the back door.

Her key didn't fit the lock.

"Fuck!" she said aloud, then bit her lip. That bitch must have changed the locks. She went around to a side door off the kitchen and tried her key there. Same thing. The only other entrance was the front door. In two minutes, Valerie was standing in front of it and cursing June again.

That woman had locked Valerie out of her childhood home–something that Valerie's father *never* would have done. But now the house belonged to June, and probably would forever. Despite her wish not to be seen, Valerie let out a small high-pitched scream and then muffled her voice. Who was June to lock Valerie out of her father's home? Was Valerie never to enter the house again without being invited?

That was simply unacceptable.

15

Stand Off

In late September, the oppressive heat of the Georgia summer was quickly becoming a fading memory.

The leaves were just beginning to turn, and in a few weeks, the city would be adorned in a color swatch of bright yellows, oranges, and reds. The air smelled fresh and light, blissfully stripped of humidity. Mornings were crisp and sometimes a bit chilly, but every day, afternoon temperatures reliably rose into the upper seventies or low eighties. Deep orange mums bloomed in the front yard of the Perkins home on Darlington Way, and the drunken, angry bees of August had graciously disappeared.

On a Thursday afternoon, Melody finished folding clothes and placed them in stacks in the laundry room. It was almost time to go pick up the children at school. As usual, the day had flown by. She always ran out of time on the weekdays, trying to get everything on her to-do list accomplished while the kids were away. She was either running errands, cleaning this room or that, or putting out constant small fires that popped up without warning like Whac-a-Mole. She started another load of laundry and heard her phone buzz.

"Is this a bad time?" asked Frank.

Melody sat down at the kitchen table. "Um, not really. What's up?"

"Bad news. I just learned that Valerie filed the suit."

"*Damn* it."

"Right. The judge is going to appoint a commissioner to go visit Sea Gem, to see if it can be divided equally. When he reports that it can't, the judge will order the property to be sold at auction."

"When the three of us talked, I thought she said the judge would order us to sell it ourselves."

"That's what she wants us to do. If we don't agree to do that, the judge will order a sale by auction. She's not going to want that, though—I'm sure she realizes that the highest bid would probably be a lot less than six million dollars."

"How *much* less, do you think?"

"I've been told that properties like Sea Gem can go for as low as half their value at auction. You and I just have to stand firm, Melody. If we do, I think she'll back off and drop the suit. She won't want to sell it for so much less than it's worth."

"Unless she really needs the money."

"Well, even if she does, I can't imagine that she'd want a fire sale as a temporary solution to some financial problem. She can always go to a bank and get herself a loan, if she needs money. Or, hey, she *could* cut her lifestyle."

"Ha! I can't see that happening. Can you?"

"She may have no other choice."

Melody frowned. "Well, if she pushes this thing and it does go at auction, we get screwed, too. What do we do?"

"We *could* just cave now. We could do what she wants, and buy her out. I don't think we'll have to, though."

"I really, really don't want to. As much as I wouldn't mind owning it just with you, I don't want to pay her a million dollars. Not that we have that much money just sitting around, ready to give her, so she can get her way." *Like she always does.*

"I don't think it will come to that. I think she won't want any less than two million dollars, and if she can't get that, she'll stop."

"But you don't know that."

"No, I don't. It's what I think, though."

"So what's the next step? I mean, what do we do now?"

"We wait for the commissioner's report. And we hope that Valerie understands how much less she would get than what she wants, if it goes to auction. But I think she already knows."

"So, to put it nicely, this is a standoff."

"I guess so. I think she'll change her mind, though."

"I hope you're right, Frank."

"Me, too."

*

That Saturday, Valerie went to Phipps Plaza to shop for a new bag at Saks. While she was there, she would also look at shoes. She wouldn't think about how much money she spent–she would just put everything on her Visa and forget about it.

Saks was one of her favorite stores, and the upscale department store was not yet a client of PriceUtopia. The startup's strategy had been to begin with the smaller discount chains, move on to retailers like Kohl's and Target, and ultimately work up to luxury department stores and chains. Now wasn't the right time to call on Saks. However, during the holiday season just ahead, all retailers would start to feel the pinch of show-rooming. Even stores like Saks and Neiman-Marcus weren't immune to the practice, whether they liked it or not.

Macy's was the first major non-discount department store to become a PriceUtopia client. Nordstrom and Belk were recent additions and were in the process of installing the technology in all their store locations. Like Josh, Valerie believed it was only a matter of time before all department stores did the same.

She found her way over to accessories, located on the store's main floor. A variety of designer bags crowded a sale table, but after a cursory glance, she quickly rejected them all. She wanted the latest style, the perfect bag for fall. One that she wouldn't regret having bought on sale simply to save a little money. She scanned the counters and shelves nearby, spying the Dolce & Gabbana bags and the new Fendi collection.

Of course, she had looked at many of them online before coming into the store–she had web-roomed. But she wanted to see them herself. She wanted to touch them, reach inside them, pick them up, and look at herself in the mirror holding them. She walked around the display to view another collection. Then she did a quick double take.

There stood June, five feet away from her, looking at a dark brown Brahmin satchel bag.

For half a second, Valerie considered ducking back around and behind the display. But before she could, June looked up and right at her.

The older woman's smile was tentative, and her tone was condescending. "Hello, Valerie."

Annoyed, Valerie feigned a smile. "Hi, there," she breathed.

An awkward moment passed as the two women stood facing each other, each at a loss for what to do next.

June broke the silence. "I just love the new bags, don't you?" She swept her eyes around the displays.

Valerie nodded and turned to view the collection, thankful to look away. Perhaps, if she stood there long enough, June would wander off somewhere and leave her in peace.

No such luck. "Looking for something in particular?" June persisted, her smile amused now. She locked eyes with Valerie.

Valerie motioned, glanced around, and then looked at June again. "Oh, you know. Just browsing. How about you?"

"Same. I do need a new bag, though." June paused. "Pretty necklace you're wearing."

Valerie's eyes narrowed. "Thank you." Her David Yurman thick gold link strand was the opposite of June's taste. How like June, to point out and compliment something she had to hate, and not admire.

Another moment or two passed. Like most women from the South, each tried to pretend that they didn't feel uncomfortable, though each fully understood that both did.

Valerie turned back to June and gave her a cold stare. *How long is she going to stand there? And why won't she just go away?*

Thankfully, a saleswoman appeared from out of nowhere and came to the rescue. She stopped a few feet from the women and seemed to read the situation somewhat. Valerie turned toward her.

"Hello," said the saleswoman. "Please let me know if I can help either of you." She flashed a smile and backed away slowly.

"Actually," called Valerie, "I think *I* would like some assistance." She glanced at June. "Have a good day." *And get out of here.*

June remained where she was, her feet planted. "You too."

Valerie stepped away and led the saleslady around a corner. On an impulse, she selected a leopard print Dolce & Gabbana bag and examined it. June had disappeared from her peripheral vision; hopefully, she'd had enough sense to make an exit by now.

At the register, Valerie handed the salesclerk her Visa card and eyed the nearby merchandise while she waited to sign. Maybe she ought to pick up another bag while she was here. She needed another black one.

"Goodness," the woman said, looking up from her device. "It seems we have a problem with your card."

Valerie turned and stared at her. "What do you mean, problem?"

The woman gave her a sheepish look. "Well, for some reason it's been rejected. Would you like to use a different card?"

Embarrassed, Valerie snatched the card away from her, put it in her wallet, and produced another one. *Did I max out on Visa last month?* Maybe, but she could figure that out later. Right now, she needed to make this purchase. She fished another credit card from her wallet.

A moment later, the woman gave her a sympathetic look. "I'm sorry, I'm getting the same thing on your MasterCard."

Valerie's face reddened, and she started to panic. *Is June still somewhere nearby, and within earshot?* She glanced around but didn't see her. "Are you sure it's not an issue on your end?"

The woman pursed her lips. "I'll try it again."

Valerie waited. *Shit. Is my MasterCard at its limit, too? There's no more room on Amex, either, since they put that ceiling on—*

"No," said the woman. "Same result. And I ran a diagnostic to make sure it's not my machine. I'm so sorry." She smiled. "What would you like to do?"

Valerie's face was rigid. *How can this be happening?*

Then she saw her stepmother loitering fifteen feet away over to the left. Their eyes met, and June threw her a patronizing look. Then June glanced away, a smile creeping on her face. Had she heard, and figured out what was going on?

It was possible.

"Ma'am?"

Valerie turned back to the woman. How dare she call her 'ma'am?' "Excuse me?" she snapped.

"Would you like to handle it another way?"

Valerie bristled. She couldn't use her debit card—she had just paid a bill from her attorney, and her checking account had dwindled to an all time low. There wasn't enough in it to cover this purchase, and she didn't get paid again until Friday. *Fuck.* "You know, I've run out of time now, and I've changed my mind, too. I think I'll just go online and buy it."

She turned abruptly and strode out of the department. *What a fucking disaster.* She had never had a credit card declined before. And—not only had June witnessed it, but worse, Valerie had had to leave the store without the bag she wanted.

In a flash, her mind traveled to an afternoon almost twenty-five years ago, when she was a teenager shopping here at Phipps. She wanted to buy an expensive designer purse that day too, but she hadn't had enough money. So she picked up one that didn't have a security tag attached, and slipped it inside the big leather bag she carried. Before that day, she had taken things from stores without paying at least a dozen times, and each time, it was easier to do. But the next time, it had turned into a nightmare.

It happened the summer after her first year in college. Frank had just graduated from high school, and had found a summer job. Their father insisted that she do the same. Reluctantly, she applied for a salesclerk job at a jewelry store in Lenox Square. Making only minimum wage plus a tiny sales commission, she counted the hours every day and almost went out of her mind with boredom.

Then one day near the end of June, she misplaced a pair of two-carat diamond earrings after showing them to a customer right before closing time. She panicked, but she didn't tell anyone while she searched for them. Five minutes later, she found them on the floor under the showcase a coworker had just locked. Instead of admitting what happened and asking the coworker to unlock it so she could put them back, she quietly dropped the earrings into her purse.

No one noticed that they were missing from the case.

She clocked out, but as she walked toward the door, a security guard blocked her way and told everyone they had to stay put. Evidently, he had seen something on the security camera. He searched everyone's pockets and bags. When the missing earrings turned up in Valerie's purse, she was immediately handcuffed and arrested.

She trembled, remembering that moment. Of course, she had lied to the police, saying she didn't know how the earrings got there. She told her father that another employee must have stolen them, panicked, and then put them in her bag.

Of course, he believed her. She guessed that he was still angry about what Owen had done to her—she had told him about that only weeks before. Her father had wanted to protect her from further humiliation. Indignant that she had been accused of a crime—and convinced she was innocent—he got the charges dropped in exchange for her resignation from the jewelry store and his purchase of the earrings. Then he gave them to her, and she spent the rest of that summer hanging out at the pool and playing tennis.

She hurried over to her car and slid behind the wheel. When she got home, she *would* go online, buy that same Dolce & Gabbana bag, and have it shipped.

As soon as she figured out how to pay for it.

167

16

A Zero-Sum Game

Ninety-one days after the failed IPO, PriceUtopia was no closer to going public than it had been on the afternoon of June 29. Josh sat at his desk on Friday, September 28, wondering what to do next.

In recent weeks, he and Graham had been busy fielding questions from the tech team and the product team. The latter was in charge of the creative side of development. Tasked with discerning client needs–and with designing the front end product to meet them–they worked closely with the tech team. Though it hadn't been officially approved, they had all been working hard on the next release. A few days ago, Graham told them to hold off for the time being. Now, both teams were anxious and confused.

Josh knew that he and Graham had exacerbated the situation with vague answers and uncertain leadership. Neither wanted to stall product improvements, but without more funding, the release would have to be delayed indefinitely.

And the funding side wasn't going very well. Just over a month ago, Swift Ventures had declined a request for $20 million.

"It's not that you don't have a good product," Julian had told Josh and Graham on a conference call that day. "You do. And you've put a lot of sweat equity into developing it. But the emphasis in tech companies has evolved over the last few years. It's not about changing the world anymore. It's not even about improving people's lives. Investing in technology is much more of a zero-sum game now. It's about knowing who else we need to *destroy* out there–and knowing how to do it. Eliminate others, to ensure our success."

During the discussion that followed, Josh felt as if he and Graham were playing high school defense against a seasoned NFL quarterback: inexperienced rookies who couldn't figure out how to hold their territory. It was demoralizing.

"I don't mean to be harsh, but I can't say this enough. Forget about trying to become some kind of an enabling force," Julian continued. "It's no longer about fulfilling a need. It's about *creating* a need, and then offering the best way to meet it–so that we can *all* get rich."

Josh and Graham exchanged apprehensive glances, unsure of what to say. Julian's assertion had irked Josh, but he held his tongue. After an awkward moment, Josh broke the silence.

"We believe we can do both–fulfill a need, *and* get us all rich. People aren't buying on impulse anymore. They buy only what they need, and they look online to save time and find deals. They want selection, less hassle, and price transparency."

"Bottom line," added Graham, "retailers have to respond to the new consumer environment. They have to be competitive to stay in business. In the past two years, the number of smartphones has doubled, from sixty million to a hundred and twenty. People are using them—and other devices—to find the lowest prices available."

"You're not telling me anything I don't know," said Julian. "We're all aware that consumers are more informed, and much savvier now. The group to reach is the millennial generation. They're more discerning, and much more likely to shop online. They're cherry pickers when it comes to making purchases. Retailers' margins are going to get worse for sure, whether they like it or not. They can't stop the process."

"Exactly," said Josh. "They're all going to have to play the game. But we can dominate the market, and crush any competitors. We're ahead of the game, Julian. We're so close now, too—we just have to stay focused right now, and not let anything throw us off plan."

A longer silence followed, and then Julian took an apologetic tone. "Josh, I admire your hubris. I always have. Success requires a certain bravado, and you've got it. But we have to say no to more money. It's not that we don't appreciate what you've done, or that we don't want you to succeed. We do. We've gotten straight talk from both of you. But we don't trust Stewart Young anymore. We *still* haven't learned why Cornucopia pulled out of your IPO at the last second. I can't *tell* you how unnerving that is, and that's putting it mildly. Frankly, it's a mystery that *you* guys need to solve, if you want to move forward and make a success of your company. Honestly, I can't believe you haven't done so yet."

Graham rolled his eyes at Josh, but kept his mouth closed while Julian wrapped up the conversation. "Look. Keep us apprised of your plans for another offering, and good luck in getting there. I've got to jump now. Just remember, we're on your side."

"Julian, we understand your concerns, but–" Josh began.

"Good," Julian said. "Gotta go now. Best of luck."

Since that afternoon, luck had not been good. Josh rubbed his wide forehead, feeling a headache coming on. He was sick of headaches–literal and figurative. The roadshow he and Graham had done to try and court more investors after Swift had declined had been a bust. Worse, when they didn't have good news to report to employees, morale had taken a further dive. Everyone was nervous now, and productivity was lower than ever.

Josh stood up and walked to the window. For weeks, he hadn't been able to shake something he had heard from the venture capitalist they met with out in Austin. The guy had seemed very interested in PriceUtopia, and was full of compliments about the product and their presentation. But he'd been ambiguous about investing in the company. When Josh had pushed him, his response was probably the most honest thing he or Graham had heard since the end of June:

"The thing is, we've heard that there are some developments going on in this space. So we need to wait and see what happens with that before we make any investment decision."

Josh couldn't get those words out of his mind. Was there a hint within them about why Cornucopia had pulled their order from the IPO? Did the Texas investor know something that he and Graham didn't?

What developments?

*

David felt that his new title was pretentious, if factual: *Advisor to Families of Significant Wealth.* But leadership at Elite Financial Planning had recently decided that neither Financial Advisor nor Wealth Manager accurately described his job.

He'd had a busy week. It was the final week of the third quarter of the calendar year, which was the same as the firm's fiscal year. He had reviewed investment and financial reports for several clients, and had met with the accountants. Yesterday, he had welcomed a brand new client, an architect moving down to Atlanta from D.C. who had bought a home in Brookwood.

David was more than ready for the weekend, and was glad his job didn't require him to put in any time on Saturdays or Sundays anymore. Families "of significant wealth" were certainly demanding, but emergencies rarely occurred outside of normal business hours. Financial emergencies, that is. Sometimes, personal issues developed on the weekends, and they had often interfered with—and interrupted—David's leisure time. But when that happened, he stepped in to help out. It was part of his job.

Rich people were complex. Executives who had earned sizable fortunes were often, not surprisingly, Type A personalities. David could deal with those types of people very well. He was a good listener, rarely became ruffled, and was adept at not wasting other people's time. The latter was an important quality in his profession, since wealthy people valued their time very highly, with good reason.

But those who had personality issues, on top of being Type A–well, those people were a challenge, at best. Each one had his own idiosyncrasies, to put it nicely; to put it honestly, each had his own specific disorders. Many were narcissists, and some of them bordered on sociopathic. But they had been able to channel their disorders into successful careers. If they weren't exactly humble, at least they knew how to charm others. And if they didn't have particularly high IQs, many possessed a high level of emotional intelligence. They knew how to feign empathy, even when–and though–they didn't feel it. They were good actors.

But having emotional intelligence didn't mean they were emotional, as long as David was generalizing. These were tough individuals–they had done much more to succeed than others had done, and they had done it for a lot longer. Some of them had sacrificed family life to do it, or if they hadn't, their relationships had suffered somewhat. But they made lots of money.

And helping them take care of their money was David's métier.

He stood up and stretched. It was almost six, and the Atlanta traffic was in full swing. The Shepherds had been clever enough–or sensible enough–to buy a home just a few miles from the office, easy to reach by navigating a web of seldom-used back roads. If he walked out the door now, he would be home by six twenty; by six thirty, he'd have a cocktail in his hand.

His phone buzzed, disrupting his plan. "Hello, June."

"Hi, David. Sorry to call right before the weekend."

"No problem. What's going on?"

173

"Well, it's not a big deal. I wanted to run something by you before I see my sister Linda tomorrow. It's just an idea I had."

"Okay. Shoot."

"Well, her son Chad is applying to a bunch of colleges this fall–he's super smart, and he'll probably get into every single one he applies to. But the only one on his list that she and Clay can afford is Georgia, and that's the one he's the least interested in attending."

"That's too bad."

"It is. I don't know why he doesn't want to go there– Georgia's a good school now, and Linda says he'll qualify for 100 percent of the Hope scholarship."

"That's terrific."

"Yes. But as I said, he'd rather go somewhere else. She told me he's applying to five or six other schools, all of them expensive, and his top two choices are Vanderbilt and UNC Chapel Hill."

"How can I help?"

"That's just it. *I'd* like to help–if I can. Jim and I talked about doing that very thing, and so I feel he would want me to. What I wanted to know from you is whether, if I paid for Chad to go to one of those schools, would I have to pay a gift tax on it?"

David paused for a second. "The short answer is no, you wouldn't, because there's an exclusion for education. But you would have to pay his tuition directly to the school. You can't give it to him, or to the family, for them to pay it."

"Hm. Does the exclusion apply to tuition only?"

"I'll have to check on that–it might include fees, and room and board."

"Would you do that? In the meantime, I want to propose the idea to my sister when I see her this weekend. I just want to give her son some more options. She and Clay make too much money for Chad to get any real financial aid or a decent scholarship. They're solidly middle class—they don't make enough money to afford the cost of a private university, or out of state tuition somewhere. She was appalled when she found out what the government said she and Clay ought to be able to afford, once they filed their forms."

"I'm sorry."

"And Chad has worked so hard—and here *I* sit, with so much money in the bank that I don't really need. The thing is, I don't want him to go out and get himself an enormous loan that would take him forever to pay off."

David smiled. Many of his clients gave generous financial gifts to charities, occasionally to underlings, or even to strangers. When they did, they rather liked to have it publicized. But, for most, generosity to extended family was rare indeed.

Unless there was some kind of string attached.

"I admire you for wanting to help him, June. But—well, I don't mean to be blunt, but in situations like this, I think it's a good idea to ask yourself some hard questions."

"What kind of questions?"

"Well, first of all, do you think that, if you do this, you'll want something in return from your nephew? Or from your sister? For example, would you expect Chad to be more in touch with you than he's been in the past? Other than thanking you, would you expect him to do anything else?"

"Oh no, I don't think so."

"What about telling you what his grades in college are? Do you think that if you paid his tuition and expenses, you'd want to know that?"

"Oh, I'm sure he'll do well—as I said, he's very smart. I know he's a hard worker, too. I don't think I'd *need* to know."

"But—would you be curious? I'm asking because I think it's good to take an honest look at your expectations, if you have any. If you don't, well, I think that's the right attitude to take. If you do, though, I think you need to recognize them, and then communicate them to your sister and her son."

"I see what you're saying, David, and I appreciate it. You always give me such good counsel. I'm close to Linda, but money does put a complication in there. When I see her, I think I need to be clear that I *don't* have any expectations."

"Good. Okay, while we're on the subject, let's consider this. What if Chad quits school before he graduates, or what if he doesn't graduate on time? From what you've said about him, I doubt either of those would happen. But maybe you could tell your sister that you'd like to pay for a four-year degree—or tell her the amount of time that it takes him doesn't matter to you, if it doesn't. And, if he *should* quit school before getting a degree, outline to her what you'd do in that case, too. I just think it's good to be open and clear."

"You're right, David. I hadn't thought about either of those, and even though I don't see them happening, you never know what the future holds. As far as grades, or being more in touch with me, I really don't have any wishes there. I just want our relationships to stay the same as they are now."

"That's a very realistic approach. One more thing. What if, once you take this financial burden off of your sister and her husband, you notice them spending a lot of money on other things?"

"What things?"

"Well, things like vacations, cars, whatever. Extras that they couldn't afford if you weren't helping in this way. Or—what if they sold their house and bought a more expensive one? Would you care?"

"Of course not! The reason I want to do this is so that they *can* do things like that! I want to do something meaningful for them, and give them more freedom."

"That's fantastic, June. Okay, let me know when and how you want me to handle things. I'll get back to you next week about whether you can pay fees and costs other than tuition. If you have any concerns after you talk with Linda, don't hesitate to call."

"Thanks so much, David. Have a great weekend."

"You, too." David clicked the phone and reached for his briefcase. June was refreshingly different from most rich people, and he was sure that her intentions were good.

He checked his watch. He would have that cocktail in his hand by six forty-five.

17

The Heebie-Jeebies

Valerie almost always got the heebie-jeebies on Sunday nights.

Her father had called it the Sunday night blues: doubts, worries, or even feelings of dread about the coming week. She called it the heebie-jeebies, because instead of feeling depressed, she usually felt nervous, anxious, and a little disorganized. To chase away those feelings, she had to do something productive. If she didn't, it was on Sunday nights that she reflected about her life. Another week was over, and she couldn't get it back. It was a morbid thought, but exactly how many more weeks did she have to *live?* How many more *years* did she have? As many as she'd already lived? Hopefully, since she was only forty-two. But not necessarily.

To distract herself this evening, she decided to reorganize her closet. Even though the season hadn't changed for good yet, she ought to go ahead and switch out her summer wardrobe for her winter clothes. In a few weeks, warm temperatures would be over until spring. The cold rainy days of November and December loomed ahead, just over the horizon. She had several coats, sweaters, and long-sleeved tops; she needed to discard the ones she no longer wanted, and organize the rest. She would leave her sleeveless tops and dresses where they were, though. She could always wear them in the winter with a jacket or a wrap. In Atlanta, you had the occasional odd winter day when the high temperature climbed into the seventies.

She pulled out a red and black patterned sweater and evaluated it. What had she been thinking when she bought this? It was ugly and unflattering, and she couldn't recall it ever being in style. She threw it in the pile. Soon she was on automatic pilot, quickly deciding whether to toss or keep item after item. As the mound of clothes grew larger, her mind began to wander.

Tomorrow was October first, and it was time for her to make a decision about Sea Gem. The commissioner had viewed the property and had turned in his report: as everyone expected, it couldn't be subdivided equitably. Any agreement to carve it up would have to be reached independently by the parties involved. That didn't seem likely, so the next step was for the judge to order it sold at auction to the highest bidder.

If that happened, it would go for a lot less than its market value, and Valerie and her siblings would be throwing away a huge chunk of their inheritance. While none had put any of their own funds into the home, as owners they ought not sell it for so much less than what it was worth. But if things proceeded, that's exactly what they would be doing.

By staying silent, Frank and Melody had called her bluff, and they had challenged her to a game of chicken. They wanted her to back off and drop the lawsuit so they could win. If she didn't drop it, she would win, but she would lose more than just a game. She would get only a portion of what she ought to receive.

She hated both of them for putting her in that position.

Whatever happened, she couldn't live like this anymore. Her salary covered only her most basic expenses. Her credit cards were at their limits, and some of her bills were more than a month past due. She had to catch them up, and prioritize her expenses. She could cut some things out, but she wasn't going to sell her condo or downsize her car—doing those things might buy her some time, but they wouldn't solve her problems.

There had to be a better way to get the funds she needed.

Her eyes fell on a silver cowl neck sweater she had bought in December. It was okay for the holidays, but she rarely wore it otherwise; more importantly, it didn't make her feel pretty last year. It wasn't very flattering, and it seemed to accentuate her rather thick neck, instead of distract from it. Would she miss it if she threw it out—would she ever want to wear it again? Probably not. This year, she would want something new to wear, anyway. She tossed it in the pile.

She couldn't afford to be impulsive about Sea Gem, though. She needed to put emotion aside, weigh her options, and make a wise decision about what to do. Though she would hate to let her siblings get their way, dropping the suit might be her best course of action. And who knew? One day, they might change their minds and agree to sell, and then she would get the funds from it that she deserved. But instead of forcing a sale now for so much lower than the home's market value, she ought to switch

DADDY'S GIRL

gears, and come up with another way to get the money she needed.

*

Josh stretched out on the chocolate leather sofa in his apartment, mindlessly flipping channels and drinking a beer.

He'd spent the weekend *not* seeing Valerie, and he felt great.

Exactly five weeks ago, he had met Aimee Lovejoy through his brother Andrew and Andrew's wife Claudia. Claudia had introduced them at Andrew's fortieth birthday party. It was the night after Josh had shown up at Valerie's with an orchid and an apology at the end of a hellish week. He had left her place quickly the next morning, barely escaping her tirade about his bathroom faux pas.

Compared to Valerie, Aimee was a breath of fresh air—actually, compared to *anyone*, she was a breath of fresh air. And Aimee was everything that Valerie wasn't: considerate, patient, and unselfish. She was also nine years younger than Valerie, and she had a sweet, girl-next-door look about her. Her dark eyes and long brown curly hair reminded him of Andie MacDowell in *Groundhog Day*, one of his favorite movies. Aimee had moved up to Atlanta from Orlando six months earlier for a new job—she was an animator at Turner Broadcasting, and she had worked at Disney for ten years.

"What was that like?" Josh had asked her.

"Really, it was amazing," Aimee said. "I started at Disney right after college. I got to see so many changes there, and learned so many new things. It was great preparation for Turner."

"That's terrific. Andrew told me Rick said you love your new job."

"I do. I miss Florida, and most of all, the beach. But Atlanta's a really nice town."

"I like it a lot here," Josh said. "It's vibrant, and there's a lot of opportunity. But the traffic sucks. What's arguably worse, I don't think the city always gets the respect it deserves."

Aimee tilted her head, and a strand of curly hair dropped in front of her eye, flirting with her long eyelashes. "What do you mean?"

"Oh, I don't know. I guess I'm thinking of our sports teams. Or maybe the fact that we're in the South, and that in itself gets misunderstood, sometimes." He meant, but didn't add, that outsiders seemed to think southerners were a bunch of hicks.

"I know what you're saying. Did you grow up here?"

"No–Charleston."

She smiled broadly. "Oh, I *love* it there!"

Josh grinned. "It's a fun town, and it's becoming a technology innovation hub. Kind of an incubator for tech startups."

"Is that what you do? Work in technology?" She sipped her gin and tonic.

Josh nodded. "Yeah, kind of. A friend and I founded a tech startup a few years ago." He sipped his cocktail. "He handles the tech side, and I handle the marketing and management side."

"That's so cool! Tell me about it."

Josh hit the highlights, being careful not to bore her or to complain about the stress. Soon they were talking about what their work had in common: creativity, cleverness, and imagination. It was exhilarating to talk with a woman who appreciated what he did, for a change. And it was a relief not having to brace himself for a random explosion about something ridiculous and inconsequential, like he'd had to do way too often around Valerie.

As they chatted, Josh was drawn in by Aimee and was intrigued by her sweet nature. There was definitely some chemistry going on there. Aimee seemed worldly enough, and as savvy as any other woman of her age. But she was also genuine, and funny. She didn't have a snarky bone in her very attractive body. As he listened to her talk about Florida, her brother, and her parents, he kept telling himself to view her only as Andrew's friend's sister. Not as a potential girlfriend–for fuck's sake, he had rolled out of Valerie's bed only hours earlier.

But Aimee's manner had communicated some kind of signal that she was interested in him, and he just couldn't help himself. Before long, he was telling her all about himself, his company, and his aspirations. Of course, he hadn't mentioned Valerie.

He got Aimee's number at the party, and they had several text conversations over the next couple of weeks. How refreshing it had been to exchange flirty texts, instead of business-y or terse ones with Valerie. Then, one Thursday evening, Josh met Aimee for dinner in Midtown. That night, he laughed more with her–and shared more about himself–than he had ever done with Valerie. Since then, they had talked or texted almost every day, and last night, they had slept together for the first time. He wasn't sure if he was falling in love with Aimee, but he knew that he had fallen deeply in lust.

What a mistake he'd made in ever getting involved with Valerie, and worse, in continuing to see her all this time. His old man had cautioned him time and again about the perils of sleeping with someone at the office. Like an idiot, though, he had paid the warning no heed.

Turns out he was right about one thing, at least.

He took a deep breath and exhaled. It was time to make a big change in his personal life. Whatever happened with Aimee–and of course, he hoped they would continue seeing each other–he would be a cad to go out with her, let alone sleep with her, if he kept on screwing Valerie. He already felt like a cad, after last night with Aimee. Of course, he hadn't said he had a girlfriend. He had justified his omission by rationalizing that Valerie wasn't really his girlfriend. She was only his sex partner.

Even so, he had to break off his relationship with Valerie, no matter what the ramifications were or what kind of hell she raised. Maybe she wouldn't go nuts, anyway–maybe she was just as tired of him as he was of her. And why wouldn't she be? They weren't emotionally close–they never talked about anything except work. They weren't intimate. Their relationship was tense, at best. At worst, it was toxic. He couldn't afford to continue in a toxic relationship with *any* woman–not personally, and not professionally.

He hadn't slept with Valerie in over two weeks–a record. Perhaps he didn't even need to tell her straight out that he wanted to stop seeing her. Maybe all he had to do was just avoid her outside of the office. He didn't have to take her out anymore, and he didn't *have* to sleep with her. Their relationship, such as it was, could just cool off naturally. He didn't think she would miss him much, anyway.

She might want things to cool off–and to end–as much as he did.

Yes, that was the answer. He would be cordial and professional with Valerie at the office, but he wouldn't be weird or distant. However, he would stop assuming they would see each other after work, and on the weekends. If she mentioned it, he would say he couldn't do it, and make some excuse. Maybe, eventually, he could get her to believe that ending things was *her* idea.

If he couldn't, there might be hell to pay.

He finished his beer and went to the head. He'd chill out tonight and watch the Eagles game. He needed to clear his mind. Then he needed to get a good night's sleep before he tackled the coming week.

*

Melody had a hundred and forty-three Facebook friends.

Many lived in Charlotte, and some were friends from Davidson College, where Melody and Jeff had met and started dating. Some were high school friends, and a few were family members. Dawn was friends with her, of course, and so were June and June's sister Linda. However, other than occasionally posting a photo of the children, Melody rarely got on her Facebook page anymore, or spent much time looking at her friends' updates.

But on Monday afternoon, she sat down at her laptop and pulled up her page. She had about ten minutes before she had to go and pick up the kids. Her most recent post was a photo of Nick, and June had already commented on it (*"So cute!"*). Melody clicked idly on June's name to bring up her page.

June's profile photo hadn't changed, but she had posted a lot lately. At the top was a photo of her and Linda that looked as if it had been taken recently. Underneath it were several Likes and comments.

Melody's eye fell on a comment Linda had made. *"Thanks so much for your generous offer! Chad's very grateful to have more choices for college next fall!"*

Melody's jaw dropped. Chad was Linda's son, and evidently he was a high school senior this year. Did this mean June had offered to pay for him to go to an expensive school? *Surely* Linda hadn't meant to make her comment a public one. Didn't she know she could send a private message to June on Facebook? Possibly not.

But, more importantly, who else had seen this?

Melody clicked over to June's friend list. *Was Valerie friends with her?* Only if they had friended each other, a long time ago. She started typing in Valerie's first name—

There she was. *Shit.* If Valerie had seen that comment, she would be incensed. Though paying for Chad's college expenses wouldn't make a huge dent in their father's fortune—and their inheritances—it *was* a good bit of money, especially if he was going to an expensive private school. The question was, if Valerie knew about this, would she have a fit? Would she accuse June of squandering the family money? If Melody had thought of it that way, even briefly, Valerie certainly would.

But why did Melody even care what Valerie would do? She let out a deep breath and glanced at the top right side of the screen. It was time for her to leave. Napoleon scampered up to her with an expectant look. She scooped the dog up, grabbed her bag, and got in the car.

186

18

Surprise, Surprise

Last night, Valerie had slept on her dilemma about Sea Gem. She had woken up feeling more resolved about what to do, and a little calmer about her financial situation. She had called her attorney first thing this morning and instructed him to drop the lawsuit.

Then she got on Facebook and saw Linda's comment to June on her newsfeed.

What was June *doing,* dipping into her late husband's fortune to pay for *her* nephew's college costs? Unless he was going to an in-state university–and the phrase about having more choices next fall suggested otherwise– she had offered to pay for a private college, or some expensive out of state university. And what would make her stop there? What if the nephew went on to grad school, and she paid for that, too? Once she established this gravy train, who knew when or where it would end?

It was unbelievable. Next thing you knew, June would be buying her sister a new car, or taking her family on a luxury vacation. Or she would buy them a new house.

What if one of June's relatives got sick, and she decided to pay all their medical bills?

Why aren't there specific restrictions on what June can do with the family money? And why is she allowed to fritter so much away on people who aren't even her husband's blood? Why is June allowed to funnel hundreds of thousands to her sister's family, yet she isn't able to lend me a comparable sum?

Valerie was furious, but not just because of what she had seen online. She was angry that she didn't know the conditions of the trust. Why hadn't her father shared them with her? He couldn't have predicted that June would do something like this. Clearly, he had intended that his fortune be preserved and passed on to his own children someday. But evidently, in the meantime, June had the freedom to do whatever she wished to do with the funds.

Valerie needed to figure out how to protect her inheritance before it diminished any further.

Over the next few hours, she walked around in a semi-daze, unable to focus on work or accomplish very much. The sales team looked despondent and seemed unmotivated, and the marketing people were freaking out. Sales had slowed to a standstill, and the implementation team was idle, too. Morale was way down throughout the office. Employees were acting nervous and worried. Someone on the finance team had been quietly crying in the break room this morning, and another person quit this afternoon.

Around three o'clock, Valerie's inbox dinged receipt of a new message. Josh wanted to see her in his office for a client update. She let out a deep sigh. How in the hell did he expect her to do her job when things were in such disarray? With nothing to do, people were now gathering in groups of twos and threes, whispering their concerns and keeping secrets. Cliques had formed, and the atmosphere was listless, even chilly. Everyone at the office knew that he and Graham had struck out when they went on their latest roadshow. No one knew what was going to happen to the company, nor did they know when—or if—it would ever go public.

Josh had been extraordinarily cool toward her recently, too. Last week, he had barely exchanged a word with her, and they hadn't slept together since the middle of last month. She had just had her period, but the week before that, for whatever reason, they hadn't seen each other outside of the office. He was probably as down about what was going on as anyone else, and with good reason. Maybe he'd been in his man cave.

Whatever. In any case, he ought to be paying much more attention to her. It was unlike him not to want to go to bed with her, especially after this long. The fight they'd had back in August about the psychological assessments could have been the start of the current chill between them. She was still upset over the way he had treated her at the meeting, and his backhanded apology had been insufficient and weak.

Even so, she missed being with him. She had had plenty of solitude lately. He wasn't perfect, but then again, no man was. He was good at lightening her mood when she was upset, and he did have some nice qualities. He was optimistic, a glass half full guy, and when she let him, he could bring her out of a funk. She didn't always laugh at his jokes, but he was patient, and a pleaser—kind of like a puppy. And he was good in bed. But for some reason, he wasn't paying her much attention lately. She wasn't going to confront him about it, though. She would be all business when they met to discuss client status up-dates. If he didn't want to have sex with her, fine. She certainly wasn't going to beg.

*

Josh looked at Graham, sitting across from him in the conference room. "I spent the whole weekend worrying. Most of it, anyway," he said.

"I did, too. I don't know *how* we got to where we are now."

Josh puffed his cheeks and raised his eyebrows. "It sucks, where we are."

Graham ran a hand through his hair and scratched the back of his head. "Did you hear back from Ferguson?"

Josh shut his eyes. "They passed. As expected."

"*Damn* it. Do we do another roadshow, do you think?"

"I don't know. What choice do we have, though? We've got to have more money. We could cut expenses—"

"You mean, people."

Josh shook his head slowly. "I don't want to do it, but it looks like we may have to."

"Man, this is *so* not what we planned."

"Plans change." Josh pushed away from the table, stood up, and put his hands on the back of his chair. The elephant in the room was still sitting there, and he and Graham had made an unspoken agreement to ignore it and hope it would go away. If it didn't, then at least the Cornucopia mystery would be solved.

But no matter what, the sooner the new release was out, the better—and at least getting that done was under their control. Then they could beat others to the market, as intended, and it wouldn't matter why Cornucopia had pulled. That would just be some blip in the past. "We just have to adapt, that's all. What if we cut some nonessential staff, like some of the admin roles? Let the others take their work, and reallocate it."

"That's not going to be fun."

"I know. But we can do with less employees."

"How about marketing and sales?"

"We should look at them, and we need to let go of some people on the implementation team. We ought to cut some of the support staff, too." Josh rubbed his forehead. "Obviously, we keep everyone who has intimate knowledge of the product."

"That includes contractors." Over half the tech team worked on a contract basis, and they were the company's highest-paid employees.

"Agreed. Anyone who's hands-on, supporting the platform, stays." He raised his eyebrows and looked his partner in the eye. "Look. We still have a great idea, and we have a fantastic product. We just have to ride this situation out. We can hire again when we have more money—"

"But when are we going to have more money?" asked Graham. "Tell me. Because once we run out—"

"We're *not* going to run out of money. Mark my words."

*

Two days later, on the first Wednesday of October, June arrived early at the club for bridge.

Lois walked up to her and squeezed her forearm. "Hey, girl. We're partners today." She grinned.

June smiled. "Fantastic! I can be assured of winning, for once."

Lois laughed. "We'll see. But, yes, I'd bet on it, if I were you." She winked.

A moment later, the women sat down across from each other at the card table. "Looks like we're up against Kitty and Nancy today," said Lois. "Angela's on that cruise, over in France."

"Oh, that's right. Lucky her!"

Lois leaned forward slightly. "Speaking of France, how's Antoine? And tell me about your *own* trip over there last month."

June lowered her chin and looked up at her friend. "It was very romantic," she said in a low tone.

"I'm not surprised. Tell me all about it."

"Now, or should I wait for Kitty and Nancy?"

Lois cocked her head. "Is word out, then? Are you two a couple?"

June blushed. "I suppose. But no, word isn't out, not to everybody. I don't mind telling my friends, but I'm not telling Jim's children."

"Good girl. Don't. They don't need to know. Keep your private life private, that's my advice."

June smiled again. "Well, it's not like I see any of them all that much. Though I did run into Valerie at Phipps, about a week and a half ago."

"What's this about Valerie?" asked Nancy. She and Kitty had walked up behind June a second earlier and were pulling out their chairs to sit down.

June turned to Nancy. "Ran into her shopping. It was awkward, to say the least."

"I'm sure it was," said Lois.

Kitty's eyes widened. "What happened?" She brushed a lock of straight, silver hair away from her face.

"Oh, it wasn't too bad. It was over quickly, anyway. We stumbled upon each other in accessories, and of course she was her haughty self." June rolled her eyes. "When the saleslady came over, she grabbed a purse from the counter and tried to buy it."

"What do you mean, 'tried?'" said Nancy. "Didn't she succeed?"

"That's just it. I walked away, but I couldn't help but overhear the commotion. Seems her credit cards were declined." June lifted her brows.

"Oh, Lord," said Lois. "So—what did she do?"

"What *could* she do? Told the girl that she'd go and buy it online. Was real bitchy to her, too."

"Surprise, surprise," said Lois.

"Do you think it was an identity theft thing?" asked Kitty. "Like her credit card was hacked?"

"Who knows? If so, I'm sure she dealt with it. In any case, she looked very embarrassed, and then she stomped off. I haven't seen her since."

"My goodness," said Nancy, shaking her head.

"Maybe she's maxed out in all of her credit cards," said Lois.

June bit her lip. If Valerie was in serious financial trouble, that could be the reason she had wanted that half million dollars.

No. Couldn't be.

Kitty turned to June. "Well, I'm sorry you had to deal with her. Now, tell us about your trip to France with Antoine. Was it just wonderful?"

June glanced around the table. "It was." She smiled.

Nancy tilted her head toward June. "So, it's going well with him?"

"*Very* well. I don't know how it's happened, y'all, but I guess he's kind of swept me off my feet."

Kitty laid her hand on June's forearm. "Are you two getting serious?"

June shut her eyes for a second. "Maybe. I don't really know! I'm very happy, though. Let's just leave it at that, for now."

Lois raised her eyebrows. "Next thing you know, you'll be engaged."

June gave her partner a look. "Marriage is the *farthest* thing from my mind."

"Currently," corrected Lois. She shot back a sly smile.

June shook her head. "Honestly. I know y'all want to marry me off, but trust me on this. If you want to call it an affair, do. Antoine is very romantic, and he and I are enjoying each other's company. But right now, that's *it*."

Nancy fanned the cards out face down, and drew a Jack. "Whatever you say, June. I'm just glad the two of you are spending so much time together." She smiled coyly. "Didn't you say he worked for the French government?"

June nodded. "He has, for some time. Doesn't have to work all that much anymore, either." She drew a Queen.

Kitty slid a card out and turned it over; it was the eight of Hearts.

"None of the French work all that much—at least, that's what *I've* always heard," said Lois. She reached over, drew the Ace of Spades, and smiled. "Okay, girls. My deal." She picked up the other deck.

June gathered the cards on the table and began to shuffle them. "Well, it's a different system over there in France. In any case, he's very comfortable, financially."

"That's nice," said Nancy. She tilted her head again.

Kitty turned to June. "I expect that you and Antoine have a lot more to learn about each other. No matter what happens, that ought to be very interesting, and *lots* of fun."

"You know, it has been, so far. But I have to be truthful with you. It still feels a little strange, being with a man who's not Jim."

"Give yourself time," said Lois. "You'll get used to it." She winked again. "Or maybe you already have. One Heart."

19

Epiphany

At three o'clock the next morning, Melody couldn't sleep.

Eyes wide open, she lay on her back next to Jeff, who was on his side, facing away from her. They had gone to bed together at ten thirty, after all the kids were asleep in their rooms. Around eleven, they'd fallen asleep in each other's arms after making love. She had felt great then and quickly dozed off, but now she was restless and wakeful, and she couldn't relax.

It was probably the wine. She'd had one glass too many, once again. It was a bad habit, but only a habit—she could cut down, and could even stop drinking anytime, if she wanted to. When Jeff was away on business, she rarely drank—at least, not too often. When she did, she always thought of Rhett Butler's line in Gone With The Wind.

"Don't drink alone, Scarlett. People always find out and it ruins your reputation."

Last night, she hadn't been drinking alone. She and Jeff had split a bottle of wine and then had opened another. After that, she had lost track.

Four hours later, she was lying here, paying the price. She didn't feel awful, physically—just a twinge of a headache forming, and she could always pop a couple of Advil for that. She did feel anxious and out of sorts, though, as if she had forgotten to do something very important, or even crucial.

But she was sure that she hadn't.

She inhaled, let out a deep breath, and tried to calm her nerves. She hated it when her mind went into overdrive like this. Random thoughts, worries, and doubts surfaced uncontrollably and wouldn't go away. She drew closer to Jeff, trying to comfort herself with his warmth. His long frame served as a body pillow, and as long as she didn't wake him, she could snuggle up to him in peace. She closed her eyes and tried to clear her mind.

It wasn't working.

She turned to her other side and flipped her pillow over to the cool side. Should she read for a while, to distract herself? No—she couldn't afford to lose more sleep. The kids would be awake in a little over three hours, and it would be the start of another busy day. She couldn't put the treadmill of life on pause tomorrow morning just because she was wakeful right now.

Her days were filled with so many tasks, some of them seemingly useless, or worse, unappreciated. But as soon as she felt it, she willed away her self-pity. She had a good life, even if busywork took up most of her time. Four young children depended on her, and she was doing her best to mother them all. The time since Pip and Neely became part of the family had been challenging, though. In truth, her relationships with the two of them were the most difficult ones in her life. Plus, she felt she had to manage their relationship with each other. They were so different, yet they were close—that was something to be thankful for. Since she had never been close to her own sister, she couldn't know what that was like.

She had tried to tell Jeff how she felt about the girls, but she had hesitated to be totally honest. They were his blood—his twin sister's children, and he cherished them. He was counting on Melody to take her place in raising them. She loved him, and because of that, she would love the girls. She and Jeff would make it through the years ahead together.

She tried to relax, but her eyes were open now. Then the phone conversation she'd had with Frank today began circulating in her mind. Evidently, he told her, Valerie had dropped her lawsuit. Sea Gem was going to stay in the family. Valerie had even been apologetic about having filed the suit in the first place, and Frank had no reason to believe she wasn't sincere. He and Melody had won the battle over Sea Gem, and Melody had gotten her way, for once.

She tossed in bed, feeling relieved and grateful, but also bewildered. Valerie rarely said she was sorry about anything, and sincerity wasn't one of her qualities. Did she have some kind of an ulterior motive?

Melody shuddered and unsuccessfully tried to banish her suspicions. Valerie never did anything without a reason, and it wasn't like her to surrender. It couldn't be because she now understood why the rest of the family enjoyed going to Sea Gem. It also couldn't be that she had suddenly become selfless. Maybe she had gotten a big bonus, or had come into a bunch of money some other way. Perhaps her business was a lot better, she didn't need the money anymore, and didn't want to fool with a lawsuit. And lawyers were expensive.

Most likely, though—and as Frank had predicted earlier—she had decided she didn't want to risk getting a lot less for her share than two million dollars, if the house were sold at auction.

It was a puzzle, and not one that Melody was going to solve tonight. She closed her eyes again, clutched her pillow against her forehead, and prayed that slumber would soon overtake her.

*

On Thursday afternoon, Dawn put Cole down for his nap, made herself a cup of tea, and called Helen.

"Hey, Sis. Is this a bad time?"

"Not really. I just got back from lunch, but I'm caught up with work, for now. Is something up?"

"No," said Dawn. "Nothing bad, that is. Valerie dropped the lawsuit."

"You're kidding."

"Nope. Frank thinks it's because she didn't want Sea Gem to be sold for a fraction of its value to the highest bidder."

"But—that's what she was threatening to get done, right?"

Dawn sipped her tea. "Not exactly. She thought that if she kept pushing, Frank and Melody would cave in, and agree to put it on the market."

"So, what does this mean?"

"Just that we don't have to worry that she'll try to make us sell."

"Ever?"

"For now. Whatever she does, I'm glad this is over now. There's just one thing, though."

"What?"

Dawn put her cup down on the kitchen table. "She told Frank that she was sorry for having filed the suit in the first place. She was, like, all heartfelt and earnest about it, Frank said. Practically cried—was all boo hoo and everything. She even apologized for what she'd said about Cole and Melody's girls not being her 'blood'—and also for what she said about us inviting you and John down to Sea Gem. She said she didn't mean it."

"Okay...that's all good, right?"

"I don't know. It's not like her. Not at all."

"People change."

Dawn smiled. Helen was trusting to a fault, often giving people the benefit of the doubt when they didn't deserve it. She had done that in a major way two years ago, and it had been a horrible and almost deadly mistake. "Not always. I don't think *Valerie's* changed."

"Well, I'm glad you don't have to worry about the beach house anymore."

"Yeah. Hey, how're you feeling? Still no morning sickness?"

"No, thank God. I'm *so* relieved. Last time, it was awful."

"I remember. Listen, do you think you guys might want to get together this weekend?"

"You mean, go out to dinner?"

"Yeah. Well, no, not out. How about we have dinner over here, either Friday or Saturday? It would be easier for me to stay home, and get Cole down early. I still haven't found a sitter I trust."

"Okay. Let me talk to John, and I'll let you know. We may leave Adele with a sitter, though, if I can get either Madison or Tatum. They're her favorites."

"Okay. Just let me know."

*

Valerie spent the weekend working on her new plan. Josh had driven to Charleston to visit his mother for her birthday. Valerie was grateful–but annoyed–that he hadn't asked her to go with him. The frosty atmosphere between them hadn't melted one bit. Was he so stressed out that he couldn't get it up?

Well, he ought to be stressed. Everyone in the office was aware that more funding wasn't coming in. Work on the new release was being stalled. No one knew exactly what was going on. Rumors of layoffs were flying around, and some people had started looking for new jobs.

And PriceUtopia was no closer to going public than it had been three months ago. If things continued along this trajectory, there was no reason to think that Valerie's shares would ever be validated. Even if an IPO did occur–and it seemed more unlikely every day–the longer it took for that to happen, the longer it would be before her six-month lock-in period would begin.

But there was nothing she could do about that. She had to focus on the things she *could* control. She needed to repair the damage with her siblings, and get into their good graces. That was priority number one.

She had called Frank yesterday afternoon, and their conversation went as well as she had hoped. She'd had to feign getting emotional, but it worked. He seemed to take her at her word and to believe she was sincere. Two minutes later, they had amicably said goodbye.

Mission accomplished.

Communicating with Melody was going to be more problematic. She was going to have to grovel. But she had to be careful not to sound fake, or to come across as insensitive. Perhaps she ought to send her a text before she called.

Late Sunday afternoon, she picked up her phone and began typing.

Can you talk this afternoon? I'd like to explain—

No, that was wrong. She deleted *explain* and replaced it with *express how sorry I am and—*

And what? She deleted the last word and put a period after *am.* Short messages were best. But she needed a finishing touch. She deleted the period and wrote *and apologize. Let me know when you have a minute to talk?*

She put her phone down and heaved a deep sigh, relieved that she'd already said—on the record—the words 'sorry' and 'apologize.' Surely Frank had let Melody know she'd dropped the lawsuit; all she had to add was that she should have never filed it. That she should have respected Melody's feelings, and been empathetic. That she—

Her phone signaled a text message. It was from Melody.

I can talk right now.

Valerie took a deep breath, let it out, and clicked on her sister's number.

"Valerie?"

"Hi. Thanks for getting back to me so fast. I'm glad you have a few minutes."

"Sure."

Valerie paused. This was going to be harder than she had imagined. "I assume you heard that I dropped the suit."

"Yes, I did."

Silence.

"So–well. I just wanted to speak to you myself, and apologize for causing so much trouble, and for probably causing you a lot of angst."

Melody's tone was brusque. "Okay. Anything else?"

"Yes. I'm sorry about what I said about the twins. They're as much a part of your family–*our* family–as the rest of us are. I hope you'll forgive me. Can we put this behind us, now? I'd really like that–if we could just move on." *Oops–does that last part sound bossy? I can't afford to piss her off.*

This time, Melody paused. "Fine."

"Good. The thing is, I understand now how much Sea Gem means to you–"

"You do? Why now, and not before?"

Bitchy, as usual. "Because I–I wasn't thinking. I've been stressed out about a lot of things. My job, for one. I don't know if you read about how my company didn't go public a few months ago–"

"Is *that* why you wanted us to sell Sea Gem?"

"Not exactly. I mean, it was a difficult situation, and it still is. I won't bore you with the details. Suffice to say, it shook me up. But things are okay. Besides all that, though, I think I was still in grief mode about Daddy. I was angry and upset at losing him."

"So, because of that, you filed a lawsuit to try to get money from us–or to force a sale of the house he left all of us? That doesn't make much sense."

"I'm sure it doesn't. I'm not trying to justify what I did, nor am I asking you to understand my feelings. But I've *changed*, Melody. I get that Sea Gem is important to you, now–and to the family–and I won't forget it. The house *is* something Dad wanted us to share. It's part of our

history, our family tradition. Which I respect. Honestly."
Slow down. Let her talk.

"Okay, look. I'm glad you've changed your mind. But how can Frank and I be sure you won't change it back again?"

"I won't. I promise."

Another pause. "I guess time will tell."

"Oh, Melody! Please trust me on this. I'm over the whole thing about owning a third of Sea Gem, and about wanting to sell it. I respect the fact that it belongs to all three of us. The only way we'd ever sell it is if we all agree to. And I don't want to sell it anymore."

"Why did you change your mind?"

"I guess I had an epiphany. I understood what Daddy wanted, and why we need to keep it in the family."

"So, does this mean you plan to go down there any-time soon? Or join us there when everyone goes?"

"Of course I will. More than that, I just want to heal the rift I caused between us. And I want to be part of fam-ily events. If that's okay."

Melody's voice softened a little. "Well, Jeff's birth-day is coming up on the twelfth. June's coming over, and we're going to celebrate at my house next Sunday night, the fourteenth. You're welcome to come, if you want to."

"I'd love to. What time?"

20

Killed

Around nine o'clock the next morning, as usual, Josh sat in his office and skimmed the technology blog posts. For several months, bloggers and others in the press had been speculating about the technology response to show-rooming. Much of the discussion was ill considered or misguided, in Josh's view; the less some of these guys knew, the more they conjectured. Those with more information were often cryptic, only hinting at what might be happening down the pike. Most of them had little real tech knowledge or experience, but almost all made predictions, and offered strong opinions about the future.

Wading through all the crap out there could drive you nuts. Things were constantly happening in the technology marketplace, with its extreme highs and lows. Something red-hot one day could be discarded and forgotten the next. It was part of the industry. Normally, Josh had Sophie sift through it all and forward only what was relevant, interesting, or intriguing. But ever since that trip to Austin several weeks ago, he had perused the blogosphere daily, looking for clues about new "developments" in the space.

As far as he could tell, there hadn't been any. Yet. But that didn't mean nothing was happening. Still, what could be going on that would really affect PriceUtopia? Competitors would be coming late to the game. Anything they were doing couldn't be a game changer. He and Graham just needed to stay the course they were on and ignore the symphony of babbling idiots spouting off on the Internet. He clicked through the links, dismissing them and eliminating worries from his mind.

Then he saw it. A piece in Digital World online magazine about a new app by Origin, a major, world-renowned tech company in Seattle. As he read, Josh's eyes widened and his pulse quickened.

With new price matching app **Savvy** set to come out in a few short weeks, customers have been impatient to download it onto their smartphones and tablets.

"Keeping quiet for the past eight months wasn't easy," said Origin CEO Tom Devon. "But we're glad we did. The time has come for consumers to have instant access to price comparisons, without having to rely on some random retailer's clunky device," Devon continued, an apparent reference to tech company **PriceUtopia**. The Atlanta startup, whose IPO was canceled at the eleventh hour on June 29, sells a price matching service to retailers, along with hardware-equipped devices which must be installed at all of their points of sale.

*"With **Savvy**, the consumer has control of purchasing decisions with information available on their own personal device," Devon added. "The app enables mobile, targeted show-rooming by scanning an item's bar code, or QR code. If retailers wish to match the price, they can."*

*Industry sources say that **Savvy** will also have a GPS feature and will allow users to sign up for text alerts for promotions and sales in nearby locations. **Savvy** will charge retailers to post promotions, but the app will be free to download on users' smartphones and tablets. However, for a fee, users can upgrade to the premium version to get its full benefits, such as advance notifications of sales and access to price comparisons straight from a retailer's website: clicking on an item will trigger a pop-up window revealing competitors' prices and availability.*

Stunned, Josh lifted his eyes and sucked in a breath. *What the fuck?*

He exhaled and stared into space. Why hadn't he–or anyone else at the company–known about this? Origin was a top player in the technology world, and once their new app was available–*in a few short weeks*–well, PriceUtopia could kiss its ass goodbye.

Josh bit his lower lip. The mystery was solved: *this* was why Cornucopia had pulled–it *had* to be the reason. They must have found out the app was on its way, or at least heard rumors, back in June. They had reneged on the IPO because they wanted to wait and see what happened over at Origin. And, understandably, they had been afraid to invest in a company whose product might become obsolete—and worthless—in a few months.

Josh pushed his chair back and stood up. He was trembling, a mixture of anger and embarrassment welling in his gut. How could his idea have been usurped—no, *seized*—by another company, and one that was so much bigger and more powerful than his?

This news was the nail in the coffin for him and Graham. Origin had killed their dream, and now there was no way they would be able to ask *anyone* for more funding.

PriceUtopia was dead.

In shock, he went to find his partner. Two minutes later, they were alone in Josh's office. He shut the door.

Graham sat down and read through the entire article while Josh paced back and forth. When Graham finished reading, he put his head in his hands.

"We've got to cancel the release," said Josh. "Immediately."

"*Fuck*. Fuck, fuck, fuck."

"I know." Josh ran a hand over his head.

Graham looked up at Josh. "Wait, though. What if this app isn't all it's cracked up to be? What if it doesn't work?"

"Seriously?" asked Josh. "You're asking that question, when it's Origin that's developing it?"

"I just think we need to know more. Before we do *anything*, we need a lot more information."

Josh stopped pacing and regarded him. "Look, man. I know you're shocked. So am I. And I agree with you that we need to find out whatever we can about this. But if that report is true, we're fucked. *Totally*."

"Maybe it's not."

"Right. Maybe it's a bogus report. Maybe it's bull-shit, and we're fine. What are the chances, though?"

"Let's spend the rest of the day investigating this. And then let's talk. Do you think Sophie's seen it?"

Josh let out a sigh. "Who the fuck knows? Maybe, maybe not." He gave Graham a measured look. "Remember a couple years ago, when she brought up the idea of doing an app?"

"Yeah, vaguely. I feel like it wasn't long after she started."

Josh rubbed his temples. "She suggested trying that, instead of going in the direction we were going. But we shot her idea down pretty quickly, and, Sophie being Sophie, she never mentioned it again."

Graham crossed his arms in front of his chest. "We own the decision we made, and we made it because we wanted to go for the retailer side, not the consumer side. We thought that was where the money was."

"I know. Retailers were running scared back then, and the smart ones were looking for a way to respond to show-rooming, to stay competitive. And they had the money to invest in it."

Graham shook his head. "You know, back then, I remember thinking it was wiser for us *not* to do an app. That, even if apps really caught on, there might be too many of them out too soon, and that would be too confusing for the consumer. That an app would be too big of a gamble, and that we wouldn't be able to make money. And later, that if we changed course, we might get lost in a sea of apps."

"And I agreed with you. Our investors thought the same thing–none of them guessed that was the way to go. Or, that someone like Origin would develop one, and would put us out of business." Josh blew out his cheeks. "If Sophie sees this, she'll freak. Hopefully, she'll come to us, instead of spreading the word. Damn it. We need to preempt her." He sent her a text telling her to drop what she was doing and come to his office, pronto.

"What's going on?" she asked a few minutes later.

"Close the door, please," said Josh.

She turned, did as she was told, and regarded the two men, her eyes questioning.

"Have you seen anything about a new price matching app by Origin coming out?" asked Josh.

"No," she said, her face clouding with concern. "Why?"

Graham pushed back from the laptop and trained his eyes on her. "Look at this." He glanced at the screen, and Sophie walked over and read the article.

"Oh my God," she said, her eyes wide. Her face was red and her body stiff.

"Yeah," said Josh. "So, you haven't seen *anything* about it? Nothing at all?"

Sophie's lips were tight. "No. But even if I had–"

"If you had," said Josh, "at least then we'd have had some warning. A heads-up."

"No one in your area, or in the office, has mentioned anything about it?" asked Graham.

She shook her head, dropped her eyes, and let out a small sigh.

"People are going to find out, though," said Josh. "Look. Don't say anything to anybody. Graham and I are going to look into it and figure out exactly what it is. Go on with your day as normal. We'll get back to you about it later."

"If you do hear anything," said Graham, "let one of us know. Immediately."

She looked up and trained her eyes on him and then on Josh. "Of course," she murmured. She turned and left the room, closing the door gently behind her.

"What about Valerie?" asked Graham. "Should we bring her in now?"

A look of apprehension settled on Josh's face. "I don't know. I guess so."

"Are things weird between you guys right now?"

"What do you mean?"

Graham shrugged. "I don't know. It just seems like something's different. I don't mean to get into your business, though."

Josh shook his head slightly. "No sweat. But–well, it's complicated."

"Say no more. If you want to talk to her about this alone, later–"

"No, I don't. Let's do call her in now. Before she sees it herself and explodes."

"Fine," said Graham.

"But–if you don't mind, you message her to come in. Better yet, go get her."

"Sure." Graham pressed his lips together, stood up, and trudged out, closing Josh's office door behind him. Josh leaned back in his chair and shut his eyes, trying to channel calm and push panic away. A few minutes later, Graham and Valerie walked in. Both sat down across from Josh.

"What's this about?" she demanded.

Josh put his chin in his hand and braced himself. "A new app called Savvy by Origin. Take a look." He turned his laptop toward her and waited.

She read the piece, looked up, and stared at Josh. Her voice was low, but her eyes glazed, and the vein on her forehead was throbbing. "How the fuck did you not already know about this?"

Josh looked at Graham, then back at her. "None of us knew. Sophie hadn't even seen anything—"

"*Sophie's* an idiot," said Valerie. "So we shouldn't be surprised. Even though it's her *job* to know what's going on."

"Ultimately, it's my job," said Josh. "But—"

"But what? Yes, it *is* your job." Valerie's tone was sharper now. She threw a glance at Graham. "Obviously, *you* had no idea."

Graham shook his head slowly. "But at least now we know why the offering collapsed."

Valerie scoffed and looked from him to Josh. "So, that's supposed to make us all feel better? The mystery's been solved! PriceUtopia didn't go public because everyone but them knew their product was a total failure!"

Josh steeled his jaw. "We don't know if everyone else knew about this. That doesn't matter, but—"

"Right," Valerie cut in. "It *doesn't* matter. What does matter is that *we* didn't know. *You* didn't know. And because of that, we're dead."

"We were never in business to develop an app," said Graham. "So—"

"So, what? You want to be congratulated for that? For not knowing that's what you *should* have been developing all this time?"

"Look, Valerie," said Josh. "You're right. We fucked up, and we both know it. We should have been aware of what was going on, even though that's next to impossible to do. We had tunnel vision, and for whatever reason, no

212

one around here questioned it. But we should have been able to foresee this, and to respond to it. Who knows? Maybe we can do that." He looked at Graham, then back at Valerie. "Graham and I are going to spend the day investigating this. We'll let you know what we find out." He crossed his arms in front of his chest. "Feel free to do your own research about it."

"I do," she said. She stood up. "This company is a disaster."

*

By three o'clock that afternoon, everyone in the office knew about Savvy. Josh and Graham had terse conversations with Adam Langford, Tony Ferguson over at FVP, and Julian Stone at Swift. As the co-founders expected, Adam had the mildest reaction to the news, as if he had written off his investment and didn't want to fool with it anymore. He wasn't happy, but he seemed resigned to cutting his losses. But Tony and Julian were both livid that neither Josh nor Graham had known about the new app until today.

"Thank God I didn't throw more money down a rat hole," Julian said to them on the speakerphone. "I still don't understand where you guys' heads have been, these last few months. Isn't it a huge part of your job to know everything that's going on in your own industry? Josh?"

"You're right," Josh said. "It is. We should have known about this, and we're kicking ourselves right now."

"You need to do more than that," said Julian. "A *lot* more. Look. Swift is not in business to fund losing ventures—ventures that don't know what they're doing, or what their *competitors* are doing. You two need to figure out what to do about this."

"What *can* we do, at this point?" Graham said, his voice rising. "Even if we had been aware of it a long time ago, that wouldn't have changed the technology we've developed, or our plan to market it. We would have proceeded in exactly the same way."

"That's incredible, Graham," said Julian. "I'm astonished that you said it, and what's worse, that you believe it."

"Just because this happened doesn't mean what we've worked on for so long is without value," argued Graham. "This company isn't a *rat hole*. We have different approach, yes, but it's the approach we all agreed on, and we all believed in. Yourself included, Julian."

Josh winced at his partner's words, and sat in stunned silence as Julian responded. "Whatever we said in the past, you've convinced me of one thing now, Graham: You're a lot less intelligent than I thought you were. Frankly, I'm embarrassed. Running a business is evidently beyond both you and Josh, and I'm a fool for believing in you."

Josh spoke up. "What Graham meant was, our product was never going to be an app on a smartphone. Nobody knows how well this new app will work, or what the effect will be. It could have lots of problems. Even if it takes off, we have paying clients already using PriceUtopia, and we're poised to go nationwide—"

"You mean they're using those clunky devices that no one cares about anymore, that are soon going to be about as useful as a VCR? I'm sorry, Josh, but I can't let you go on trying to justify an inferior product and wasting my time. My advice to you both is this: accept reality.

You had an idea, but it wasn't the right one. I applaud you for trying. But trying isn't succeeding. I think we can all agree that success has eluded you in this business, once and for all. Look. I wish you both well in your future endeavors, but the verdict is in, for me. We're done, guys."

The call ended shortly afterward, and the conversation with Tony Ferguson was a redux. When it was over, Josh felt battered and broken, and as if he had been sucker-punched to death.

*

On Thursday morning, Josh and Graham called a company-wide meeting.

Valerie stood in the back of the room, leaning against a side wall. Her five sales staff was clustered on the opposite side, also in the back. From here, she could see their profiles and keep an eye on them. A low, anxious chatter echoed in the room, bouncing around like stray ping pong balls hitting metal.

The last few days had been a true nightmare.

At the office, reactions to the news were all over the place. Some people were angry, some were sad, and some were shocked and bewildered. Most people had openly started looking for new jobs. Some were naive enough to believe that PriceUtopia would be okay—that the company would adjust and reprioritize. Or, worst case, that Origin would come in and buy the company. PriceUtopia had collected its clients' internal pricing data, which Origin would need. But a company like Origin could have already gathered that information from retailers—if not, they probably would have little problem doing so. Nobody at the startup was working on the new release, nor had any-

215

one received direction about what to do next. Of course, sales had come to a screeching halt.

Josh stood up in the front of the room. The chattering faded to whispers and then to silence. He clasped his hands in front of him and cleared his throat.

"By now," he began, "you're all aware of Origin's new app coming out, and that's not what we're here to discuss." He dropped his hands to his sides and glanced steadily around the room, making brief eye contact with this person or that. "We're here to talk about what this means for all of us, and for our future. As most of you know, we haven't succeeded in securing new funding over the last couple of months."

Valerie bit her lip. What a jackass he was. And what an idiot *she* had been, for trusting him. She shut her eyes for a moment and forced herself not to get upset. She looked down at her nails. She needed a manicure.

"Because of that, and because we're looking at ways to respond to the situation we find ourselves in now, we've decided to cancel the new release." He shot a glance at Graham and then looked back at the group.

No one made a sound. Then, a tall thirty-year-old redhead and member of the finance team half-raised her hand. Josh looked at her and motioned a go-ahead.

"What does that mean for all of us?" she said.

Graham looked at Josh and nodded.

"For now," said Josh, "it means we may bring it back later, with modifications. However, we have to adjust to reality. Everyone knows that we eliminated some positions recently. Today, we're announcing a layoff 20 percent of the remaining staff."

A few people gasped, and one or two quietly shook their heads in dismay.

Josh held up a hand. "This afternoon, everyone will get an email stating whether their job has been cut. If yours has, the message will contain an appointment time with me or Graham. We'll sit down with you and go over the details of your package."

Valerie was disgusted. What a mess. Only one of her staff was being fired—the most junior person—but many nonessential employees in other areas were. Several people on the implementation and issuer teams were getting canned, and so were some marketing people. A majority of the contract employees had been let go yesterday.

She glanced at the salespeople, none of whom looked in her direction. Then she surveyed the rest of the room. First the IPO was canceled, and now the release. It wasn't exciting to work here anymore. Fear and anxiety had settled in, and had replaced the optimism and energy of earlier days.

As for her stock options, and for what might have been—well, all of that was permanently out the window. The millions she had been promised had gone up in smoke. This place was a burning, sinking ship, and it was time to jump.

21

Changing Ways

"Does she know June's coming?" Jeff asked Melody early on Saturday morning. He poured a cup of coffee, turned, and leaned against the kitchen counter.

Melody nodded and dropped four slices of bread in the toaster. "I told her she was."

"So—do you think Valerie wants to make nice?"

Melody raised an eyebrow at her husband. "Well, she said she wanted to be part of, quote unquote, family events. It's just that—that's so not like her." Melody grabbed some eggs from the fridge. "I don't know. It's almost like she has some kind of an agenda."

Jeff cocked his head. "You're a pretty suspicious sister."

"After a lifetime of observation, yes, I guess I am." She began breaking the eggs into a large bowl. Honestly, when had Valerie *not* had some type of agenda? And didn't Jeff realize that if anyone knew she did, it was Melody?

"Maybe she's turned over a new leaf. Or maybe she's feeling lonely, or stressed out." He shrugged. "Think you should give her the benefit of the doubt?"

Melody dropped her shoulders and gave him a look. "I've done that before, and it was always the wrong decision. But hey. For the kids' sake–and for the family's sake–I will."

"Have you told June that she's coming?"

"I called her yesterday and told her. She was surprised. And she sounded a little tense about it."

"I can imagine." He pulled the toast from the toaster, stacked it on a plate, and popped in four more slices. "Where's the butter?"

"On the table," said Melody. "It's just–I can't help but think that Valerie wants something."

"What, though? I mean, she's dropped the lawsuit, and she's also apologized. Maybe she just wants to make amends now."

Melody smiled. "Maybe so. I wouldn't bet on it, though. In any case, we'll see what happens tomorrow night." She slid the panful of scrambled eggs into a bowl. "These are done."

Jeff looked in the direction of the den, where all four kids sat watching TV. "Breakfast is ready!" he called. "Come and eat."

*

June stepped out of the shower and wrapped herself in a plush white bath towel.

Last night, she had gone out to dinner and a movie with Antoine. He stayed overnight, and this morning, after an hour of lovemaking, he had risen, showered, and was now in the kitchen making omelets. Tonight, they were meeting Angela and Hugh for dinner at Paloma's, a restaurant in Midtown.

Her old friends were enthralled with Antoine, and ecstatic that she was seeing him. Angela even seemed a little jealous—or maybe she was just wistful. She and Hugh had been together for decades, and they had always seemed happy. But the contentment of a long marriage was nothing like the romance of a budding, new relationship.

June knew that now, firsthand.

She dressed in white cropped pants and a turquoise top, and then sat down to do her makeup. She was looking forward to the evening, and to spending part of today with Antoine. Tomorrow afternoon, he was leaving for the west coast, and he wouldn't be back until Thursday. Then he planned to be in Atlanta until the week of Thanksgiving. She was glad she would be seeing Melody, Jeff, and the kids tomorrow night, but now that Valerie was also coming—

Well, it would be awkward, but it would probably be okay. According to Melody, Valerie had asked to be included at the birthday dinner. Valerie had never been fond of Jeff, so the request seemed strange, and on the phone, Melody had voiced suspicions about her sister's motives. June had listened sympathetically, but had offered no opinion. Whatever Valerie chose to do—however she chose to behave—well, Valerie never worried about how she affected others.

Jim had defended his older daughter time and again, and June had never completely understood why. Of course, she knew about Beverly, and about the awful time Jim had gone through after she killed herself. When he was raising Valerie, had he had some underlying concern that she might become depressed as well, one day? That she could have inherited some kind of mental instability from her mother? Had he given Valerie special treatment in an effort to protect her from ending up like Beverly?

Jim had confessed that he felt terribly guilty about what he might have done to prevent Beverly's suicide, and that he hadn't dealt with it very well. After he married Ginger—who was one of Beverly's not-so-close friends—the two of them had gotten rid of all the photos of his first wife, including her and Jim's wedding album. Perhaps it was exactly what Jim needed then, to be able to move forward and process his grief. But those photos would have provided a link for Valerie to her mother. What a thing it must have been for her to find out the truth the way she had, and not until the woman who had raised her was dying of leukemia.

Jim had always said that blood was thicker than water. Although he had adored Dawn and Jeff, his unspoken attitude was that neither of them was blood; each were valued and even loved, as long as they made his children happy. Both seemed to understand that, and that they couldn't earn his unconditional love, but each appreciated his affection and respect. When Valerie learned that Ginger wasn't her real mother, and that Frank and Melody were only half-siblings, it must have been a shock.

Valerie didn't know it, but a long time ago, Jim had told June about what had happened to her in college, too. Of course, he had been furious, and very upset. He was also unhappy about his daughter's decision not to report it. He had respected her wish, but he was frustrated that, powerful and wealthy as he was, he could do nothing to bring the perpetrators to justice. Even worse, the so-called boyfriend was the son of Jim's college friend and fraternity brother, Bill Crawford. Fortunately, Valerie hadn't turned up pregnant, or been infected with some

awful sexually transmitted disease. But for years afterward, Jim had agonized about what that horrible experience had done to her, emotionally.

In June's view, *that* was why he had spoiled her.

"Chérie," called Antoine from the kitchen, just down
the hall from the master bedroom. "Everything is ready.
Come join me."

"Be right there." June finished her mascara and regarded herself one last time in the mirror. She stood up
and fluffed her hair, then turned and walked out of the
room and toward the kitchen. She let out a deep breath
and tried to push thoughts of Valerie from her mind. That
girl had been through so much, and it certainly *was* awful,
what had happened way back then. Such a crime was more
than horrendous. How in the world could those boys have
even done it? In June's generation, men were gentlemen,
and were brought up to respect women. At least, southern
men were.

Oh, well. Life could be very tough, unforgiving, and
unfair. Sometimes, it was downright tragic. But did what
had happened decades ago give Valerie license to behave
the way she did today—so abominably, and so selfishly?

No, it didn't. And it was about time that she
changed her ways.

*

It was going to be easier to cut it off with Valerie than
Josh had believed.

After the meeting on Thursday, she had avoided
him. Neither of them brought up the idea of seeing each
other this weekend. On Friday, she walked around the
office with a "mad on," just like his old man used to do.

When she left for the day, Josh had been grateful to see her go. If she had already decided to dump him—and all signs were, she had—it would be a blessing. Maybe she had begun looking for another job, too.

Over the last few weeks, her attitude about working at PriceUtopia had definitely changed. Hell, hopefully she had already found another job and was about to quit. There was nothing for the head of sales—or any salespeople—to do anymore. Now that Origin's new app was about to come out, no retailer was going to sign a contract with PriceUtopia and pay to have its "clunky" devices installed in their stores.

Josh lay in bed now, feeling depressed and hopeless. He had gone out with Graham last night and gotten drunk. They stayed out late—Josh couldn't remember exactly what time, or even what they had said. Fortunately, he had taken a cab home. But that meant that he had to go back and pick up his Audi today. He hoped to God it hadn't been towed. That would be the last thing he needed right now.

Aimee was down in Florida for the weekend, visiting her folks. Though she knew his company was in trouble, he hadn't yet told her the murderous news. He would, though. At some point.

He rolled over in bed, trying to will his hangover away. He had a mild headache, and he felt thirsty and achy. He'd pop some aspirin, get some breakfast, get the car, and come back home. Then he would lie around. He needed a little solitude today, some time to think.

He had to get a new game.

Graham was going to be fine—he and all the tech people would be. Developing the technology for PriceUtopia was no black mark for them; if anything, it was a badge. Some other company would scoop them up, and soon. Graham' skills and experience were in demand. He would probably get a new gig in no time.

But—Josh wouldn't.

Both of them were out their founders' equity—fifty grand apiece—but that was fine. Nothing you could do about it. The sweat equity they had put in, though—the years of work, of passing up on other opportunities, more secure futures, better jobs—that was something else. How was Josh going to emerge from this disaster?

Who would take a chance on him now?

Thinking about that wasn't going to help him. All he could do was to go on and try to do something else. He ought to take a few months to figure out exactly what. It would take that long to recover. He could live leanly while he got his mind wrapped around the end of PriceU-topia, and as time healed his wounds.

Obviously, he should have been paying more attention to what was going on in the marketplace. He shouldn't have counted on Sophie, or anyone else, to keep him informed. He should have known about the new app coming out. And over two years ago, he and Graham should have listened when Sophie brought up doing an app. Even if they had still eschewed it and gone in the direction they had, they might have guessed that someone else would do an app. But they had been shortsighted about the future, and had been of the same one-track mind when it came to product philosophy. And Josh had been so busy trying to get funding and thinking about planning another IPO that he'd had blinders on.

He and Graham had come so far since the early days, back when everyone loved hearing about their concept for a price matching device. If the IPO had gone through as planned—if there had been no such thing as Savvy, or Origin itself, for that matter—things would be so different now. Money—and accolades—would be flowing in. Success would be certain. Josh would be looking at making millions, or more. He'd be able to help his mom financially, and maybe buy her a nicer house. He and Graham would have had the freedom to work on their next brainchild, and would be accepted as visionary and cool by other tech CEOs and CTOs. It wouldn't matter that Josh wasn't brilliant, that he had gone to a third-rate college, or that he hadn't earned good grades.

His phone buzzed, jarring him out of his thoughts. He had a text from Aimee. He smiled weakly. She missed him. He responded immediately, with the same message.

He *did* miss her—she was the one bright spot in his life. Thank God he met her when he did, and was seeing her now. As the saying went, you *did* become like the five people you saw the most in life. He was grateful that Aimee was becoming one of them in his, and that Valerie was departing from it. Spending so much time with her this past year had not been good for him. In little ways, he had found himself picking up some of her bad qualities, and even her tone. She had rubbed off on him way too much, and now it was time to wash himself clean of her.

Aimee would be back tomorrow evening, and by then, he had better know what he was going to tell her about the company. The truth, of course, but without any self-pity, anger, or sadness. He felt all three of those right now, but he couldn't keep on feeling them. He had to reinvent his future, starting today. Or, at the very latest, tomorrow.

Without a toxic woman in his life.

22

Lies

On Sunday evening at seven o'clock, Valerie knocked on the Perkins' front door carrying a bottle of white wine.

A moment later, Matt opened the door. "Hi, Aunt Val."

"Hey there. How's it going?"

"Great! Come in. Everybody's in the den."

Valerie followed her nephew into the room, where Pip and Neely sat on the floor, working on a jigsaw puzzle. Nick was perched on the sofa next to his father. Melody sat in an armchair, a glass of wine in her hand.

"Hey, Valerie. Welcome," she said.

"Thanks." She glanced at Jeff. "Happy birthday!"

"Thank you!"

Valerie held out the wine bottle to Melody. "Do you like sauvignon blanc?"

"Sure–that's perfect." She smiled and took the bottle. "Would you like a glass?"

"That would be great." Valerie smiled back. She followed her sister into the spacious kitchen.

Melody grabbed a wine glass from the cabinet. "I already have a bottle open, so I'll put this one in the fridge for later, okay?"

"Sure–fine." Valerie took the wine glass, held it up over her head to check for dust, and then rinsed it and set it on the counter.

"It's clean," said Melody. She paused. "But–whatever. I'm glad you could join us tonight." She poured wine into the glass.

"Glad to be invited. Didn't you say that June's coming?"

Melody nodded. "She ought to be here soon. Hope you like ribs."

"Of course."

They went back into the den and sat down. A moment later, June walked in the door with a bottle of champagne, a gift, and a birthday card. Valerie shut her eyes for a second. *How did I forget to buy something for Jeff–or at least, get a card?*

"The champagne's for both of you," June said to Melody. "Save it for another night." She grinned at Jeff and handed him the small gift bag and the card. "Happy birthday."

"Thank you! You shouldn't have."

"Oh, it's no big deal. I didn't know what to get the man who has everything, so I went over to Cook's Warehouse in Brookhaven and got you something you probably already have. It's a cork pop–like a corkscrew, but without the screw." She grinned.

Jeff reached in the bag. "Oh, wow. No, we *don't* already have one of these." Valerie had two of them. They *were* convenient: you just inserted the needle straight down into the cork and pushed the top of the device down with your thumb. The thing emitted gas like a burp and popped the cork right out.

"Cool," Melody said. "We can always use another wine opener!"

"Speaking of which," added Jeff, "would you like a glass of wine, June?

"Sure." She turned to Valerie, smiled, and raised her eyebrows. "Nice to see *you* again, Valerie."

Valerie flashed a plastic smile. "You, too." *Has June told Melody about that day at Saks?*

Awkward periods of silence were punctuated with bits of small talk as the alcohol began to do its job relaxing the adults. Valerie wondered whether Melody had started drinking before everyone arrived.

Probably.

"So, how was your trip to Nice, June?" asked Melody.

"Oh, fantastic." June's cheeks colored a little. She kept her eyes trained on Melody. "You know, the Côte d'Azur is *so* lovely in the fall. We had a wonderful time there."

So that's where she was. "Did you go over there with a group?" asked Valerie.

"No...I went with a friend of mine." She turned and gave Valerie a measured look, then blinked. "Antoine Dugast. He's French—originally from Grenoble."

"Oh. How did you meet him?" asked Valerie.

"Through some friends," June said in a singsong voice. She let out a breath and turned back to Melody. "So, how's the school year going? Do the kids like their teachers?"

For the next twenty minutes, conversation revolved around the Perkins family and, specifically, their children.

As everyone chatted, Valerie half-listened, her mind pre-occupied with June's disclosure. Was the man she had traveled to France with her new boyfriend? What man would you do that with, if he *weren't* your boyfriend? Unless he were either gay, or decades older than June. But– June had *married* someone decades older than she was.

Valerie simmered inside, but resolved to keep silent and to try to learn as much as she could. Evidently, Melody knew what was going on in June's personal life–did they often talk on the phone? Maybe they met for coffee or lunch, too. Since neither had a job, both had plenty of time to waste.

Before long, some of Valerie's unspoken questions were answered. Antoine *was* June's significant other, and though they had met only two months ago, they were getting serious. Valerie looked at June's hands. She was wearing her gold wedding band and the diamond engagement ring Jim had given her on her right hand. Her left hand ring finger was bare, but there was an unattractive indent where she had worn the rings for almost twenty years. Apparently, June was completely over Jim's death.

Does this Antoine have any money? Or–is he a gold digger?

Jeff must have been wondering the same thing. "What does Antoine do?" he asked.

June tilted her head. "He works for the French government."

"Ah–a civil servant," said Jeff.

"He's quite well off, though," June hastened to say. "Evidently, a lifetime of civil service in France is very rewarding, financially."

"Things are different over there, aren't they?" asked Melody. "In the society, I mean. They have so many free services."

"But taxes are exorbitant," said Jeff.

Valerie's mind wandered as conversation continued. *How much money can a French civil servant make? And does he know how wealthy June is?*

None too soon, dinner was served buffet style in the kitchen. Everyone traipsed out to the deck, where the adults sat at one table and the children at another. Jeff offered the women another glass of wine.

June raised a palm. "I'll have a little, but not too much. I have to drive home."

Valerie watched June pick up her glass. Her two-carat diamond ring sparkled on her right hand.

Is she avoiding even looking at me?

"So, June," said Jeff, "when's your next trip to Europe with Antoine?"

She blushed. "Actually, we're going to France in December."

Melody raised her eyebrows. "Christmas in France? Lucky you!"

"Not Christmas. Well, we may stay through the holidays, but I'm not exactly sure yet. We're talking of going over there a couple of weeks after Thanksgiving."

"Which is early, this year," Melody interjected.

"Yes, it is. Antoine will be in France all of that week, then he comes back to Atlanta, and *then* we're going. The French don't have Thanksgiving, you know."

Valerie repressed a smile. Yes, they all knew that. "How fun!"

"What *about* Thanksgiving, then?" asked Melody. She looked at Jeff, who nodded at her. She turned back to the other two women. "Since we didn't go to Sea Gem last spring, should we spend Thanksgiving there together? I spoke to Dawn earlier, and she said they'd come down if we all do. What do you think, June? Would you like to go?"

"Sure—that would be lovely!"

Melody turned to Valerie. "How about you? Can you come?"

"I'd love to," she lied.

"Great!" said Melody. "Then it's settled. The kids are off for the whole week, so our family could go down early, to avoid the traffic."

"We ought to go down the weekend before," added Jeff, glancing at his wife. "We can do the food shopping when we get there, and get the kitchen organized."

"When can Frank and Dawn arrive?" asked June.

"Dawn said they could book a flight for Monday of that week, or Tuesday at the latest."

"I probably shouldn't wait until Wednesday to drive down," said June. "The holiday traffic will be terrible."

No one spoke for a few seconds. Then Valerie broke the silence. "That's true. I need to look at my schedule to figure out when I can get down there, though."

"Of course," said Melody. She lowered her chin and threw Valerie a sideways look. "But—is there *really* that much business being done during the few days before Thanksgiving? I wouldn't think—"

"I'm sure you wouldn't," Valerie cut in. She tossed her head. "Since you haven't worked in years, I mean. In *my* business, though, it's a very busy time."

If I were working for a company that wasn't about to collapse, that is.

"Right—it's the big lead up to Black Friday," said Jeff, grinning and throwing his wife a glance. "But is that day as important now as it was in the past? What with Cyber Monday, and all that?"

"Yes, it's still big, even though the holiday shopping season has already begun."

June shook her head. "It seems to start earlier every year. Kind of maddening, in my view."

"You know," said Melody, "I buy everything online, and I don't pay much attention to dates. I just get it done when I can."

Valerie gave her a look. *How does she not know that no one cares? But now she's pissed at me for that comment about her not working—so insecure.* "Well, you're not the typical shopper. You're much more affluent. Most people look for sales, especially around the holidays."

Jeff turned to Valerie. "Speaking of sales, I thought I read something about a new app coming out that's right up your alley. A deal finder, or something like that, where people can find the lowest prices on their phones?"

Valerie nodded. "It's called Savvy. Not sure how successful it's going to be, though."

"Really?" asked Jeff, a bemused smile on his face. "I've heard it could actually be pretty big. Especially since Origin has developed it. Has it changed things over at your company?"

"No," Valerie lied again. "There's so much going on *all the time* in technology—so many changes. It's hard to keep up with, unless you're in the industry." She smiled.

"Well, it's good that it hasn't affected *you*," said June.

"How about some birthday cake now?" asked Melody. "And some more wine?"

*

A few hours later, Valerie lay under the sheets, alone in her condo. She closed her eyes, stretched her legs, and thought about the evening at Melody's.

It had been awkward, but somehow she had gotten through it. It was the first step in finding the opportunity she was seeking. It was troubling news that June had a boyfriend, and worse, that she was going to France with him for a few weeks in December. Valerie wondered why she hadn't suggested they all spend Thanksgiving at Sea Gem herself. But it was much better that Melody had.

Melody was normally insufferable, but every once in a while–inexplicably–she did exactly what Valerie wished her to do.

23

Seeing Someone

After she put Cole down for his afternoon nap, Dawn made a cup of tea and called Helen.

"So, we'll be back at the beach a month from now," Dawn said. "Frank was like, why are we going down there *again*, and for the second time in three months? He hates the hassle of flying into Jacksonville and then driving up. But since you guys are going to John's brother's house for Thanksgiving, I pushed the idea."

"It'll be fun for you guys," said Helen. "And nice to be there while it's not so hot."

"Yeah. That is, if I can survive the week, surrounded by the whole family."

"Is *everyone* going, then, you mean? Including Valerie?"

Dawn let out a sigh. "I'm afraid so. But Melody told me she's being all nicey-nice now. If you can believe it."

"Oh, Dawn. Is she really that bad?"

"Not all the time. Just most of it. And it's a little disturbing that she's suddenly decided she wants to hang out with the family at Sea Gem. I mean, why?"

"Well, maybe she's gotten through with grieving about her father, and she's started to think about how short life is. Maybe she's turned over a new leaf."

"Possibly. But I wouldn't bet on it." Dawn took a sip of tea, and then put her mug down on the kitchen table. "I think it's more like, she has nowhere else to go for Thanksgiving this year."

"Isn't she seeing someone? Or do you know?"

"I don't. She may be, though. But according to Melody, she's driving down to the beach by herself."

"And so is June."

"And so is June," confirmed Dawn.

"I don't know—after everything you've told me that's happened between them, maybe Valerie wants to bury the hatchet with her, too. Didn't you say Melody was worried that Valerie was going to get in June's face about that thing on Facebook? That message June's sister posted about paying her son's college expenses?"

"Yeah, Melody *was* worried about that. But Valerie didn't say a word to June, or to anyone else. At least, not that I know of. But I'll bet she was pissed about it. Even though something like that would barely make a dent in June's money."

"I swear, Dawn. I can't even *imagine* having that kind of money."

"You know, I don't think June's ever really gotten comfortable with it herself. I mean, she spends money, don't get me wrong—but she's not a spendthrift. She likes getting a good deal, just like we do. I would even say she's frugal. But she's also very generous."

"I'll say. What a nice thing to do for her nephew."

"I know, right? But Jim was generous, too. I'm sure he would have been in total agreement with her about doing that."

"So why did Melody think Valerie would care?"

"Probably because it *is* a lot of money–and because it's going to someone in *June's* family, and not theirs. Not their blood."

"What does Frank think about it?"

"Oh, God. *He* doesn't care. He knows it's June's money, to do whatever she wants to with it. Plus, he knew his dad wanted him to make his own way, and not count on his inheritance."

"Do you think Melody feels that way about it, too?"

"I don't know, but I think so. Jeff makes a good income, and they're solidly upper middle class. Or higher. She's been a stay at home mom since their oldest kid was born, and they have a big, beautiful house in a really nice neighborhood. You should see it."

"But you've always said that Melody doesn't act like a spoiled, rich person. No offense–and not to generalize–but you know what I mean."

"Yeah, I do. She's not, though. Despite the fact that she grew up in a rich home, she's so, I don't know–*normal.*"

"Like Frank."

"Right. And she's been through a lot over the last year."

"Well, it's good that you and she get along. Too bad you have to deal with the family tension over Thanksgiving, though."

"Oh, I'll make it. But when we all sit down to eat Thanksgiving dinner, it could be a bit stressful."

Helen laughed. "Who's doing the cooking?"

"Me and Melody. I'm sure June will help, too. Hey, how are you feeling? Have you felt the baby kick yet?"

"No–it's still too early for that. But I'm fine. Nothing like last time."

Dawn took another sip of tea. "Are you eating enough?"

"God, yes. I'm hungry all the time. When we hang up, I'm going to eat lunch in the break room."

"Okay. I'll let you go, then. Have a good day, and call me later on this week, okay?"

*

On Wednesday evening, Josh left the florist shop on Peachtree Road carrying a dozen pink roses.

He slid behind the wheel of his Audi and carefully laid the bouquet on the tan leather passenger seat. He loved the idea of surprising Aimee with the flowers. He had bought them on a whim, just to be romantic. It wasn't her birthday or anything–she had turned thirty-one back on June 30. A couple of weeks ago, just to be safe, he had asked her if she liked roses, because, who knew? Valerie might not be the only woman who didn't, and he certainly didn't want to make that mistake twice.

But of course, Aimee had said she did like roses, and said she was surprised he'd asked. He'd made something up about an aunt who he thought didn't like them, but who he'd later found out was allergic to them. It was a total lie, but it made sense, and it had come out of his mouth before he knew what he was saying.

It was the only falsehood he had told Aimee, though, and he wasn't going to do it again. He had been upfront with her about the company, not sugar-coating anything, and in the short time he had known her, he had bared his soul to her. He even revealed that he had recently emerged from a relationship with a woman who worked for him at PriceUtopia.

If it wasn't exactly the truth, it wasn't a lie, either. He and Valerie hadn't seen each other in weeks, and he didn't plan to see her again.

Ever.

"That must be so awkward for you, now," Aimee said the night he told her, when they had a drink together after work. "I hate that you're having to go through it, and deal with her at the office."

"It *is* a little weird," he'd said. "She's very driven, though. I feel like, any day now, she'll come in and say she's gotten a new job, turn in her resignation, and leave."

"I hope so," said Aimee. "You need less to deal with right now, not more." She touched his arm.

God, she was empathetic—she reminded Josh of himself in that way, only she was more so. She was also like him in that she was an eternal optimist. When he described his apprehension about finding another job after PriceUtopia ceased to be, she had quelled his fears with soothing assurances.

"Of course you'll find another job," she said. "With your background, experience, and work ethic, it won't be hard at all. I'm sure of it."

"I hope you're right." He offered a sheepish smile and took her hand, clasping it in his. "However difficult it is, I've got to make it happen."

Tonight, they were going out to dinner at a Greek place on Piedmont Road that had recently reopened. It had gotten good reviews, and it wasn't too pricey. Unlike Valerie, Aimee wasn't a spender, and she didn't expect the

most expensive everything. She was a good person, too—
the kind of person who could bring out the best in him.
The kind of woman Josh could see himself wanting to talk
to and hang out with every day. He didn't want to get
ahead of himself, but who knew? She might even be a
good wife and mother, one day.

He tapped his brakes and slowed to a stop behind a
silver Mercedes on Peachtree. Crap. He hadn't been paying attention, and now he was caught in this lane behind a
guy turning left during rush hour. If Valerie were sitting
next to him, she would be steaming—or screaming at him
to change lanes. But she wasn't there, thank God.

Life was too short to get pissed off all the time about
trivial matters.

No, he had to focus instead on the important things:
his professional life, and his developing relationship with
Aimee. He glanced at the roses on the seat next to him.
He couldn't wait to see her tonight. Their evenings together were keeping him going right now. But he
couldn't afford to do anything wrong. She was the best
thing that had come along in his life in years, and he
didn't want to blow it.

The guy in front of him finally made his left, and
Josh accelerated. The turn to Aimee's place was less than a
mile away, and it was also on the left. He glanced at the
dashboard clock. He had plenty of time. Instead of trying
to weave around the other cars, he stayed in his lane, and
drove on.

As he approached his destination, he flipped on his
left turn signal and slowed to a stop, to wait for a gap in
traffic so he could make his turn. How nice it was to do a
simple thing like drive the way he wanted to, without

Valerie sitting next to him, giving him orders. Life was better without her, and he wasn't going to miss her.

24

Betrayed

Two weeks later, Graham entered Josh's office and sat down.

It was Monday, October 29, exactly four months after the IPO had been pulled. In three days, Origin would release Savvy, and the hype was incredible.

"Even though everyone knows it's against policy," said Graham, "people have been asking me if they can work from home now. But nobody has any work to do. They're spending all their time looking for jobs, and they're starting to talk about it openly."

"I guess we can't blame them," admitted Josh. "Everybody knows the end is near."

"So, I'll tell them the policy's changed. They can now 'work' from home." He made air quotes.

"And, we're still paying them." Josh grimaced.

"They're also asking me how much longer they're going to be paid."

Josh crossed his arms in front of his chest. "Not much."

"So—we're agreed, then? One more month."

Josh nodded, and then sighed. "You know, *we* were the ones breaking new ground in this technology. It was just—our timing was off."

"No shit. By a few years."

"I mean, if PriceUtopia were now in place *everywhere* out there, if we had gotten more merchants on board, more quickly—and if we'd been able to raise funds faster and earlier, to grow the company—it could have all been different."

"For the merchants, there was a big learning curve with our product—"

"As there is with any new technology."

"Right. But still. Three years ago, we had no idea so many people would have smartphones now, or that a tech giant would come along and displace us—beat us at our own game with a free app."

"We should have predicted it. We should have approached and solved the show-rooming issue from the consumer's viewpoint, not the retailer's."

"Well, we didn't. That was never the direction we discussed. Unfortunately." Graham frowned. "I mean, when you look at it objectively, though, these merchants were agreeing to pay for something that was untested. Something they weren't convinced they even needed. Something they'd have to invest in training costs to teach their employees to use. User education isn't easy, either."

"And something they thought would hurt their bottom line, initially. If we had just had more time, to prove that it was going to help them, not hurt…"

"Yeah, well, time—and timing—is huge in the tech world," said Graham. "We've always known that."

Josh shook his head. "I almost feel like we should close down three weeks from now. Nobody's going to come in to the office the week of Thanksgiving, or the week after, for that matter. We pay them through November 30. That's the package. But the last day is Friday, the sixteenth."

Graham nodded. "I'm with you. But—what are *you* going to do next, man?"

"I don't know yet. Probably take some time to regroup. Get through the holidays, and get ready to search for a job, come the first of the year."

Graham put his chin in his hand and covered his mouth. He trained his eyes on his partner and raised his eyebrows, but said nothing.

"What is it?" said Josh. Then a look of understanding came over his face. "You've already got a new gig, don't you?"

Graham nodded slowly. "I didn't want to tell you yet."

"It's okay. Where are you going?"

Graham hesitated for a second before speaking. "It's—it's a division of Origin—"

"You're shitting me."

"No, man. I feel like I'm betraying you. They contacted me last week, and the offer was too good to turn down. I'm sorry."

"When do you start?"

"They want me on Monday, December third."

*

Valerie unlocked the door to her condo, dropped her keys on a table, and changed into yoga pants and a stretchy lime green top.

The office was too depressing, so she had left early, just before five o'clock. There was nothing to do, and it was pointless to look very hard for another job until the start of the new year. No one in the industry was hiring at her level at the moment. Their entire focus was on the holiday season. Even seasonal workers had already been hired weeks ago. When she found a new job, though, she would be able to command a much higher salary than she was making now. That was comforting, but a better paying position wasn't the answer to her problems.

The answer was a lot more money than what she could earn in a year.

But—maybe she *could* find a really good job right now, and dig herself out of her financial hole through hard work and focus. It would be what her father would want her to do. She had plenty of experience, and the failure of PriceUtopia wasn't her fault. She had done her best, and because of other factors, the company was about to dissolve. Like so many other startups did. In fact, her decision to take a risk on this one could be viewed as a major positive. It showed that she was forward thinking, and young in outlook. It added to her background, and didn't take away from it. Despite the fact that the founders had produced something that, ultimately, nobody wanted.

She poured herself a diet ginger ale and sat down on the sofa. It was good to be alone, but for weeks, she'd been wondering what was the matter with Josh. She assumed he was in super overdrive about the company, and that he must be worried about money, as well. But their relationship had cooled so much that now it was downright icy. He treated her respectfully and professionally at the office, but he avoided being alone with her, and he hardly even made eye contact with her. It was a little baffling. She knew he needed the release of sex, so maybe he'd been jacking off a lot.

How disgusting.

She chased the idea from her mind. She hadn't cared that much about not seeing him on the weekends lately, nor did she really miss sleeping with him. In all honesty, the sex wasn't *always* great, anyway. She could take care of her own physical needs, too. And exercise helped a lot. It distracted her mentally, and just like anyone else, she enjoyed the endomorphin release. And constant exercise was key in maintaining her shape and firmness. She worked out at her fitness club on Peachtree Road at least four times a week; lately, she'd gone almost every day after work. She was going again in a little while. There was a yoga class a half hour from now, and afterward she would work out on the machines.

Around eight o'clock, she was done at the club and on her way out the door. The sun had set about an hour ago, and she walked into the parking lot under a dark, clear sky. There was a chill in the air, with the temperature hovering around fifty–pretty normal for Atlanta in the fall.

Halfway home and sitting in the right lane at a red light, she saw them. Josh was ten feet ahead on the sidewalk next to her. His back was to her, and his arm was around another woman.

Valerie's eyes widened as she caught her breath and gripped the steering wheel. She watched them standing at the entrance of a bar. Then Josh pulled the woman in to him and kissed her playfully–something he had never done with Valerie.

They looked like two people in love, or falling in it.

She could see their silhouettes now, as they looked at each other and laughed. The bitch was only a few inches shorter than Josh, but she was wearing heels. She was slim but not skinny, and she had long, unruly, hideous hair.

Then they turned and disappeared inside the bar before the traffic on Peachtree moved. After a few seconds, the car in front of Valerie edged forward. She kept her foot on the brake, staring at the entrance of the bar.

It was obvious that Josh hadn't just met the woman. He must have been seeing her for weeks, if not months.

Apparently, he had been cheating on Valerie.

The car behind her honked and startled her. Still in shock at what she had just seen, she looked up at the traffic light. It was green. She accelerated, but drove slowly.

So this was why Josh had cooled toward her. He was getting sex elsewhere, and he didn't want her anymore. She felt betrayed, and very rejected. What an asshole he was. Evidently, like other men, he wanted a younger woman. Like her own father had wanted, after his second wife passed away. Like he had found, in a matter of months.

She began breathing evenly, trying to fight away the tears. She did her best to stay attractive: she worked out, took care of her skin and hair, and wore the best makeup. She had had her last Botox injection a few weeks later than it was scheduled. She ought to have major work done, probably. She was getting older every day, and putting that off wasn't helping any. The fact that women had to worry about aging, whereas men didn't—Josh didn't— was incredibly unfair.

If either of them was going to decide to part ways, it should have been her. But here he was, going out with someone else and acting as though he were unattached.

It was dark, and Josh hadn't seen her, but he wasn't exactly sneaking around. Evidently, he didn't care if she found out. Like a fool, she had trusted him, and she couldn't fathom why. All this time, she had assumed their relationship was exclusive. She didn't want to be with him forever, but she didn't want to be cast aside, either.

In a fog, she arrived back home and stepped in the shower. She had recovered somewhat, and had decided she wasn't going to tell him yet that she had seen him with another woman. But he was going to pay for betraying her. At some point soon, she would confront him, and he would regret having treated her this way.

As of tomorrow, she was going to stop going in to the office. Why should she? She would send Josh and Graham an email stating that she was now working from home. They would have to keep on paying her until the company dissolved. And as a top executive, she would get a much better severance package than most everyone else.

She turned off the stream of hot water and wrapped herself in a towel. She had to compartmentalize Josh's infidelity for now, and turn her attention to other, more pressing issues. A new job, no matter how highly paid, wouldn't solve her problems. She needed to focus instead on the plan she had devised. In a few weeks, her world would completely change. She would finally get what she should have gotten almost a year ago. Then it wouldn't even matter if she found a new position. She had already contacted a few companies, but if things went the way she planned, she wouldn't have to work if she didn't want to.

She could retire, and live the life that she was meant to live.

She pulled on a bathrobe and went to the kitchen. She would have a glass or two of wine before she went to sleep. She opened the fridge and picked out a bottle of chardonnay. She fished in a drawer for one of her cork pop openers and removed the plastic shield from the needle.

She stared at it before inserting it into the cork. This was the weapon she had been fantasizing about, ever since the birthday dinner at Melody's house. She could get June drunk—if she knew she wasn't driving, June could easily drink a bottle and a half of wine. After she passed out, Valerie would pierce her carotid artery with the cork pop needle. No need to push the top of it to emit the gas. It would be a bloody mess, but she could take measures to prevent that woman's blood from getting on her.

She just had to figure out exactly how to do it without going to jail.

25

Disclosures

Melody's least favorite holiday was Halloween.

Unlike some moms she knew, she detested having to figure out what the kids' costumes would be. Last year had been the worst. Pip and Neely were barely past the shock of losing their parents, and were still getting used to living with the Perkins. Nick and Matt hadn't quite accepted them as members of the family. Jeff had taken all four of the kids out trick or treating, but he'd had to bring Nick home early.

And it had rained.

She checked the weather on her phone. Tomorrow was supposed to be clear. But with Halloween falling on a Wednesday, the kids had to go to school the next day. They would have Halloween parties at school tomorrow and then go out for candy. It would be all she could do to get them to eat a decent dinner before they left. All four kids would probably overdose on sugar.

She planned to ration their candy, and she knew they would pout. But too bad. Matt had already had his first cavity, and all the kids went crazy with sugar highs. She would count out ten pieces for each of them when they got home, and then she would let them pack two pieces of candy a day in their lunch. Maybe after a week or two, they would get through everything they liked, and no one would notice when she tossed out the rest. By then, she would be busy getting ready for the trip to Sea Gem for Thanksgiving.

Frank and Dawn had booked flights for that Monday, and they planned to arrive at the beach in the evening. Melody was looking forward to seeing her brother and Dawn. Over the last year, her sister-in-law had been very supportive. Dawn was close to her sister, and she had been a great source of advice about Pip and Neely.

Dawn and Helen hadn't lost their parents, but their father abandoned the family when they were very young. They'd had to cope with a narcissistic, alcoholic mother who somehow found a second husband a few years later. He adopted the sisters and provided the stability they needed. The family struggled financially, and both girls became independent early. But Dawn had never forgotten what it was like when her entire world was in free fall—before her stepfather came along and righted things.

With Pip and Neely, it was different, of course. They had grown up in a stable, loving home out in California, until one horrible day when that was gone forever. Within a week, they were living in North Carolina, and less than a year later, the family moved to Atlanta. Jeff and Melody were nothing like their parents, personality-wise, and neither had had a clue about how to raise girls. They'd been muddling through though, and things had gotten easier, little by little.

Melody checked the time. She had only a few minutes before she had to go pick up the kids. She had just walked Napoleon, and now he was taking a nap in his crate. She decided to leave him in there while she was gone.

Her phone buzzed. "Hi, Frank."

"Hey. Just wanted to tell you about something going on down at the beach."

She picked up her car keys and headed to the garage. She could talk to him on the way to school. "Okay. What is it?"

"Mick called and said there's been a rash of burglaries and some vandalism in the area recently. Just last weekend, someone broke into the Kane house next door, and damaged their pool."

Melody got in the car and fastened her seat belt. "Somebody broke into Sugar Kane? Oh my God. I assume they called the police?" She started the car and backed out.

"They did, and they haven't caught the burglar yet. But there have been several other incidents in the last few weeks in the neighborhood. Mick suggested that we change all the locks at the house, reconfigure the garage door openers, and recode the alarm system. He's the only one who knows the current code to it, but still."

"I guess that would be smart."

"Me, too. I was thinking, though, we might want to get security cameras installed inside the house, too. All we have now are a few motion detectors. We have the outside cameras, but we don't have any video monitoring in the interior."

"Do you really think we need that?"

"I'm just thinking, if someone does get inside while we're away, it would help the cops catch them."

"Where would we have them installed?"

"We could have the motion detectors changed into cameras. There's only three of them, but it might be prudent."

"Okay. Fine with me. This is kind of creepy, though."

"I don't know what else we can do."

"I guess you're right. I say go ahead. But since we're getting down there before anyone else for Thanksgiving, I'll need my new key to the house before we leave, and the new code."

"Right. I'll tell him to go ahead and have the cameras installed inside, and I'll have him FedEx you and me our new keys, garage door openers, and the new security code."

Melody stopped at a red light. "What about Valerie?"

"I'll let her know, and have Mick send her a set, too. I can't imagine that she'll object."

*

Around four o'clock, Frank called Valerie.

"Glad I caught you," he said, somewhat surprised that she picked up.

"I'm in between meetings right now. What's up?"

He repeated Mick's report. "Melody and I talked a little while ago, and she and I think we should follow his advice. He can get all the locks rekeyed, redo the garage door openers–"

"Fine."

"–and reset the security code."

"He knows the current code, right?"

"He's the only person who knows it, but he suggested that he change it now. If we think we need to, we can reset it again when we get down there."

"Okay."

"I'll have him FedEx you the code, your keys, your garage door opener—"

"Good."

"When are you getting down there?"

"Not until Tuesday or Wednesday. I'll let you know."

"Okay."

"Look. I'm busy, and I've got to go. See you soon."

She hung up, and Frank put his phone down. Problem solved. He would get a message to Mick this weekend, and would tell him to get started on the security cameras. He and Melody could let Valerie know about them when she arrived at the house.

*

Three days later, June sat down to eat lunch with her friend Angela at Bistro Niko, a French restaurant in the heart of Buckhead. Angela and Hugh had just returned to Atlanta from their European river cruise.

"So, bring me up to date," said Angela. "I want to hear all about you and Antoine. What all happened while I was away?"

"Well," June said, smiling. "A lot." She lowered her chin and raised her brows.

Angela's eyes widened. "Did you—are you two *together* now?"

"I guess so. Yes, we are." June placed her napkin on her lap and looked up at the waiter, who had just walked up.

Angela regarded him. "May I have an unsweet tea, please?"

"Same for me," said June.

Neither woman had looked at the menu yet. The waiter nodded, turned, and trotted away.

"So?" said Angela. "This is killing me, June! Tell me!"

June offered a mischievous smile. "It's all good. And I'm so glad that you and Hugh introduced us."

"Is he romantic? Do you two have a lot in common? What's he like in bed?"

"Angela!"

"Well?" She cocked her head. "Don't tell me you haven't—"

"I *won't* tell you," said June. "But I don't want to talk about that—if you don't mind."

Angela humphed. "All right, if you insist. It's just that he's so *sexy*…"

"I agree. To answer your other questions, though, yes, he's very romantic. And we do have a few things in common. More important than that, though, he knows how to make me laugh."

"Are you in love?"

The waiter appeared with their drinks and set them down on the table. The women began studying their menus.

"Let us have just a few minutes, please," said Angela.

"Of course." He vanished.

Angela gave June an expectant look.

"You know," said June, "honestly, I'm not sure if I'm in love. But I haven't felt this way in years, Angela. I loved Jim—you know I did—and I still do. But now, well, it's just so *different* with Antoine. I can't explain it, really. It feels strange, but wonderful at the same time."

Angela smiled. "I know you loved Jim, and honey, he *adored* you. But since he's gone, well, I'm just glad to see you so happy."

"Really?"

"Yes, really. You deserve it! I say, enjoy yourself with Antoine. Life is short, and if you find love, you've got to grab it with both hands!"

"Well, we certainly enjoy each other's company. I never imagined I would feel that way about another man, but I do. And so far, he seems to want to be with me, all the time."

"Why wouldn't he? You're gorgeous."

June cocked her head. "You're my friend, and you're being kind. But I'm not young, Angela."

"So what? You're not old, either! And you look *fantastic*. So does he, for that matter."

"He is very attractive, isn't he?"

The waiter reappeared and stood next to the table. "Have you decided, ladies?"

Angela looked down at the menu, then back at June. "Do you know what you want?"

June looked up at the waiter. "Yes. Bring me the *salade niçoise,* please."

Angela closed her menu, put it down, and smiled at her friend. "Make that two. I'll have what *she's* having."

26

Future Endeavors

Josh felt relieved.

He stretched in his office chair and let out a deep breath. He hadn't seen Valerie in over two weeks. With almost all of her sales staff gone, she had decided to work from home. Her only remaining direct report was a thirty-something woman named Nicole, also working from home. However, Josh was certain that both women were spending all their time looking for a job.

It didn't matter, though. Today was Wednesday, November 14, and next Thursday was Thanksgiving. Valerie would find a new position soon. She had loads of experience and lots of industry contacts. She would disappear from his life. The sooner, the better.

He and Aimee were spending the holiday with Andrew and Claudia. Josh and Andrew's mom, Colleen, was flying in from Charleston to join them. Last year, Josh, Andrew, and Claudia spent the holiday there, with her. That weekend, Valerie's father had passed away suddenly, and the next few weeks—between Thanksgiving and

Christmas–had been intense. That's when he had first begun to understand who Valerie really was.

At the time, he thought her shock had quickly been displaced by anger. That she didn't mean to be so sharp or nasty. That her behavior was almost normal, as the next stage of grief. But when she continued to behave badly, he began to pick up on her true nature. When she was stressed, she didn't curb her tongue at work anymore, nor did she care when she was ugly toward others or obnoxious. Privately, he tried to excuse her, hoping she would move through her grief over the next few months and that it would fade. But that never seemed to happen. Not as far as he could see.

Looking back, he wasn't sure whether her dad's passing was the catalyst for some kind of dreadful sea change in her or not. Perhaps, before then, he had just been blind to her nature because of his own ego, and his lust.

If only he had never hired her–he would have ended things with her, way back then. Looking back, he was a bit baffled as to what he had seen in her. Maybe every man had to date a woman like her once in his life, just to know what he didn't want. In any case, he and Valerie were done, and he was very happy now to be seeing Aimee.

He had to figure out what he was going to do professionally, but he was feeling a little better about that lately. Surely something would open up in a few months. Until then, he could assess his situation, and explore opportunities. Graham and he would remain friends, and although there was nothing for Josh at Origin, you never knew what might transpire in the future. Plus, Josh had a ton of contacts, some of whom must be impressed with what he had accomplished at PriceUtopia, despite what happened.

He stood up and looked out the window. It was chilly today, and dark clouds threatened a thunderstorm, something not all that unusual for November in Atlanta. The weather seemed to fit the anxious mood felt around the office. In forty-eight hours, the company's doors would close for good.

Josh sighed. How had success eluded him, once again? Why hadn't he known about what was going on "in the space?" Even if Graham wouldn't have done anything different, why hadn't he intuited a long time ago that consumers were going to be the ones in control when it came to finding the lowest prices—by using their own personal devices?

The ubiquitous smartphone.

He had almost gone crazy, asking himself these questions. Maybe Julian Stone was right, and he just wasn't smart enough to succeed in this industry. Graham was brilliant at what he did, but Josh was no match for him, on the other side of the business.

Maybe Josh should have listened more and talked less. He definitely should have read more, and studied more—not just back in school, but ever since. He had fucked up, believing that he could do something nobody else could do, and assuming that no one else had thought of his idea. And now, he had missed his chance.

Julian had been right about it being a zero-sum game now. His words haunted Josh daily: *"It's about knowing who else we need to destroy out there—and knowing how to do it. Eliminate others, to ensure our success."*

He sat back down at his laptop and put his face in his hands. Then he looked up and absently clicked his in-box. He had several new messages. One was from Gary

Trigger at Lallique–Valerie's old boss. What could that guy want?

He opened the email. Gary only wanted to touch base and to wish him well in future endeavors.

Then Josh's eye fell on his final few sentences:

> I wanted to let you know that Valerie Mitchell has contacted me for a reference. Not sure if you knew, but her reputation in the industry has been seriously damaged by our experiences with her. Had you not hired her last summer, we were about to dismiss her without a reference. Perhaps she will have some luck in the tech industry and/or in the growing Atlanta startup community.
>
> Best,
> Gary Trigger
> SVP Lallique
> lallique.com

Josh read it twice. Whoa. What exactly had Valerie done to burn her bridges? From what she had told him after joining the company, Gary had been a bad boss—insecure, jealous, and uptight, and a big change-his-minder. She claimed he was more concerned about his image than about results, and that he hadn't made good use of her experience. Josh believed her, but later on he wondered how true her version of the story was. He'd only heard her side, and, maybe because he was so taken with her at the beginning, he hadn't doubted her. Gary probably was a jackass, but Valerie must have pissed him off when things came to a head, if not before. Even so, why would anyone but a jackass send Josh an email like this one?

But if Valerie couldn't find a new job in that industry—if Gary had blacklisted her—it wouldn't be good. What would she do? She would have to look elsewhere for a position. There were lots of technology startups, but they were looking for people who were a lot younger than her, and more tech-savvy. And cheaper.

Josh shook his head. Valerie always claimed that she could have done Gary's job much better that he did it. Apparently, though, she'd been identified as toxic before she ever came to work at PriceUtopia.

But that wasn't Josh's problem. She would figure out something. God knew, he had his own issues to deal with.

*

That Saturday night, Antoine and June went out to dinner at Maurice's, a French restaurant near Piedmont Park.

It was their last night together until after the Thanksgiving holidays. Antoine would be back in Atlanta on Wednesday, November 28, and the two of them were on a flight to Paris on Friday, December 7. They would stay for a week, and then take a train to Provence.

"We could go west, after that," said Antoine. "Travel over to Languedoc, since you've never been there."

June smiled and picked up her glass of champagne. He had told her a lot about that part of France. "That sounds lovely."

This man could propose almost anything to me right now, and I would probably agree. She inhaled deeply and gazed into his sexy, green eyes. As they chatted, random thoughts of Jim popped into her mind. He had been so different from Antoine, yet in some ways, much the same. The way Jim had made her feel, back when they began dating, was very similar to the way she felt tonight, and to the way she had been feeling for weeks.

Jim had truly loved her. Despite his wealth and status, he had accepted her for who she was: an ordinary schoolteacher with a humble background. Jim had also grown up in a middle class family, and had gone to a small college on a football scholarship. During his second year, he'd had a knee injury, lost the scholarship, and had to work his way through. He and his first wife had married young and lived frugally, and as he built his career, neither had taken their good fortune for granted.

When he lost Ginger, of course he had been devastated. But within a year, he and June began seeing each other. Jim hadn't cared one iota that she wasn't terribly sophisticated or smart. Her inability to have children wasn't an issue, either—with his kids reaching adulthood, he didn't want any more. But now he was gone, and June was with another man who made her feel as desirable as Jim had.

"*Chérie?*" Antoine asked. "Of what are you thinking, with such a serious expression?"

June blushed. "Oh, nothing. Just of how happy I am." She smiled.

"*Ah, moi aussi.* Which makes me want to ask you something that is also quite serious."

She raised her eyebrows. "Yes?"

Antoine reached across the table, took her hand, and smiled. "I was going to wait until later this evening. But now, I think, is the right time. At least, I hope it is."

What could he be talking about? They had already made their plans to go to France.

He looked into her eyes. "June, I'm in love with you, and I hope that you feel the same. Rather than spending our time apart, why don't we spend it together? Not just when it's convenient, but always?" He glanced at her right hand. "I'm not familiar with the American custom regarding engagement rings when you marry for the second time, but—"

"Antoine—"

"June. Will you marry me?"

27

Ulterior Motive

"I'm texting Melody," Dawn said when the plane touched down in Jacksonville late Monday afternoon. Frank was holding Cole, who had done well on the flight. Slipping her phone back into her bag, Dawn reached for the baby. "Here, I'll take him."

Frank handed Cole to his wife. He pulled his own bag from underneath the seat in front of him and powered on his cell phone. Fifteen minutes and a diaper change later, they were at baggage claim, and after another half hour, they were on the road. It was still light out, but it would be dark when they arrived at the house. Hopefully, Cole would sleep on the way, but would also settle down for the night later on. Fortunately, he was rarely fussy, and he was a good sleeper.

He did sleep in his car seat for most of the way. When Frank pulled the rental car into the drive and put it in park, Cole stirred, but he didn't cry.

"Hey, sweetie," Dawn said to him. "We're here."

The outside lights cast a bright glow on them, and Melody, Jeff, and the kids streamed out through the front double doors to greet them. June waved from the porch. After words of welcome and hugs, most of the group sat down together in the spacious great room just off the two-story foyer. The Perkins children went to watch television in the den, on the other side of the kitchen.

"Cole is more adorable now than ever," Melody said to Dawn. "And he's grown so much!"

Dawn smiled. "He has a great appetite."

"How old is he?" asked June.

"Eight and a half months," said Dawn. "He just mastered holding his own bottle."

"That's great!" said Melody.

Dawn nodded. "It does help a lot."

"He's going to be walking—and then running—before you guys know it," said Jeff.

Frank smiled. "I'm sure he will." He looked at his wife. "Well, I'm ready for a drink. How about you?"

She glanced around. Melody and June were drinking white wine, and Jeff was drinking a beer. "I'd love a glass of wine."

He disappeared into the kitchen, and Dawn turned to June. "When did you get in?"

"Oh, about three hours ago. I left town early this morning. Traffic wasn't too bad, luckily."

"It wasn't bad on the way up from the airport, either," Dawn said. "Our flight was fine, too. But I'm glad we got out of Chicago before the holiday rush."

A moment later, Frank returned with a glass of wine for Dawn and a gin and tonic for himself. He sat down between his wife and his brother-in-law, and turned to his sister. "Did you say that Valerie's getting in tomorrow?

Melody nodded. An awkward silence passed as family members avoided each other's eyes. Evidently, no one was impatient for Valerie to arrive.

Jeff came to the rescue. "It must be nice to escape the cold weather up north for a few days." He grinned at Frank.

"It sure is," said Frank.

The men began to chat about work and business, and the women fell into their own conversation about the next few days. After the three of them agreed about who would prepare what for Thanksgiving dinner—without assigning anything to Valerie—Melody poured each of them another glass of wine.

"The company she works for is going out of business," said Melody. "Jeff said he read an article about it in the *Atlanta Business Chronicle*."

Dawn shook her head. "Wow. That's too bad."

"I know. But she didn't seem concerned when we saw her at our house for Jeff's birthday."

"Did the subject of her company come up?" asked Dawn.

Melody nodded. "She acted like everything was fine."

June sipped her wine. "Well, I bet she'll find herself a new job in no time. She always seems to land on her feet." She smiled.

"So how was it, over at your house that night?"

"Oh, fine," said Melody. "I mean, things went as well as I expected—no better, but no worse. She did manage to say something about me not having 'worked' in years, though." She made air quotes.

Dawn rolled her eyes. "Like staying home with your kids isn't work."

"I'm used to it," said Melody. "She's not the only person I've ever come across who thinks it isn't work."

"Well, even though I've never done it, I *know* it's a full-time job," said June. "Honestly, I don't know how you all do it."

"You know, at one point, Jeff and I talked about me going back to work after a few years. But now, with the girls—well, with four kids, it's like running a marathon, just to get everything done every day! I can't imagine it's going to get much easier anytime soon." She took a sip of wine. "Don't get me wrong. Life is good, all things considered. But me fitting in an outside job on top of everything else I do—well, it's pretty much impossible."

"I don't see where you could find the time," said June. "You don't need the money, anyway."

"That's another thing," said Melody. "I'm thankful that we don't, and most of our friends *know* we don't. Even so, sometimes I feel judged for not working outside the home. Not by friends, but by society."

"I know what you're saying," said Dawn. "I mean, look at me, with only one child. When I decided to quit my job, most people at work were incredulous. Some were even kind of judgy."

"My goodness!" said June, looking at Dawn. "After everything you've been through, that must have been hard to take."

"I guess it could have been. But I couldn't care less what people think. I think it's a shame when people criticize moms for staying home, especially when it's other women who do it."

"Me, too," said Melody. "Most people don't say anything blatant, though. More often, it's like, when I'm at a party or somewhere and the subject comes up, people—

usually career women–look at me as if I'm a Martian. Or like I'm too stupid to have a career. It's irritating."

Dawn took another sip of wine. "Those women don't know how much work we really do. I've only been home with Cole for less than a year, but I can't imagine juggling an outside job with being his mom." She put down her glass. "And I know it was really hard for my sister, working full time when Adele was little."

"How is Helen?" asked Melody. "When's her baby due, again?"

"Late April. She's doing great. She plans to quit her job and stay home after he's born."

"They know it's a boy?" asked June.

Dawn nodded and smiled. "They're thrilled."

"That's wonderful," said June. "Well, I think we women all need to support each other's decisions. People have all kinds of reasons for what they do, and it's no one else's business. I applaud anyone raising little kids, whether they work outside the home as well or not."

"I know, right?" said Melody. "I'm glad Mom stayed home with us, and I always thought she was happy she did. Whether you have to work, or you choose to do it, I respect your decision. I just wish I felt that same respect for my choice to stay home."

Dawn put her hand on Melody's arm. "Who cares what 'society'–or *anyone*–thinks? Those career women who pay someone else to raise their kids aren't any smarter than you are, Melody. This one woman at my office had boy-girl twins a few years ago. She hired a Spanish-speaking nanny and went back to work full time. But she forbade the nanny to speak Spanish in front of her kids. Evidently, she doesn't realize that the best way to learn another language is when you're very young."

"What an idiot," said Melody. She glanced at June, then back at her sister-in-law. "I'd have loved for my kids to learn Spanish the same time they were learning English. But back to Valerie, since she's not here yet. What do y'all think about her wanting to come down here and spend Thanksgiving with us?"

"I was surprised," said June. "I can't remember the last time she spent Thanksgiving with the family."

"Me, neither," said Melody. "She normally disappears for it. I hate to say it, but I feel like she must have some kind of ulterior motive."

"Like what?" asked Dawn. "Are you thinking she wants to bring up selling Sea Gem again?"

"No, no, nothing like that," said Melody. "I don't know what I think, really. I just feel like she has an agenda."

"Well, I dare say we've all felt that way about her, at times," said June. "But maybe she just wants a feeling of belonging and acceptance. With Jim gone for a year now, I wonder if her own mortality is starting to hit."

Dawn shrugged. "Maybe. Life is short, after all."

*

Valerie arrived at Sea Gem the next day at four thirty.

She hated the drive down. Traffic hadn't been too bad, but it was boring being on the road for over five hours. She'd stopped four times to distract herself. She much preferred flying, which she always did first class, of course. Coach was out of the question; she'd never done it before, and she didn't plan to.

She pulled her BMW into the driveway and parked in front of the house. No one came outside to greet her.

She grabbed her suitcase and her bag, and walked in the unlocked front door.

The house was silent. Maybe they were all out by the pool, or down at the ocean. Wherever they happened to be, she was very happy not to have to see any of them yet. She had stopped at a supermarket about twenty minutes ago to pick up the coffee creamer she preferred, and some of her favorite foods. All the bedrooms here at Sea Gem had a small fridge, a microwave, and a Nespresso coffee maker. She rolled her suitcase into her room, dropped her purse on a tan leather chair, and went back to her car to get her groceries.

After she put them away, she unpacked her bag. The weather was supposed to be sunny and warm this week. She planned to go outside and exercise every day, not only to feel good, but to get away from everyone. Otherwise, she'd go crazy.

It was going to be all she could do to get through the next five days. But no matter how hard it was, she simply had to be a very good actress. She had to make everyone believe that she liked being here and that she enjoyed their company. She had to act interested in them and in their lives. She had to make them think that being with family was important to her, and make them wonder why they ever doubted it was.

She took a look at herself in a mirror and evaluated her expression. Unlike her sister, she could mask her emotions very well. Really, she could have easily been a Hollywood actress. She certainly had the looks for it, and she had talent that only needed to be developed. If she had stayed in California and pursued acting, by now she would have all the money she had ever wanted. She would have been famous, and been worth millions.

But—because of what other people had said and done to her—she hadn't been able to follow that dream. She'd been afraid that her father wouldn't approve, that he would say it was a lark and was a waste of time and money. She had followed another route, simply to please him and to make him proud of her. Then, while she was out west, busting her ass just to prove that she could be successful in the business world, he had made the biggest mistake of his life.

He had married June.

That mistake had changed Valerie's life, and at the time, she had no idea how much. But over the years that followed, she never lost any sleep about her inheritance. Her father was a well-known, wealthy executive, and she felt assured that one day, she would receive her rightful portion of the family money. She looked up to him and kept seeking his approval, if not that of his ill-bred, tacky wife. Then, suddenly, he was gone—and his wife was still here.

Now it was time for her to go, too.

Not this week, though. This week was only a dry run.

28

Perfect

Ninety minutes later, over cocktails, June made her announcement. She had waited for Valerie's arrival so she could tell everyone in the family at the same time.

She put her wine glass down and cleared her throat. "Everybody, I have some news," she said. Conversation stopped abruptly, and she glanced around the room. Her eyes rested on Melody, and she smiled. "Antoine and I are eloping."

Melody started. "You mean, you're getting married?"

June nodded.

"Oh my God! That's wonderful!" exclaimed Dawn.

"Yes, it is," said Valerie, smirking. "But—what do you mean, you're eloping? You're not sneaking off to get married, if you're telling us *ahead* of time—"

June gave her a measured look. *Why does she have to be snarky?* "I mean, we're going away to get married."

"When?" asked Melody.

June lifted her eyebrows, paused, and braced for reactions. "Next month, when we go to France. We're getting married over there."

Jeff spoke up. "Well, this is great news!" He raised his glass. "To the bride–congratulations!"

The others raised their drinks in the air and repeated his last word.

"So, June," said Frank, "how long have you and Antoine been seeing each other?"

Here it comes. "We met in August. So, since then."

Melody tilted her head. "Goodness. I had no *idea* that you two were getting serious. But I'm very happy for you!"

"Thank you." June looked from Melody to Dawn and then over to Frank. "It's just, when you know, you know. At my age–"

"What do you mean, at your age?" asked Dawn. "You're only ten years older than Valerie!"

June shot a glance over at Valerie. You had to love Dawn for always speaking the truth, and for not being afraid *who* it annoyed. And it looked like Valerie was extremely annoyed. "I'm just saying, at my age, it doesn't take long to know what you want to do."

No one spoke for a second or two. Melody glanced at June's bare left hand. "Is he going to give you an engagement ring?"

June paused for a second. "We've decided on a combination engagement ring and wedding band. He's giving it to me when we marry." She blushed. "I'm still going to wear the diamond your father gave me, though." She held up her right hand. "I think Jim would want me to."

"Has Antoine been married before?" asked Dawn. "I don't mean to pry, but–"

272

"That's okay. Yes, he was, when he was in his twenties. But his wife passed away after a few years, from a sudden illness." June sipped her wine. Anticipating the next question, she added, "He has no children."

Valerie picked up her drink. "Will you two live in Atlanta?"

"Actually, we plan to live in France for half the year, and in Atlanta for the other half." June put down her glass. "We've decided to stay in France from this December through May. Then we'll come back over here, to avoid the summer tourist season." She paused, and then cocked her head. "I'd invite you all to our wedding over there, but it's going to be very small, and very soon. That's what I meant about eloping." She glanced at Dawn and Valerie. "My sister and her husband are coming to visit us afterward, in mid-January. They've never been to Europe."

"Oh?" asked Valerie. "I'm surprised that you and Daddy never invited them to go there with you."

"You know, the summer before he died, we talked about taking them with us on a trip to Italy. But we never got a chance to do it." She sighed. "So I'm really glad they're both able to take a little time off from work to come visit us in France."

"How long are they staying?" asked Dawn.

"About a week." She glanced around the room. "Of course, you're all welcome to come over and visit anytime. I'm so glad to be able to see y'all here all together this week, before I leave."

"I know we're all glad to have you here," said Frank, looking around.

"*I* certainly am," said Melody. "You know, I don't mean to bring up something unpleasant, but I can't believe somebody broke into Sugar Kane next door."

"Do you know what was stolen?" asked Valerie.

"No," said Melody, "but I know they also vandalized the pool. Good thing the Kanes weren't home at the time. What if there had been a home invasion instead of just a burglary?"

"According to Mick, there haven't been any home invasions in the area," said Frank. "Thank goodness." He picked up his drink.

Jeff stood up. "Would anyone like another drink?"

*

Valerie spent the next twenty-four hours considering her options. Late Wednesday night, she came to a decision.

She had to do it here, at Sea Gem. She would do it tomorrow night. She had decided against the cork pop, however. Piercing June's carotid artery would be too messy, and she wasn't entirely sure she could do it on her first try. Plus, she may not die quickly enough. Instead, Valerie would do something that was a lot easier, and wasn't bloody. She wasn't sure exactly what yet. But whatever it was, she would make it look like an accident.

She had originally planned to do it over the Christmas holidays, but that was before she found out June was about to get married and leave the country for the next six months. She couldn't allow her to go through with her plans. If she did, things would get way too complicated, and could get out of hand.

What if June buys an expensive chateau in France, and starts blowing the family money on her new lifestyle? What if she isn't getting a prenup? What if she names her new husband as sole beneficiary to the funds? God knows what the terms of the trust are, or what it allows.

Valerie lay in bed and closed her eyes. She had never considered that June would meet someone and decide to get married. Not only was it dismaying, it was embarrassing, and even tacky. Valerie couldn't afford to let it happen. She had to do this now, while she had the chance. While June was still single, and her late husband's fortune wasn't at risk of being siphoned away by a stranger.

It was half past eleven now, and the house was quiet. Hopefully, tomorrow night everyone would go to their rooms early. They would start drinking before dinner, and by ten, they should all be ready for bed.

She would do it after everyone else went to sleep.

She would have to create a reason for June to stay up to talk with her. She played out the scenario in her head. After June was drunk enough, Valerie would tell her she wanted to talk to her alone, before they went up to bed. She would say that it might be the last time they would see each other for months.

Maybe she would tell her that, before she went to France, she wanted to clear the air between them. She would apologize for letting herself into the house on Sherwood Circle last December. She would say that losing her father weeks before had dredged up her deep feelings of grief about Ginger's death, and even her grief when she found out that Ginger wasn't her real mother.

If she had to, Valerie would also talk about her job. She would say that she had been under a ton of stress during the last several months. She would talk about how much she had loved her father, how much she still missed him. She would assure June that she knew he would be

275

fine with June's decision to remarry. She would ask June a lot of questions and get her talking about herself. With enough wine, it ought not to be that difficult.

Whatever she had to say to keep June up, she would say it.

She turned on her side and let out a deep breath. This had to work. She had to make it work. Tomorrow was the perfect time to do it. And once it was done, her life would instantly change for the better. She could feel safe again, and feel secure about her future. She would have the money she was entitled to. Her father would want that for her. She couldn't allow herself to consider anything else.

*

Valerie slept in the next morning.

She got up around ten thirty. After she'd had her coffee and a Greek yogurt, she went downstairs. Melody was in the kitchen, already busy cooking.

Why they couldn't just have Thanksgiving dinner catered, Valerie had no idea. No—actually, she knew the reason. It was because Melody wanted to control everything, and then be able to complain about it.

"Good morning," Valerie said.

"Hi," said Melody. "Happy Thanksgiving!"

"You, too. Where is everybody?"

"Jeff took the kids to the beach, and I'm going down to join them in a little while. I think everyone else is sitting out by the pool." She slid two pies into the oven, set the timer, and then turned around to face her sister. "Would you like a Bloody Mary? I just made another pitcher."

"No, thanks. I'm going for a run. See you later."

"Okay. Have a good one."

Valerie stepped outside the back door and pulled on a light jacket. It was about sixty degrees and sunny.

She began running down the driveway, crossed the street, and followed a path going north. The air was crisp and clear, and the terrain was flat as a table, a welcome change from the steep hills of Atlanta. As she ran, her thoughts raced.

What if something went wrong tonight? What if the others didn't go to bed when she needed them to go? What if June went to bed too early, or didn't drink enough?

She simply had to manage all of that. She couldn't miss this chance to accomplish her goal. Late last night, after ruling out using the cork pop, she had briefly considered poison. There were several choices, all readily available, right here in the house. But in the end, she decided against it. Like with the cork pop, it would be too difficult to escape blame if she poisoned June. Then, she figured out the perfect way to get the job done.

She couldn't believe she hadn't thought of it before.

It was simple, and more important, it would work. She wouldn't be accused, nor even suspected. When it was done, everyone would be shocked and upset. However, she was doing them all a big favor. Once they got over it, they would be very happy to get their money, too.

29

Halftime

After Valerie stepped outside, Melody went over her cooking schedule. Everything was on track at the moment, but she still had a lot to do to get dinner ready. She was in charge of the turkey and two other dishes, and she was baking two of the four pies.

She picked up her Bloody Mary and took it with her to her bedroom. She put some sunscreen on her face, dabbed on some lip gloss, and then studied her reflection in the bathroom mirror. She had a few wrinkles around her eyes, but she didn't look bad, especially for almost thirty-eight. Her birthday was just a few weeks from now, conveniently midway between Thanksgiving and Christmas.

She pulled on a hoodie, went back to the kitchen, and sat down to finish her drink. When the timer dinged, she carefully removed the pies from the oven and set them on the counter to cool. Later on, when she finished cooking, she would change into the new dark grey pants and the bright red V-neck top she had recently bought online. The Mitchell family always dressed up for Thanksgiving dinner, and having it here at Sea Gem was no exception. Last year, everyone except Valerie had spent the holiday at the house on Sherwood Circle.

Melody had been equally dismayed and relieved at her absence that day. What was more important than spending Thanksgiving with her family? On the other hand, it was a lot easier last year, not having to walk on eggshells around Valerie all day. Melody let out a sigh. Everything was so different now. Her father was gone, and June had found happiness with another man.

This might be the last Thanksgiving that June would spend with the family. But since the French didn't celebrate the holiday, maybe they could establish a new family tradition. They could invite June and Antoine to spend Thanksgiving with them each year. The couple ought to be in America in November; June had said they would be back by the end of May, and would be here for six months. Perhaps they would keep the same schedule going forward, and not return to France until next December.

She would mention the idea to Jeff later. She finished her drink, walked out the door, and headed over to the beach.

*

A few hours later, everyone gathered in the large media room to watch football. No one cared much who won the games, but everyone liked watching. It also gave them something to do before dinner. And halftime of the Cowboy game was the unspoken, unofficial time to start drinking.

From her spot on an ottoman, Neely turned to Jeff. "Where's Napoleon?"

"I think he's in his crate in the kitchen. Why don't you go take him for a walk?"

She grabbed her sister. "Come on, Pip. Go with me."

"Don't go too far," Melody called as the girls dashed off. "And try not to let him get dirty."

Neely glanced back at her and rolled her eyes.

Frank stood, picked up Cole, and looked Dawn. "I'll change him and put him down for his afternoon nap."

"That would be great, babe."

When halftime began, Melody quietly scurried off to the kitchen. A moment later, she reappeared, carrying a full glass of white wine. A country club pour.

She sat down in a yellow armchair next to the long leather sofa, sipped her wine, and glanced around the room. Valerie was sitting in an armchair on the other side of the room, engrossed in her iPad.

"I think it's time for a beer," said Jeff. "Anyone else want a drink?"

Dawn glanced in Melody's direction. "I wouldn't mind a glass of wine."

"How about you, June? Valerie?" asked Jeff.

June shook her head. "Thanks, but I think I'll wait a bit."

Valerie looked up. "I'll wait, too."

Jeff retreated to the kitchen. A few minutes later, he returned with Dawn's wine and his beer. He looked over at Melody.

"I just heard the oven timer go off."

"Oh—that's my broccoli dish." She walked into the kitchen, grabbed a mitt, and opened the lower oven.

Clang! The glass dish hit the floor and broke into several pieces, spewing broccoli and cheese everywhere.

"*Damn it!*" Melody cried.

"Are you okay?" called Jeff as he hurried over.

"I'm fine. When I pulled out the rack, the damn thing slid off. The rack slipped or something. It wasn't level."

Dawn and June came in and helped pick up the pieces and clean up the floor.

A moment later, Valerie followed them into the kitchen. "Need any help?" she said from the doorway.

"No, thanks. I think we've got it," said Melody. She glanced at the others, who were still mopping up melted cheese with paper towels. "Well, I guess that's one less dish to clean!"

A few seconds of awkward silence passed.

"Oh, well. Who needs broccoli on Thanksgiving, anyway?" asked Jeff. He put his arm around his wife. "We've got more than enough to eat without it."

"We don't have a green vegetable now, though," she said.

"Who cares? I'm sure it was delicious, but the kids weren't going to eat it anyway." He tilted his head. "Doll. I know it took a while to make, but—"

"It doesn't matter," said Melody, fully recovered from the mishap. "I just don't know how that happened! I guess I can make it again some other time."

When the floor was clean, everyone wandered out of the room and back over to watch the game. It was still halftime. The boys were sprawled on the rug in front of the TV. Nick was playing with a few of his favorite toy matchbox cars.

Frank walked into the room and sat down next to Dawn. He leaned toward her and murmured, "Cole's asleep."

Melody sipped her wine. "So, Jeff's going to carve the turkey," she announced, looking around. "The pies are all done, and now I only have two other dishes to cook." She smiled wanly. The extra dressing and the potatoes would be easy to prepare, and she could get them done later.

"I'm going to fix my sweet potato casserole," said June.

"Watch out for the lower oven shelf," Melody advised.

Dawn threw a glance at her husband, and no one spoke for a moment or two.

"You know, I think I'll have that glass of white wine now," said June, glancing at Jeff. "After all, it's a holiday."

He smiled. "I'll be happy to get it for you."

"Thank you, Jeff."

"You ready too, Valerie?"

"Sure. Thanks."

He trotted away, returned with the glasses, and looked at Frank. "How about a beer?"

"Sure. I'll get it, though. Need another?"

"Yeah, thanks." Jeff sat down.

The third quarter began, and conversation dwindled as the adults started to relax. A few minutes later, the girls burst in the back door and into the kitchen.

"Clean his paws," called Melody.

Jeff gave her a look. "Mel, he's a dog."

"I don't want him tracking sand and dirt in!"

Jeff sighed and got up to oversee the twins and Napoleon. A few minutes later, he was back. "Matt, after the game, I want you to go and help Pip and Neely set the table."

"Make sure you all wash your hands first," said Melody.

"We *will*, Mom," Matt said tiredly. He rolled his eyes. "Don't freak out!"

June smiled and threw a glance at Dawn. "Little boys are so cute," she said quietly.

Melody let out a deep breath. All ten of them were going to eat Thanksgiving dinner at the huge rectangular table in the dining room. She would tell Jeff and Frank to sit at either end. She had chosen not to do place cards this year, but now she was beginning to regret that decision.

However, after another glass of wine, she probably wouldn't care that much. But she would make sure not to sit next to—or across from—her sister.

30

Truth Told

June sympathized with Melody, but she wished that she would let go of her feelings toward Valerie.

Having witnessed the drama of the sisters' relationship for the last two decades, she knew that she wouldn't miss it when she was in France. As for the six months a year she and Antoine planned to spend back in the States, well, she would make sure that they filled their time with people and activities they enjoyed.

It wasn't that she didn't care about Jim's children. But, truth told, she was through with worrying about whether they got along. She wasn't going to miss hearing Melody moan about Valerie's latest affront. Yes, Valerie was a very difficult person to be around, and since Jim had passed, she seemed to have gotten worse. June didn't appreciate her constant snarky remarks, and her tone yesterday about June's use of the word 'eloping' had been rude.

But weren't they all used to Valerie by now? And what could you do about her behavior? You had to live your own life, and let her live hers, however she chose to. Melody had always been kind of a whiner. As the youngest of the siblings, she often seemed resentful of her sister for stealing the spotlight that she might have thought she deserved. June felt a pang of guilt for judging her; she had been through quite a lot. Growing up, she had been caught in the middle between her mother and Valerie, who, according to Jim, never got along. Both of them wanted Melody's allegiance and support, but neither realized the position they were putting her in. June wasn't surprised Melody had grown up to be someone who tried to control everything. Her insistence that they all somehow become a perfect family now was unrealistic.

It just wasn't going to happen.

Frank was the most stable one in the group. He was a dutiful, kind stepson, and his wife was a darling. Living so far away had to be helpful for them, when it came to getting along with the extended family. Their visits were short and infrequent, and their interactions were limited. The situation was kind of sad, when you thought about it. But June's mother Peggy had felt much the same about her family of origin. June and Linda had grown up overhearing comments and stories about Peggy's siblings, Uncle Bob and Aunt Marie, both alcoholics who eventually drank themselves to death. Then there were some distant cousins who had what June believed were mental disorders. None of them were ever diagnosed, but one had ended up in jail.

She pushed the memories from her mind, picked up her wine, and tried to focus on the game. The others cheered occasionally, and she enjoyed watching NFL games as much as anyone. But she didn't get too much into a football game unless the Falcons were playing. She and Jim had attended several games at the Georgia Dome over the years, often with friends.

There were so many things June missed about the life they'd had together: their social life, their intimacy, their companionship, and even their daily routines. Jim had given her his love and devotion, and he had always put her first in his life. Of course, they'd had their disagreements–like any other married couple who was honest with each other. But they'd never let anything come between them. *Nothing* had been more important than their relationship.

Would it be the same, between her and Antoine? She hardly knew, but somehow she believed the answer was yes. He was like Jim in so many ways, yet so unlike him, in others. And if Jim's children didn't accept him or understand her choice to marry him after only a few months, so what? She and Jim had only known each other for about the same amount of time before they got married. No one had opposed their union then–except Valerie.

But Jim hadn't paid any attention to his older daughter's opinion. He and June had rarely talked about her; their unspoken agreement had been to let him deal with her. June couldn't say that she loved his children and grandchildren, but she had grown to care for them. However, she was always acutely aware that they were his relatives, not hers. She and Linda had remained very close, and Jim had loved Linda like a sister.

June let out a small sigh. Maybe Jim had been a better person than she was–or maybe Linda was just a lot easier to love than Jim's children were. Linda was a good, honest person with a heart of gold. She and Clay worked very hard, and while June felt sure that the adults surrounding her today did that also, they had been raised with advantage and money. All of them, that is, except Dawn. June felt a sort of kinship with her. Dawn was a very direct person, bless her heart. But she seemed to understand June better than the others did, and they shared more than a few inside jokes and attitudes.

June blinked and looked up. Jeff was standing a foot away from her, a wine bottle in his hand. "Can I top off your glass?"

She held it out for him. "Sure. Thank you."

He poured the wine and then refilled Valerie's glass. June looked over at Melody. Her glass was empty; Jeff refilled it.

June shot a furtive glance back at Valerie. Like the other women, she was semi-dressed up for dinner; unlike them, she wasn't wearing flats, but clunky wedge sandals instead. The men looked nice, too. Valerie was engrossed in one of her devices, and wasn't watching the game. Hanging around her neck was that tacky, thick gold link chain she had worn that day they ran into each other at Saks. It was an overpriced, designer piece, the kind that Valerie favored but that June detested. Valerie's earlobes hung with heavy earrings, and she wore an expensive and chunky matching bracelet.

June had seen that same necklace in a picture in a magazine, but the model had worn it doubled up, letting it fall attractively right below her collarbone. But Valerie had her necklace lying on her chest in a single rope. With her thick neck, she probably couldn't double it up; if she did, it wouldn't lie at the collarbone, but would choke her instead. Her mother had had the same issue with her neck, according to Jim, but—as with Valerie—it was hard to detect unless you were looking for it.

It was only five o'clock, and the plan was to eat dinner at seven. June would make this glass of wine her last one until then. Frank had bought some champagne to drink with the meal; it was a family tradition. This could be the last Thanksgiving that June would spend with this group. If so, that would be just fine.

*

Dinner was ready at seven twenty.

Frank opened the champagne and filled the flutes, while Melody and Dawn set the casserole dishes on the wide granite island in the kitchen. Jeff carved the turkey, and after some confused shuffling–and directions from Melody–everyone found a seat at the dining room table. Dawn was next to Frank, who sat down at one end; June was to Frank's right, with Valerie sitting on her other side. Jeff sat at the other end of the table, next to Melody, and the kids filled in the middle seats on both sides of the table. After Jeff said a quick grace, everyone began to eat and conversation lulled.

Valerie had been keeping track of June's alcohol in-take. Hopefully, June would drink two glasses of champagne at dinner, and at least two more drinks afterward. She wouldn't eat too much–even on Thanksgiving, that wasn't like her. But so much the better. That way, it would be easier for her to get drunk. If she didn't get sloshed–well, that was okay, too.

But if Melody got drunk–and she was well on her way–that might present a problem. One the other hand, it might be the best way to get rid of her. Once everything was cleaned up, Jeff would get her to go to bed early. Embarrassingly, Melody had sometimes been known to fall asleep sitting up when she drank too much wine. The last time Valerie had seen that happen, Jeff had been morti-fied. A redux was certainly possible tonight.

288

Frank and Dawn would go to bed early, as they usually did. They took their baby up to their room, got him to sleep, and then crashed. Their bedroom was at the end of one of the two long halls upstairs, and was right next to June's. Valerie's room was on the other side of June's room, and was next to the top of the wide, curved staircase. The kids' bedrooms were down at the end of the other hallway, on the other side of the stairs, and their parents' bedroom was closest to the stairs.

What if the kids stayed up too late? Nick probably wouldn't, but the others might. But if they were all safely in their rooms—or even if they were still downstairs, watching TV in the den—Valerie would be able to get the job done.

It would only take seconds.

She sipped her champagne and silently listened to the others chatter as she watched them. No one gave her more than a perfunctory glance. None of them really cared about her. She knew her father had loved her, but she realized a long time ago that none of these people did. They only tolerated her, and they felt that they ought to be congratulated for doing that.

She was sick of feeling cast aside, of being ignored, and of being treated like an undesirable member of the family. If her family couldn't accept her, especially now, after she had groveled to them, well then, fuck them.

Fuck them all.

31

Crime Show

"Anyone ready for dessert?" asked Melody.

Jeff pushed back from the table. "Not me. I ate so much, I think I'll wait a while."

"Me, too," said June. "Everything was delicious."

"It certainly was," added Jeff. "I didn't even miss the broccoli. Who needs a green vegetable, anyway?" He shot a sideways look at Melody and grinned.

"I do," she said, and frowned. "But I guess it wasn't meant to be."

June turned to Melody. "Well, I'm sure it would have been very tasty. Let me do the dishes now."

"I'll help you," said Dawn, rising.

"Y'all don't mind?" asked Melody.

"Of course not," said June. "You go sit down and relax."

Valerie rose and began to help clear the table. "I can help."

Conversation was minimal as the three women rinsed the plates and loaded the two dishwashers. Everyone who cooked had cleaned up after themselves, so it didn't take long to get everything done and to tidy up the kitchen.

"Should I make coffee?" asked June.

Valerie hesitated. This was the last thing she wanted her to do. "I don't know. Should we see if anyone else would like some, first?"

"I don't care for any," said Dawn. "It might keep me up." She smiled at June. "But if you'd like some—"

"Oh, no, that's all right. I don't need it."

"I'll ask the others," said Dawn, stepping out of the room.

"You know, I think I'll have a little more wine instead," said Valerie. She looked at June. "Would you like another glass?"

June shrugged. "Oh, what the heck. Why not?"

Valerie took another bottle from the fridge.

"Here's an opener," said June, handing her a cork pop. "I just love these things. They're so much easier to use than a corkscrew."

"Me, too," said Valerie, smiling.

Dawn peeked in the kitchen. "No takers for coffee."

"Thanks," said Valerie.

Dawn disappeared, and Valerie inserted the cork pop needle in the cork and pushed the top of it down with her thumb. Out popped the cork. She filled June's glass and her own.

"Thank you," said June. "Should we go join everybody?"

"Yes. But I'm kind of footballed out, now."

"I am, too. A whole day of it gets rather long."

Valerie nodded.

Can I really do this, in just a few hours? And is it better to use a cork pop, after all? It would be quick, and wouldn't be that hard. Could I get away with it? But—the blood could be a problem. It would spurt out—

"Coming?" June looked over her shoulder at Valerie. "I'm right behind you."

Almost an hour later, everyone who wanted pie had finished eating. It was even easier now to refill June's glass. By Valerie's count, she'd had more than a whole bottle of wine, including the champagne. But, like the others, she'd had it over a period of several hours. No one was really drunk except Melody, who had now begun to slur her words.

Valerie sat back and watched Jeff deal with his children and his wife. Around nine thirty, Melody fell asleep on the couch. Jeff woke her up and made her and all their kids go upstairs to bed.

Thank goodness.

After another half hour, Frank and Dawn said goodnight. "Hopefully, we can get Cole to sleep soon," said Frank.

"Good luck," said June. "I think I'll stay up a bit longer."

Valerie smiled at her brother. "See you guys tomorrow."

Now was her chance. Whether June was sufficiently drunk or not, she could try to get her to start talking. Or she could do the talking. Whatever she had to do to give the others enough time to fall asleep upstairs.

"I wonder if there's something good on TV," said June. "I wouldn't mind watching a show for a while, and then going to bed in about an hour. How about you?"

Valerie nodded. "Sure. I'm game to watch something."

That will keep her busy, and I won't have to figure out what to say to her.

"How about this?" asked June, tuning the television to a crime show. "I haven't been following it, but a friend told me it's really good."

"Perfect." Valerie trained her eyes on the show. This really *was* perfect. When it was over, they would walk up the stairs together and say goodnight, and then—

"Have you been watching this one?" asked June.

"Oh—no. But that's fine. I don't care."

They settled down to watch the episode in silence, each sipping wine from time to time. An hour later, the show was over. June turned off the TV, got up, and carried her wine glass to the kitchen. Valerie followed, carrying hers. It was ten after eleven, and the house was quiet.

June turned to face Valerie. "What a nice Thanksgiving Day."

Valerie nodded and smiled.

"I'm so tired," added June. "Do you plan to go back to Atlanta tomorrow, or Saturday?"

"I'm not sure. How about you?"

"I'm thinking about going home tomorrow."

The women began to walk toward the foyer.

June paused at the foot of the stairs, put her hand on the banister, and looked up. "This staircase is my favorite part of the house."

"I've always liked it, too," she lied. June's touches were all over the place, and Valerie couldn't stand any of them. *I'm about to get poetic justice, though.*

The older woman started up, with Valerie at her heels. June held the handrail all the way.

At the top, Valerie made her move. "June, before we go to bed…"

June turned to face her. "Yes? Are you okay?"

Valerie cocked her head. "It's just that–I just wanted to wish you the best of luck in your marriage. Congratulations."

"Oh, thank you. I really appreciate that." She smiled. "I didn't know how you and everyone else would feel about it–"

"I think we're *all* very happy for you." Valerie looked directly into her eyes and stepped to the side. June moved just a hair closer to top of the stairs. "Let me give you a hug before we go to bed," said Valerie.

June hesitated for a second. They weren't a hugging kind of family. But Valerie leaned over, put her arms around her, and pulled her close. In the process, she moved June so that her back was to the stairs.

She squeezed her, and then pushed her as hard as she could.

June reflexively reached for Valerie and pulled her in. Valerie scrambled to get away, stumbled, and then desperately tried to catch herself.

32

Snapped

"Frank!" cried Dawn. "Did you hear that?"

He rolled over. "I didn't hear anything."

She sat up. "I'm going to go see what it is."

Frank stayed in bed while Dawn crept out, shutting the door behind her. The house was silent again. She walked down the long hallway toward the staircase.

Then she stopped dead in her tracks and screamed.

"Oh my God! Frank!" She turned and ran back to the bedroom.

Frank was already out of bed and on his feet. "What is it?"

She started to hyperventilate. "It's—it's Valerie!"

She pulled him into the hall and switched on the light.

He stopped short, on the landing. "Jesus!"

Valerie was hanging on the other side of the banister, her neck lodged between two of the iron rails. Her chain link necklace dug into her throat, and her head was awry. Frank ran to her and reached over the banister to try and free her, but he couldn't do it. "Go get Jeff!" he shouted.

Dawn took off down the hall, and five seconds later, Jeff appeared. "What the–oh my God!"

Jeff leaned over the rail and tried to help his brother-in-law pull Valerie's up. They lifted her body a little, but her head wouldn't budge from its position. Her face was blue.

Dawn was shaking. "I'm getting my phone and calling 911."

Frank looked up for a second. "Hurry!"

Dawn came back with her phone in her hand. "Yes…there's been an accident…" Her voice was panicky as she gave the address. After she hung up, she looked down at the bottom of the stairs.

"Oh my God! There's June!"

Dawn ran past the men, down the stairs, and over to June. She was unconscious, but breathing. Dawn looked up at Valerie, flanked by the men trying to free her.

June opened her eyes as Dawn crouched at her side, holding her hand. "What happened?" she asked.

"Help's on the way," said Dawn. "Don't move."

The next few minutes felt like years. Melody came out to the landing, gasped, and started to cry. Jeff told her an ambulance was coming, and told her to go and shield the children from the scene.

When EMS arrived, they went right to Valerie and tried to dislodge her head. They couldn't do it.

"I'm sorry," one of them said to Frank. "Her neck is broken. I'm afraid that she's dead."

"Oh my God. Can't you do anything?" said Frank.

The tech shook his head. "No, sir. It looks like it snapped when she fell. She probably died instantly."

"But–how did this happen?" Frank persisted.

"It almost looks as if she flipped completely over. I'm wondering how the other woman ended up down there."

Another tech squatted beside June. "You're showing signs of a concussion, ma'am," he said.

"My knee hurts," June whimpered.

"It may be broken, and you have bruises on your face and arms. We're going to get you to the hospital, where you can be treated and taken care of."

"Can I go with her?" asked Dawn.

The man looked at his colleagues. One of them shook his head. "They all need to stay here and wait for the police to arrive. I've already called it in." He turned to Frank. "They're going to want to ask you all some questions to figure out what happened."

"But my sister is dead!"

"I'm sorry for your loss, sir. Don't worry. Some of us will stay here with you, while we all wait for the police." He nodded at the tech taking care of June. "He'll take your other sister–"

"My stepmother."

"Your stepmother, then. They'll get her to the nearest emergency room."

*

The security video revealed exactly what happened: Valerie did what she did, on purpose.

She had braced one foot against the top banister as she pulled June in for an awkward hug. Then she pushed the older woman, who tried to hold onto her to keep from falling. Valerie turned her ankle, tried to right herself, and caught her long necklace on the newel post at the top. She stumbled down two steps and reached for her neck, but one of her hands got entangled in the necklace as she tried to pull away.

Meanwhile, June toppled down the staircase, hitting her head and knees and banging her shoulders and arms. Valerie grabbed wildly at the banister with her other hand, but somehow her momentum flipped her body completely over it instead. That arm didn't go with her, but cracked at the elbow and got pinned behind an iron rail. In an instant, her head was pulled up and to the side, lodging itself between two rails, and her neck snapped.

She didn't even have time to scream.

Then Dawn appeared in the hall, stopping a few feet away.

The video answered all the cops' questions, and cleared everyone of any wrongdoing. It was obvious that Valerie had tried to kill June—or at least, badly injure her—by pushing her down the stairs.

But she had killed herself instead.

The police were curious about why the camera had been installed where a motion detector had been placed previously. However, they seemed satisfied when Frank told them that Mick, the house manager, had told him about the rash of break-ins nearby.

"There *have* been some burglaries in the area," one of the cops had said. "Actually, it was prudent of you to install a camera. Not that it was meant for a situation like this, but it has helped us quite a bit."

June was released from the hospital on Friday evening, and on Saturday, they all drove back to Atlanta. Frank turned in his rental car and drove June's car; she rode in the backseat, next to Cole. One of her kneecaps was cracked, and she had suffered a mild concussion. She wore a brace on her leg to keep it immobile. Frank and Dawn changed their flight home to later in the week, so that they could stay in town to attend the funeral. Melody handled the arrangements.

There would be a visitation at the funeral home, and because Valerie wasn't a member of any church, the funeral would be there as well. The public story was that Valerie had slipped and turned her ankle at the top of the stairs, and that her death from a broken neck had been a freak accident. June's injuries were explained as accidental, too: she had lost her balance and fell down the stairs.

Both stories were basically true.

Frank, Dawn, and Cole were staying with June and trying to help as she recovered.

"How is she doing?" Melody asked Frank when they spoke on the phone.

"Pretty well, all things considered. Antoine gets back tonight, and June says he's going to the funeral with her tomorrow."

"Good. We'll see you there."

Melody put her phone down. Everything felt so unreal right now. Surely—no matter what was on the video—Valerie wasn't a murderer. Surely she hadn't *really* meant to kill June. She must have pushed June involuntarily, and only to try to keep from falling herself. It had to be an accident. And both of them had been drinking all day.

Melody shook her head and shuddered. It was just so hard to believe that Valerie could have been a criminal. But—what if she had been? What if she had hated June so much—and had wanted her inheritance so badly—that she tried to do away with June? What if she planned to do it?

What if she had waited for the right moment, and then taken advantage of it?

Whatever she had done—or not done—Valerie was her blood. They had the same father. Melody knew that Valerie had done some awful things in her life. She knew that she had stolen things, and that she had lied a lot. She had manipulated their father and had caused him a lot of grief and stress. She had never felt that the rules applied to her, like they applied to everyone else. She had demonstrated a total disregard for right and wrong. She had been abrasive and hostile, and had never been truly remorseful about what she had done or said.

But no one knew the whole truth about what had happened on Thanksgiving, and maybe no one ever would.

33

Falling Dominoes

David Shepherd attended the funeral, which took place at eleven o'clock on Wednesday. Josh Wilson, Graham Woodcock, and Sophie Prejean were also there, but no one else from the company attended it. Several of Melody's and Jeff's friends attended, as did many friends of June's. Afterward, David walked outside the building with Frank and Dawn.

"My deepest condolences," said David.

Frank shook his head. "Thank you. I still can't believe she's gone–it just hasn't sunk in yet."

David let out a deep breath. "Melody said the same to me earlier. It's truly a shock, and so very tragic. I'm glad that June's going to be okay, though."

"Yes," said Dawn. "It's a miracle that she survived that fall, and that she didn't get more badly injured. She has to do physical therapy for her knee, but she said she can do it over in France."

"Do you know if she still plans to leave the country next week?" asked David. "I haven't had a chance to speak with her."

"I don't know what her exact plans are," said Frank. "We go back to Chicago tomorrow, though."

"Good to know. Oh, I see her over there. Excuse me?"

He stepped toward June, who was holding one crutch and standing next to Antoine.

"How are you doing?" asked David. "Are you in pain?"

"Oh, no. Not too much, anyway." She shrugged. "Pain medication is helping a lot. Our flight to Paris is a week from today, and my doctor said I'd be fine to go by then."

"Good," said David. He looked at Antoine. "Do you two still plan to get married next month?"

"But of course," said Antoine. "I will take very good care of her." He smiled at June.

"I'm sure you will," said David. He turned to June. "So, I'll be in touch soon about the changes that we discussed."

"Thanks so much, David," said June. "You've been just wonderful."

"It's been my pleasure. Take care, and let me know when I can be of service."

*

Josh climbed into his Audi, grateful to be alone again. He felt numb. He was glad he had come to pay his respects to the family, but now he was ready to get out of here.

When he heard the news that Valerie was dead, he was stunned. And when he heard about *how* she died, he was astounded. What a way to go—and what a horrible, freak accident. How had she managed to hang herself and break her neck? What a horrific scene it must have been.

He had come alone to the funeral, and he was relieved that Graham and Sophie decided to attend it too. It might be the final time the three of them would be together, and it could be the last time he would see Sophie, who had found a job at a small public relations firm specializing in technology companies. They'd all been shaken up when they found out about Valerie. Sophie had been the most emotional.

Josh slowed for a red light and stopped. It was weird that the woman he had slept with for the past year was now gone, and gone for good. He had never wished anything bad to happen to her—and he certainly never wished her to die.

He let out a deep breath and accelerated after the light changed. He was on his way home to change clothes and get on with his day. He and everyone else at PriceUtopia had moved out of the office suite, and the last paychecks would be issued on Friday. This Saturday was December first. Over the next few weeks, he had to get in gear to find a job, come January. He had been updating his resume, but he needed to get busy contacting people who might be able to help him find a new position.

Despite what he had been through—and the black mark of PriceUtopia's demise—he ought to be able to find something with relative ease. His partnership with Graham was a plus, and their foray into business together was a positive in his background. People recovered from all kinds of issues in business, and the word failure no longer had such a stigma. For some, it was even a badge of honor. It showed that you were fearless and a risk-taker—two qualities that many businessmen valued highly. Josh had many other attributes, too, and a background filled with success in other ventures. Somehow, he would land on his feet, and he would be a better man.

Ten minutes later, he headed into his apartment. In a little while, he would get online and send out some emails. He was looking so forward to seeing Aimee this evening–she would be a welcome antidote to the mood he was in right now. Thank God he had stopped seeing Valerie months ago, and that he was now in a relationship with a wonderful and very different woman.

A random thought popped into his head. What if he hadn't gone to his brother's birthday party that night? If not, he may never have met Aimee. In that case, would he still be seeing–sleeping with–Valerie? And would she have gone down to the coast to be with her family over Thanksgiving, or would they have spent the holiday together? It was impossible to know. But if they had done that, maybe she would still be alive right now.

He shuddered. It was all serendipity, and he was lucky he had met Aimee when he did. Even if that event was the first domino to fall in the last few months of Valerie's life.

*

On Monday, January 7, David stepped into his office, sat down at his desk, and wrote an email to one of his favorite clients.

Dear June,

Happy New Year, and I hope that you are well and are enjoying life in France.

I wanted to summarize what we discussed on the phone recently. According to the terms of the trust, since you have remarried, the funds will now be split equally between you and Jim's two surviving children, Frank Mitchell and Melody Perkins.

As you requested, I will continue managing your income from the trust. The home on Sherwood Circle in Atlanta stays in your name, to be passed on to Frank and Melody upon your death.

I send you my regards and best wishes. Please do not hesitate to call if I can be of any assistance.

Best,

David Shepherd
Advisor to Families of Significant Wealth
Elite Financial Planning

Acknowledgments

I'm extremely grateful to Mark Christopher and Josh Coughlin for taking the time to educate me about the world of startups, venture capitalists, and IPOs. Much of what they taught me is not included in the pages of this book, but was absolutely necessary for me to know and understand, in order to tell the story.

I thank Maureen Benjamin for sharing her knowledge about technology firms, and for explaining what it's like to work in one that has no choice but to dissolve. Big thanks go to Kevin McDermott, who answered several key questions about the retail industry's response to showrooming, the research about customer behavior, and current online shopping practices and trends. I'm grateful to Cathy Darland and Jocelyn Ralston, who provided key information about luxury beach properties.

I thank author James Huskins for his wonderful feedback and suggestions, and Elen Christopher for her unwavering support. Thanks go to Wendy Lamb for finding several errors, and for her excellent advice. I thank author Susan Crawford for her support, and for catching a few typos. Thanks to Mary McDermott for cheering me on, and for her help with June's bridge playing scenes.

I am grateful to my fantastic editor, Laura Ownbey, who pushed me to develop the characters in *Daddy's Girl* and to sharpen the story. Thanks also to Michael S. Faron for his patience and his work to produce a terrific cover.

I thank my children, who believed in me and offered their love and encouragement. As always, I'm grateful to my husband Dennis for his constant support and encouragement, and for his unending and unconditional love.

About the Author

Julia McDermott is the author of psychological suspense *Underwater*, French travel/"new adult" romance *Make That Deux*, and creative nonfiction/memoir *All the Above: My son's battle with brain cancer*. A native of Texas, Julia grew up in Atlanta and graduated from the University of North Carolina at Chapel Hill, where she studied Economics and French. She lives in Atlanta with her husband and family. Visit her online at juliamcdermottbooks.com.

Made in the USA
Middletown, DE
30 January 2017